Praise for

THE RUNAWAYS

"In this suspenseful and engaging book, Sonya Terjanian looks at issues of class and intimacy, of the chaos that is youth and the uncertainty that is middle age. Written in lively, vivid prose, the novel is very hard to put down, by turns charming and disturbing."
—Andrew Solomon, National Book Award–winning author
of *The Noonday Demon*

"Beautifully observed, deeply empathetic, and harrowing in the best possible way, *The Runaways* is a story for anyone who has ever felt lost, isolated, or fantasized about reinventing herself—and isn't that all of us?"
—Jenny Rosenstrach, *New York Times* bestselling author
of *Dinner: A Love Story*

"In this superb psychodrama-thriller, Terjanian reveals her great talent at storytelling and uncanny attention to detail. I could not put it down."
—Jan Vilcek, author of *Love and Science*

THE
RUNAWAYS

Sonya Terjanian

A NOVEL

Published by Sourcebooks Landmark, an imprint of Sourcebooks, Inc.
P.O. Box 4410, Naperville, Illinois 60567-4410
(630) 961-3900
Fax: (630) 961-2168
sourcebooks.com

Library of Congress Cataloging-in-Publication Data

Names: Terjanian, Sonya, author.
Title: The runaways / Sonya Terjanian.
Description: Naperville, Illinois : Sourcebooks Landmark, [2018]
Identifiers: LCCN 2017040618 | (softcover : acid-free
   paper)
Subjects: LCSH: Self-realization in women--Fiction. | Interpersonal
   relations--Fiction. | Life change events--Fiction.
Classification: LCC PS3603.O2257 R86 2018 | DDC 813/.6--dc23 LC record
available at https://lccn.loc.gov/2017040618

Printed and bound in the United States of America.
VP 10 9 8 7 6 5 4 3 2 1

For Pierre, who makes everything possible

—
I
—

The Shell station was selling road atlases for $19.95, which was too much. But they had every state in there, and Ivy figured a lot of them probably fell somewhere between Pennsylvania and Montana. She glanced at the spray-tanned cashier, who was paging through a magazine and probing her ear with a long, fake nail. Ivy knew the atlas would fit under her jean jacket, around the side and under her arm, but she couldn't decide if that was the way she wanted to go with this. Getting busted for shoplifting—barely two hours after her big getaway—would be a shitty and depressing way for this to end.

She opened the atlas, scanning the overview map for the line where Pennsylvania pressed up against the underbelly of New York, the so-called Southern Tier. She wondered how far she'd gotten that morning; she remembered seeing the WELCOME TO PENNSYLVANIA sign about an hour ago. Was she in the Poconos? Halfway to Philadelphia? She had no idea.

Ivy closed the atlas and held it against her stomach. It took a little getting used to, this new way of doing things: Stealing. Running. Doing what needed to be done, and to hell with everyone else. She felt like she'd been split down the middle and turned inside out, the real Ivy finally set loose on the world. The Ivy who didn't care what was right or what was wrong. The Ivy with the black heart.

The cashier looked up from her magazine. Ivy put the atlas back on the shelf and picked up a smaller, cheaper map of Pennsylvania, which she brought to the counter with her Slim Jims and chocolate milk. "Don't be a dumbass," Gran would say. For now, she'd take things one step at a time. Put some distance between herself and Good Hope, wait for things to blow over before taking any more risks. She watched the cashier struggle with the register keys, her hand splayed, bejeweled nails threatening to push all the keys at once. Some people, Ivy thought. If you absolutely have to have nails like that, why in the ever-living fuck would you get a job that involved pushing buttons all day?

Back in the car, she sucked on a Slim Jim as she scanned the map and thought over her money situation. She was down to $62.84, and McFadden's Buick drank like Gran. She needed to buy as much distance as possible, spend less on food. Maybe she could find a Chinese supermarket, like that place outside Binghamton, where she and her friend Asa used to fill five or six grocery bags with noodle packets and pork cake for a few dollars. A little water in the teakettle and *bam*—a feast for two, salt exploding in their mouths like Chinese firecrackers.

Or maybe she could find herself a soup kitchen or a food pantry. Keep an eye out for a long, slumpy line of half-asleep people, wait her turn, and fill up on charity. But those church people always knew everybody in their line, and if they didn't, they would want to. Ivy'd have to make up one of her stories.

She nudged the car awake, rolled out of the lot. No

Chinese groceries around here, that was for sure. Just a couple of vinyl-clad antique shops, an M&T Bank, a hardware store with cheap plastic sleds and some shovels piled out front, not even chained up. In the middle of town, a four-sided traffic light dangled from a drooping wire, flashing yellow. Ivy couldn't remember what to do when it was flashing yellow. Stop? Proceed with caution? She stopped, to be on the safe side, then turned right.

A row of shoebox houses in ugly old-person colors, a chaotic jumble of body shops and high chain-link fences laced with shreds of pink plastic, and then the town just kind of gave up. The sidewalk crumbled into the dirt shoulder and guardrails appeared. Up ahead, thirsty woods met the gray sky in a blurry line. A sign in the shape of a football read CONGRATULATIONS, CARBONVILLE MARMOTS, and a bigger sign read WELCOME TO THE ENDLESS MOUNTAINS. Ivy could see the brown wrinkles in the distance, thin and repetitive. She imagined growing up around here—forties in back seats, bruises, feral cats, football. "Fucking endless is right," she said, the Slim Jim waggling between her teeth like a cigar.

She checked the rearview, startled by her own voice. She eased off the accelerator. Getting caught in a speed trap would be another stupid way for this to end. Anyway, she needed to stay away from these ugly coal-country towns, with their bored cops and loitering mechanics, their eyes so quick to follow an unfamiliar car. She needed to burrow to the end of those Endless Mountains, speed across the vast rectangle of Pennsylvania to…what was next? Michigan? Then push through the tall grass of the Midwest until she finally got someplace worth looking at.

Thank God she'd never told McFadden about Montana. She'd only told Asa, and there was no way his spongy brain had managed to hold on to the information this long. That day when Ivy had shown him the newspaper clipping, he'd just finished smoking a huge bowl, so he'd found it alternately hilarious and confounding.

"Is that a deer?" he'd asked, gripping the scrap of newspaper between his enormous fingers. "On a telephone wire?"

"It's a baby deer."

"Hanging by its armpits from a telephone wire. Well, I'll be goddamned." He'd let his hand drop to his lap, tilted his head back, and shuddered with silent laughter. Ivy hated talking to Asa when he was like that, but lately he hadn't given her much choice.

"It's a real picture," Ivy said, snatching the clipping from him. There was a utility worker in a cherry picker rising up to meet the deer, which was slung over the wire like a pair of old sneakers. The headline read "Fawn Causes Power Outage."

"Guess how it got up there."

Asa stopped chuckling and squinted his eyes. "Wings. Baby deer wings."

"Yes. Baby deer wings." Ivy rolled her eyes. "My point is, this is what Montana is like. Fucking baby deer dropping out of the sky. Okay? Glaciers. Geysers. They have a road called the Going-to-the-Sun Road."

"Whoa."

"Can you think of a single road around here anyone would want to call Going-to-the-Sun Road?"

"Umm…that road with the tanning salon? Route 17?" More silent laughter.

"There's this job people have out there. Smoke jumpers. They jump out of planes and fight forest fires. Okay? They jump *out* of airplanes *into* forest fires."

"Is that what the deer was doing?"

4

"Can you think of a single person around here who's ever done something like that in their entire life?"

"C'mon, Ivy, how'd the deer get on the telephone wire?"

Ivy pulled a Dorito out of the bag sitting on the floor between them, snapped off a corner between her teeth. "An eagle dropped it. Duh."

There was a time when Ivy would've asked Asa to come with her to Montana, but over the past year, he'd gone like the rest of Good Hope—into a trance. In Asa's case, it was a pot and video game trance. For her sister, Agnes, it was a hair and makeup trance. Her brother, Colin, was in a basement weight-lifting trance. Those people who opened that antique store downtown were in an antique trance, sitting there all day among the rhinestone brooches and jelly glasses, not even noticing that nobody ever came through the door, just paying rent so they'd have a place to sit between meals.

Ivy wanted to snap her fingers in their faces, shake them by the shoulders, scream at the top of her lungs. *Just go*, she wanted to yell at Agnes; go find a town that has the job you studied so hard for. *Move out*, she wanted to scream at Colin; our basement has no windows. Most of all, she wanted to burst into that antique store and swing a chair around the place, just pulverizing all the cake stands and mason jars and Hummel shit. *Snap out of it!* she would scream, throwing the chair into a case full of pocket watches and Fiestaware. You're just selling the same cracked, ugly old crap again and again, year after year, just waiting till people die and wiping off the dust and selling it again. What the *hell* is the point in that?

But instead, she stole McFadden's car. Ivy had to admit, she enjoyed imagining McFadden out in the high school parking lot, standing slack-jawed in front of her empty spot. *How could anyone do this to me*, she'd be thinking. *After everything I've done for this town.* And of course she'd find a way to get a new car for free. Ivy was sure of that. The town would band together and raise the money, everybody handing over a chunk of their tips, their welfare checks, their prison work pay, so Saint McFadden could get a sweet ride.

Ivy batted at the graduation tassel hanging from the rear-view mirror. She'd tried telling McFadden she had a plan, that she didn't need to take the SATs. But McFadden wouldn't listen. As the guidance counselor with the highest college acceptance rate in the entire Southern Tier, McFadden had a reputation to maintain, and she wasn't about to let some slacker kid ruin it for her. How many times had Ivy already ridden in this very car, against her will? Going to SAT prep. Going to the actual SATs. Going to more SAT prep.

That's how it was with McFadden. If you didn't show up for test prep, she'd come to your house and pick you up in her car. If you weren't in any clubs, she'd get you magically added to the yearbook committee. If you couldn't figure out what to write for your application essay, she'd pull one out of this giant file she kept and say, "Use this for inspiration." She'd already done it to Colin and Agnes, and the way Ma acted when they got those acceptance letters, it was like they'd been awarded the goddamn Nobel Prize by the pope himself. Both times, Ma bought them ice-cream cakes and balloons, and both times her raggedy lungs failed to blow up a single balloon and she had to get Ivy to do it.

Colin went to Alfred for social work, Agnes went to Tech for hospitality, and now they were both living at home and working at Chili's and Wegmans, respectively. And they weren't the only ones. Half of Colin's and Agnes's friends were back in their old rooms, sleeping among their stuffed animals, closets full of polyester uniforms, mailboxes full of payment coupons, and nobody had the guts to say, *You know what? The emperor is walking around with his goddamn junk hanging out.*

The sun was sinking now, striking the tops of some leafless branches, leaving the rest in chilly shade. The cracked two-lane road was rolling through patches of farmland alternating with one-story houses, pickups in the driveways framed by painted tires looping out of the ground, and collapsing barns looking like tents after a rainstorm.

Ivy fumbled for the headlight switch; the dashboard glowed orange. She wondered what Ma was going to make for dinner. Probably tomato soup, which she and Gran would eat in front of the TV, beer cans at their sides. Ivy didn't exactly miss it, the ashtray smell and the ceiling light blackened with bug carcasses, the sandy scratch of the old couch under her thighs. There was an ache, though—for the funny banter between Colin and Agnes, maybe, or for the warmth of soup sliding into her empty belly, shreds of saltine cracker dissolving on her tongue. Ivy unscrewed the cap of the chocolate milk bottle with one hand and drank what was left, letting the slimy sweetness coat the inside of her mouth.

Of course, nowadays Colin usually worked the dinner shift, and if Agnes wasn't working, she could generally be found at Hank's Elbow Room, drinking with her new boyfriend. A lot of times, Gran wouldn't even come out of her bedroom for dinner. Recently, Ivy had found a half-empty bag of pretzels and a forty in Gran's closet. Gran said it was for when she got hungry in the middle of the night, but Ivy knew Gran was spending days on end in there, sleeping too much, drinking too much, eating too little. Ivy had dragged her over to the couch and made her eat a grilled cheese sandwich, wondering why she always had to be the one checking on Gran, keeping her alive, sitting through her tirades about the men, long dead, who'd left them all up shit creek.

And now even Ma was wanting Ivy's help with things like vacuuming and carrying in the bags from the Food Bank, because her lungs couldn't take it. She wouldn't ask; she'd just stand in the doorway, trying her best to stuff some air down her throat, one hand gripping the doorjamb, the other stretched toward the floor as if it wasn't too late to stop the cans of creamed corn from slipping from the plastic bag and rolling under the kitchen table. She wouldn't ask, but she wouldn't have to, Ivy being the only one around.

It was like that more and more. Ivy could see the future coming at her like a freight train, although really it was the opposite of that. It was like a light moving backward through a tunnel until it disappeared, leaving her alone in the dark. Agnes's boyfriend had an apartment on the other side of town, and she'd already started leaving some of her clothes over there. Colin was starting to keep odd hours, answering his phone in the middle of the night and rushing out of the house, missing shifts and generally acting shady. Ivy wasn't sure if he was dealing or taking action or what, but she knew he was headed for time at the Pen. That was just kind of how things went in Good Hope: if you didn't end up working for one of the town's three prisons, you ended up inside one of them. Or else you got a different kind of sentence, like a sick ma who needed you more and more, her need like a chain around your neck.

Up ahead, Ivy's headlights picked up a brown sign with carved lettering: GARDNER STATE PARK. Ivy turned onto the dirt road, bumping past a sign that said, "Park closes at dusk." The road split, wrapping itself around a small, darkened guard booth, and ended in a parking area next to some picnic tables and trash cans. Ivy stopped the car and turned off her headlights, peering through the purple gloom for signs of life.

Did park rangers patrol the woods at night? She wondered if they were a type of cop. The ones they always interviewed on *I Survived* wore gold badges and big hats that looked a lot like state police uniforms. On the one hand, she didn't want one shining his flashlight in the car and asking to see an ID. On the other hand, it would be nice to know someone was out there in case of bears or wolves or whatnot. Ivy had thrown her cell phone out the car window on her way out of Good Hope, because she didn't want anyone tracking it—which meant now she had no way to call for help.

The car made faint ticking noises. Ivy unfastened her seat belt and lifted the armrests between the front seats, stretching her legs across. If she fell asleep soon, she could wake up early and get back on the road before someone reported to work in the guard booth. She buttoned her jacket to her chin, put up her hood, and tucked her hands under her armpits.

It was pretty funny, the idea of spending the night in McFadden's car. Funny and kind of annoying, since Ivy could feel her everywhere: in the tassel hanging from the rearview, in the disgusting sheepskin wheel cover, in the faded East Good Hope stickers on the back window. A decal on the glove compartment door had the school's motto on it: "Home of the Eagles." That irritated Ivy more than anything. She knew for a fact that nobody had seen an eagle anywhere near Good Hope for at least a hundred years.

She pulled out her wallet and found the folded newspaper clipping—the one with the deer on the telephone wire. She'd cut it out of *USA Today* about a year ago; the picture had snagged on her brain, and she couldn't get it out. The brave heartlessness of it; the uncomplicated math. It felt like

9

a doorway to something bigger than herself, to a world without walls or boundaries or questions about right or wrong, to a place where it was all about survival, and you were either a baby deer or a badass eagle. Seeing that picture was the start of her whole fixation on Montana—what had sent her to the library computer to find out where, exactly, it was; what had led her to find out about smoke jumping. That was pretty much all she needed to know. The farthest place she could imagine from Good Hope, New York, was an airplane over a Montana forest fire.

She slid the clipping back into her wallet and blew on her hands, rubbing the insides of her knees together. She reached up and yanked on the graduation tassel, trying to rip out some of the silky threads. They were firmly knotted, though, so she just slapped at it in frustration. She understood that McFadden wasn't completely to blame for everyone's problems; she wasn't the only one who'd created this town-wide hallucination about the magical power of college. It was the moms and the dads and the grans, worn to a nub by years of warehouse and prison work, blinded by the shine coming off those glossy brochures and the heavy, manila-colored promise of the acceptance letter. The ice-cream cake was long gone by the time they got the next letter, the one about tuition, and by that time, no one could bear to turn back.

Ivy was sick of it, and she didn't mind saying so. She'd said it just that morning in the guidance office. But McFadden just kept feeding her the same old line about how she did her best to help kids rise above their circumstances, but she couldn't control what they chose to do with their opportunities.

"You mean the opportunity to pay back eighty grand while making nine bucks an hour?" Ivy'd laughed. And McFadden had muttered something about kids growing up without role models in the home. Which caused a pellet of rage to burst behind Ivy's eyes. She'd had to grip the armrests of her chair to keep herself from leaping across the desk and clawing McFadden's lips off her face.

Really, the only thing that kept her in her chair was the promise she'd made to Colin a few weeks ago, to stop getting into fights. He'd told her she was going to wind up on the wrong side of the prison bars one of these days, and even though Ivy wasn't sure there was a *right* side to those bars, she didn't want to give him the chance to say "I told you so."

So she hadn't jumped McFadden, but the minute McFadden walked out to make a copy of something, Ivy had found the counselor's purse under her desk, plunged her hand inside, and grabbed the keys. And as she roared out of the parking lot and flew toward the Pennsylvania border, she'd been filled with a soaring, laugh-out-loud kind of joy that she never, ever got from punching somebody.

It was fully dark now. Ivy tried not to think about what might be lurking in the woods, watching her. She tried to keep her mind from imagining a cold hand slipping around her ankle, or a hook scraping across the roof of the car. Colin had always made fun of her for being afraid of the dark; he'd mocked her Little Mermaid night-light until Ivy finally ripped off the cover and just used the bare bulb. But on the nights when she couldn't sleep—when a nightmare jolted her awake, or strange shadows moved across her window shade—Ivy knew she could climb into Colin's bed, where her fears would be muffled by his deep, rumbling snores.

She could barely make out the guard booth a few feet away. It looked like something a little kid would draw: peaked roof, window, door. She wondered what it would be like to have that job—sitting on a stool in a tiny house for hours, ass aching, just dying for someone to drive up and ask a really interesting question. She imagined a young kid all excited about joining the Park Service, so proud of his cop-like uniform, his brass name tag, all ready to tromp around in the woods counting owls and whatnot, only to be shipped off to fuck-all Pennsylvania to sit in a four-foot-square little house handing out trail maps. "You have to pay your dues," they'd tell him. "Put in your time, and eventually you'll graduate to sitting at the front desk at the nature center."

Ivy imagined the kid sitting in the booth, seething with disappointment. Then one too many tourists would ask him one too many questions about where to buy beer or where to go to the bathroom, and he'd just snap. He'd grab his Park Service–issued rifle and march into the woods and start shooting owls out of the trees… *Blammo! Blammo! Blammo!*

Ivy chuckled half-heartedly. She wondered if the little house was heated. She got out of the car and ran stiffly through the darkness, the cold air like a steel door slamming on her body. She got to the little house and tried the door. Locked, of course, but it was just a push-button lock. She ran back to the car and got her driver's license, then returned and slid the card down the crack between the door and the jamb, angling it slightly, feeling for the click.

Inside, she flicked on a light switch and looked around. There was a padded stool, a ledge with a rack of maps and brochures, a small radio, and at the bottom of the wall, a miniature baseboard heater with a dial on it. Ivy set her license on the ledge, then twisted the dial on the heater and held her palms out, waiting to feel something. It didn't take long. She knelt in front of the clicking, animating heater, her fingertips burning as blood bloomed inside them.

She got up on the stool and spun around a few times, her

breath leaving trails in the still-chilly air. She pulled a map from the rack, idly perused the names of trails and lookouts: Pleasant View, Hopewell, Piney Point. So far, Pennsylvania seemed pretty ho-hum. Ivy was impatient to get further west, to see something worth writing home about, like the Rockies. The key was to do it all without getting caught. She wasn't sure stealing a shitty old Buick would land her in the Pen or the Supermax, but one way or another, getting caught would lead to some sort of confinement. And if there was one thing Ivy absolutely could not risk, it was that.

Ivy flicked off the light and sat on the floor next to the heater with her back against the wall. She reached up and turned on the radio, which was tuned to an oldies station. She circled her knees with her arms, lowered her head. The DJ's voice came on, low and soothing, and Ivy let her thoughts drift just out of reach, her forehead heavy on her knees, a well of breath and body heat warming her face.

At some point, she must have turned off the radio; at some point, she must have slid all the way down to the floor. She didn't remember doing it, but that was the state of things when the door to the hut whooshed open, sending a gust of freezing air across her legs and onto her face. Ivy sat up fast, barely catching a glimpse of a man's darkened face haloed in morning sunlight before the face withdrew and the door slammed shut again.

Ivy stood up, steadying herself against the ledge as her heart struggled to get blood to all the right places. She blinked out the window. There was an old man outside, not in a park ranger outfit, just green work pants and a tan canvas coat, backing slowly away from the booth. He met her eye through the window and stopped moving. Then he squinted and walked resolutely back to the hut, jerking open the door.

"You're not supposed to be in here."

"Sorry."

"How did you even... Is that your car?" Ivy shrugged. The man studied her, his face tired and uncertain. "You a runaway?" She shrugged again. "Well, where are you—"

Ivy darted forward, and the man, taken by surprise, moved back half a step. She pushed past him and ran to the car. The keys were still in the ignition. She backed out of the parking spot fast, making the man jump aside; then she clunked the car into Drive, sped toward the main road, and turned right.

Just around the bend, she pulled onto the right shoulder and swung around in the other direction, almost going into a ditch as she made the U-turn. She wasn't sure if he was going to radio the cops, but she might as well head off in the opposite direction of where he thought she was going. There was no sign of him as she passed the park entrance. She drove a few miles, turned onto a dirt road, and bumped along for a while, her heart still motoring in her chest. It was early; the landscape was blurred with morning mist. She lowered the armrest and leaned on it, trying to calm down. She noticed her wallet sitting on the seat, open.

"Oh, Jesus." Ivy picked up the wallet, slammed it back down. "God fucking damn it God fucking damn it motherfucker mother*fucker*!" She pounded the heel of her hand against the steering wheel harder and harder, screaming through gritted teeth. Her license. She'd had to use her fucking license. And she'd had to leave it on the ledge. Now it was only a matter of time before they connected her to McFadden and called Ma and put out an APB for a skinny teenage runaway/car thief.

The dirt track met a two-lane paved road, and Ivy turned left. She had no idea if she was headed east or west at this point; she just needed to get the hell away from Gardner State Park and not go near any interstates or tollbooths. The two-lane road climbed to a long ridge where the trees became bent and scrawny, black heaps of coal rising behind them. Up here, the morning light flattened out, leaving the landscape indifferent and dull. Something on a nearby ridge was pumping out black smoke, and down below she could see clumps of small, dusty-looking houses, close together but closed up. The map she'd bought filled the whole front seat when it was open; how much sooty hopelessness did it contain? This place was no better than Good Hope.

The road finally hairpinned down off the ridge, making her ears pop, and rolled into a town that, according to the sign she passed, was called Forks. Ivy liked the sound of that: forks, knives, spoons. Pancakes, coffee with cream, hash browns, bacon. She had the money. She'd be able to think more clearly with some real food in her stomach. There was a diner on the right, the mostly empty parking lot wrapping around to the back where she could park out of sight. But as she slowed and got ready to turn, she saw a cop car parked at the side of the entrance. She kept going.

There was a strip mall with a dollar store and a liquor mart just beyond the diner. Ivy pulled in, her belly cramping hard. She'd be quick.

Afterward, sitting in the parking lot, she swigged from a two-liter orange soda bottle and moaned as sugar surged through her bloodstream. Mashed cookies were packed into her molars and the roof of her mouth. She knew in twenty minutes she'd turn all heavy-lidded and slow, but she figured fear would keep her heart on the job. She capped the bottle and backed quickly out of the lot.

It wasn't until she was a mile outside of town that she

looked in the mirror and saw the cop car, bulging hood and broad windshield staring her down, about a car length back. "Fuck," Ivy muttered, taking another cookie from the package on the passenger seat. She became painfully aware of her driving, accelerating smoothly up every hill, braking carefully on every down slope, keeping her speed just a few ticks above the limit so as not to appear paranoid. The cop car matched her every move, even when she carefully eased onto a side road that wound up into a piney neighborhood of vacation rentals. "Fuck," she muttered again, watching the mostly empty driveways go past. She could turn into one of them, pretend she'd reached her destination, and maybe the cop would just keep going. But what if he pulled in behind her? What if he asked to see her license?

The road was branching here and there, leading deeper into the development. Ivy picked a random street; the cop followed. She rounded a turn and cursed: a cul-de-sac. It was now or never. Park and be confronted, or act lost and prolong the game. She rounded the cul-de-sac, headed back out. Behind her, a blue light began to flash.

"Nooo…no no no," Ivy wailed. She pretended not to see it for a few moments, continuing as before, but then the cop car chirped at her, loud and commanding. "No!" Ivy hollered. She wasn't ready. She was just getting started. She clenched her teeth, stomped on the gas, and leaped down the hill out of the development, feeling something inside her start to spread its wings.

She fishtailed back onto the main road, the cop now whooping close behind, lights whirling. Ivy came up hard on the tail of a green pickup, then did something she never would have imagined doing before this moment. She pulled into the other lane and roared around the pickup, narrowly missing an oncoming station wagon. This bought her nothing, however, as the pickup swerved to the right to let the cop by, and in seconds, he was back on her tail. Now she came up on a black SUV. She whipped around it, and this time the cop came with her into the other lane, screaming past the black car. This is it, Ivy thought. This is how it's going to end, like one of those dumb cop shows, crashing her car and bolting out of the driver's seat, only to be tackled in someone's backyard, her stupidity caught on video by the helicopter that should be appearing at any moment. Handcuffs, shackles, a toilet with no seat, and beatdowns in the yard.

Ivy pressed the accelerator as far down as it would go. The road had been pretty straight for the last few miles, but now it began bending and humping, making it hard to stay in her lane. She rounded a curve with a shriek, then swerved left to avoid another pickup that had suddenly appeared in front of her, practically at a standstill. Ivy's head jerked back at the sight of what was lumbering toward her in the other lane: a cement truck, as tall and wide and fastened to the earth as a mountain. Ivy screamed again, jerked the steering wheel to the right without checking if she'd cleared the pickup, then winced at the sound of tires screaming back at her. In the rearview mirror, she could see the cement truck and pickup skidded sideways in the road, blocking her view of the cop car. She could still hear sirens, though, from many directions, getting louder. The cop was gone from her rearview, but there were more on their way, closing in fast.

Ivy slowed down and turned left into a modest housing development, then left again, trying not to go too fast so she wouldn't attract attention, fear clawing at her insides. It was early; the neighborhood was quiet. Behind a row of one-story houses, beyond the carports and clotheslines and trampolines, she saw a muddy field edged by thick woods, and a gap in between that could be a dirt road or, just as easily, a ditch. She followed it with her eyes to a break in the trees. Might as well find out.

She yanked the wheel to the right, then stepped hard on the gas. The tires bounced energetically over the field's caked furrows and grassy mounds, throwing Ivy up and down in her seat like a rubber ball on a wooden paddle. At the edge of the field, she found what was neither a road nor a path. It was something in between, but it looked like she would just fit. She eased the car down into it, then rolled hopefully toward the break in the woods where—yes—the track turned toward the trees. She felt the forest close around her like the softest, warmest blanket in the world. "Praise be," she muttered, sounding like Gran.

The track turned out to be less of a road and more of an impression, picking its way through blank spots in the trees. Here and there, she could make out two ruts where someone's tires had been, but mostly it was covered over with a thick layer of pine needles, dead leaves, and ferns. Eventually, she figured, the track would lead to a road, which would empty out into a state park or maybe a town far, far away from Forks.

After a while, the road became more clearly dug out of the side of a hill, climbing a little, tall weeds making a line up the middle. She came across a fallen branch that looked too big to drive over, so she got out to clear it away. Pausing by the warm hood, she thought she heard the sound of a highway in the distance, faintly constant and hopeful. She shoved the branch down the hill, then squinted and cursed under her breath. At the bottom of the slope, glinting sharp and clear among the bracken and sounding very much like a highway—but offering a lot fewer options for escape—was a creek.

"Ah, shit." She got back in the car and started driving as fast as she dared. She rounded a bend and stopped abruptly. A tree was lying across the road, and it wasn't the kind she could just push out of the way. She got out of the car and shoved the tree with her foot. Its trunk was almost three feet around, and its upper branches were braced against two pines, wedging it in place. She took hold of a branch stub and yanked uselessly in the direction of the ravine, then kicked it again.

The road at this point was just a narrow, flat interruption in the steep downward progress of the mountain. Turning around was not an option. Ivy walked back around the bend to see if there was any change in the situation behind her, but she would have to drive backward for a long time before finding a wide spot. She walked back to the tree and studied its roots, which fanned dramatically out of the slope just above the road. She thought about pushing the tree with the car, but the roots were so big she knew that even if she got the tree pushed parallel to the road, the roots would never clear it.

Exhaustion began to creep across the edges of her mind. Ivy got back in the car, shivering, and clunked it into Reverse. The engine made an adenoidal whine as she started going backward. She strained to see the road over her shoulder, but the trees were throwing thick, disconcerting shadows across the way. When she came to the bend, her hand hesitated on the wheel, then yanked it to the left, but the car jerked toward the ravine, so Ivy pulled quickly in the other direction, which just made the car swerve into the hillside. She tried stopping, but her foot was confused by all the backwardness, and instead of stomping on the brake, it stomped on the accelerator at the same moment that Ivy overcorrected her turn. The back wheels bumped heavily over the edge of the road into the forest floor, and the car tipped like a seesaw, the soda bottle rolling under the passenger seat and Ivy's stomach rolling along with it. She lunged against the brake pedal, putting all her weight on it, but the ground was soft and the angle was steep, and for a few long moments, the car seemed to be considering its options.

2

Mary Ellen sat on the edge of the hotel bed, fully dressed and ready to go, watching her daughters sleep in the bed next to hers. Shelby was on her stomach, one arm hanging over the edge, her pillow pushing her slack mouth into a lopsided grimace. Sydney was on her back, her mouth also open, breaths struggling wetly past her unusually large tonsils. Mary Ellen was enjoying the chance to watch them like this, unguarded and uncomposed, elbows and knees going every which way, long blond hair hiking itself out of their ponytail holders. A rare chance to get a good look at them without being met with an affronted *What*.

They were so cute when they were asleep. Awake was a different story. Awake, the twins were extremely tall—a mysterious surfacing of genes, probably from Matt's side of the family, that made it feel like a pair of Swedish exchange students had come to stay on a permanent basis. And they were moody. The moodiness was combined with a stubborn opaqueness, so Mary Ellen never knew which mood she might be dealing with, or what might cause that mood to suddenly change.

She reached out to tap Shelby's arm, then changed her

mind. It was still early. She was excited to start the campus tour, but she wanted to start it on the right foot, and waking the twins prematurely usually wasn't a good idea. She pulled her phone from her bag and sent the girls a text: "Having breakfast downstairs. Come down when you're ready."

The breakfast room was full of families, and as Mary Ellen looked around at the other high school seniors, she regretted having come downstairs without her daughters. At home, they always seemed to be on different schedules, eating separate meals, but this trip was supposed to be different—a chance for mother-daughter bonding. A chance for her to show the girls her alma mater and try to explain the formative power of her college years—years that had begun flooding into Mary Ellen's consciousness with startling, sun-dazzled clarity ever since the UNC viewbook had arrived in the mail.

That was all so long ago, but now it seemed like a terrible oversight that she hadn't ever told her girls what she'd been like in college. Could Sydney and Shelby even begin to imagine her as that careless, overall-wearing art major, a girl without a thought in her head about the real world, dancing like a snake in a basket, hypnotized by the music of the here and now? A child, really, who loved smearing paint around and playing Frisbee on the quad and availing herself of the unlimited soft-serve ice cream in the cafeteria.

Mary Ellen took some low-fat yogurt from the breakfast bar and poured herself a cup of coffee. That girl would be unrecognizable to anyone who knew her today—pearl-wearing, feet-on-the-ground Mary Ellen, with her tailored jackets and her sculpted hair; her proficiency with PowerPoint and conference room projectors; her command of pharmaceutical positioning statements. She sat down and peeled the top off the yogurt, scraping the underside of the lid with her spoon. She'd done all right for herself in the end, thanks to her parents' wisdom and encouragement.

At her father's funeral last year, someone had said, "You were the best daughter he could have asked for," and it was true. She was, in fact, the *exact* daughter he had asked for. Her father had made a special point of coming to Chapel Hill toward the end of her sophomore year, taking her to dinner at L'Auberge and gently suggesting that it was time to switch to her "real" major. Over a meal of steak au poivre and green beans sprinkled with sliced almonds, he'd wondered aloud whether, given her creative spirit, marketing might be a good fit.

Mary Ellen had seen the wisdom in this right away, had come to her senses without any fuss. Her parents had friends in biotech, so introductions were made and internships were lined up. She'd landed a job at Gallard right after graduation, and now here she was, thirty years later: vice president of marketing, in charge of the world's leading analgesic, Numbitol, a product whose blue-and-yellow caplets brought comfort and relief to millions of Americans every single day.

She left the breakfast room and sat on a sofa in the lobby, marveling at the way life can turn on a moment, a conversation, a dinner, and how utterly unaware you can be while it's happening. Had there been white tablecloths on the tables? Probably. Her father had massaged his earlobe while reading the menu, as he always did, and Mary Ellen had teased him about his suit—always so formal! She was pretty sure she remembered candlelight and wallpaper, but was she making that up to fill the gaps? It felt important to know.

She got up and asked at the front desk if L'Auberge was still around. It was; they would be happy to make a reservation for that evening. She hesitated a moment before agreeing, worried about the other memories, the more recent ones, which would probably intrude on her evening with the girls. But she was pretty good at keeping those thoughts at bay. Besides, tonight wasn't about the past; it was about kicking off an exciting new phase in the girls' lives. It was time to celebrate.

Where were they? She took out her phone and called the room; one of the girls, her voice fogged with sleep, answered after the twelfth or thirteenth ring.

"Are you up?"

"We are now." It was Sydney.

"Get dressed and come to the lobby, all right? It's getting late."

"Why didn't you wake us up?"

"That's what I'm doing."

"No, I mean—" Sydney made an exasperated sound. "Never mind. Goodbye."

It was easier for Matt. He and the girls had sports—the glue that bonded them into a tidy, inseparable package. Ironically, this was Mary Ellen's fault. When the girls were small, back when they still adored her, Mary Ellen had seen athletic activities as a way of leveling the playing field for Matt, giving him an opportunity to connect with the two long-haired, princess-and-pony-obsessed mini Mary Ellens. She was the one who'd signed them up for peewee soccer and volunteered Matt as assistant coach.

But before long, the field had tilted heavily in the other direction, and by the time the girls were twelve, sports had become all consuming. On most weekdays Matt would feed them an early dinner, then take them to practice, and Mary Ellen would come home to a house piled high with the evidence of family life—bulging backpacks, dirty dishes, and great, tangled drifts of shoes—but no actual family.

And in truth, she didn't always hate it, the opportunity to mix a martini in an empty house after a long day of meetings and conference calls. But it had taken its toll over the years. Travel meets, team dinners, scrimmages, summer camps... The distance between herself and her family had widened slowly over time, like the gap between the first two steps of their marble stoop—barely noticeable at first, then more concerning as it filled with ice in the winter and sprouted weeds in the summer, until one day, to Mary Ellen's shock, she came home to find their first step tipped forward onto the sidewalk, a lawsuit waiting to happen.

But really, what was the point in dwelling on the past? She'd made sacrifices, yes, but somebody had to do it. Otherwise, how could this life ever have come to be? Who would have paid for Penn Charter and ski lessons and the trips to Mexico? Who would have bought their five-story row house in Center City Philadelphia and financed the new kitchen and bathrooms? Not Matt, God bless him; his free-lance writing had never even pulled in enough to pay their Whole Foods bill. Instead, he provided man-hours: overseeing the renovations, planning the vacations, taking the girls shopping for book bags, Valentine's Day cards, and cleats.

The arrangement was seldom spoken of, with both of them afraid to upset the delicate balance: Mary Ellen trying to protect Matt's ego, Matt trying to keep anything from changing, which appeared to be his goal in life. And somehow, it worked. At least, it worked better than what Mary Ellen had seen in those families with two working parents: kids raised by nannies, dogs walked by dog walkers, husbands and wives conducting marriages over Skype from hotel rooms and airport lounges.

The elevator chimed and the girls finally emerged, dressed

in their usual sheepskin boots and leggings, mouths slick with lip gloss, jaws working away at wads of gum. "There you are!" Mary Ellen exclaimed. "I thought I was going to have to send a search party."

She hurried the girls through breakfast and into the rental car. Turning onto South Road, she felt her pulse quicken at the sight of the familiar brick buildings and stone walls, the gracious walkways busy with young people. "My freshman dorm was over there!" she exclaimed, pointing toward a tree-lined quad. "And the library... Oh wow, look at all these new buildings." She was disoriented for a moment, until she passed the rec center and the Hanes building. "That's where the art studios were," she said. "Did I tell you I started out as an art major?"

"Yes," the girls answered in unison.

Mary Ellen parked and gestured toward another stately, columned building. "Carroll Hall. Advertising and marketing." She twisted around to look at the girls. "This is where it all began."

"Awesome," said Shelby, her thumb busy on her phone's screen.

"It looks really nice, Mom," Sydney said correctively from the back seat.

Mary Ellen led them up the wide stairs and through the double doors, the girls keeping their heads down, hands stuffed in their pockets, uncharacteristically shy in the presence of so many college kids. "Pretty soon you'll be one of them," Mary Ellen said with a smile, reaching out to tuck a stray lock behind Sydney's ear. Sydney ducked away from her touch.

"Mom, I don't think we're going to take marketing," Shelby said.

"I know. I just wanted to show you where I spent so much of my time when I was here." Mary Ellen looked around, trying to get her bearings amid the hurried throngs of laptop-clutching students. "They renovated," she said. She peeked into a lecture hall where students were watching a video on a large screen. None of it felt familiar; the light was flatter, the ceilings lower, and there was something off about the proportions of the place. She led the girls down another corridor, looking for details to furnish her admittedly vague memories of Intro to Communications Strategy and Product Development 101. "I think I took data management in here," she said, pulling open a door. A bearded man looked up, startled, from his desk. "Oh, excuse me!"

"Mom!"

"Anyway," Mary Ellen said, turning back the way they'd come. "It was all so long ago. Kind of a blur, really." She peered through a few more classroom windows, wondering what, exactly, she was looking for—some heady surge of nostalgia? She'd attended classes here, taken notes, met with her study group, but there was nothing so magical about that. She'd come here wanting to give the girls a sense of the wide-openness of it all—the thrilling expanse of possibility that she somehow associated with her college years. This particular building, with its drop ceilings and fluorescent lighting, wasn't up to the task.

"Let's walk around outside," she said, turning to her daughters who, she realized, were no longer with her. She made her way through the crowd of chattering students, muttering "Excuse me" while scanning for a pair of blond ponytails. She scrabbled in her bag for her phone, feeling a reflexive twinge of maternal worry, but then the crowd thinned and she caught sight of the girls at the other end of the corridor, leaned against a wall, heads bowed like a pair of swans over their screens.

"There you are," Mary Ellen said. In one long, fluid matching movement the girls pulled their gaze up and outward, blackened their screens, and slipped their phones into their pockets. "What are you doing?"

"Nothing."

"What do you say we go somewhere a little more interesting?" She gestured toward the door with her head, and the girls obediently levered themselves away from the wall and followed her into the brassy autumn sunshine.

The lower quad, upper quad, the Old Well, the library. Mary Ellen was relieved to find them all pretty much where she remembered them, still manicured and picturesque. All around them, young people either strode purposefully down the brick walkways or lounged in sunny patches on the walls and stairs. Mary Ellen searched the girls' faces for signs of interest, but they were in full slack-faced camouflage, hiding behind a veil of nonchalance.

She found herself in front of the Hanes Art Center, its brick crenellations and vast window grids a tribute to the factory-obsessed eighties. "Let's take a look at the art studios," she said, not bothering to check if this merited any change in her daughters' facial expressions. She pushed through the glass doors and sunlight followed them in, spreading itself across the floor with proprietary ease.

Mary Ellen climbed the stairs and found an empty studio with a circle of chairs arrayed around a low platform. "Oh," she said, slowly entering the room, her hand on her chest. "I remember this. The models, they would sit there, all…you know." She looked back at Sydney and Shelby and mock-whispered, "Naked!" The girls stared at her curiously. "Well, we didn't see that kind of thing as often as…you know." She waved toward their phones. "It took some getting used to."

"You mean they'd sit there for you to draw?" Sydney asked. "Like, live?"

"Live, yes. It was called life drawing."

The twins furrowed their brows. "I think I'd be too embarrassed to move," Sydney said. "Much less draw."

"Really? It's not so different from a locker room, is it?"

Shelby made a face. "Yeah, but you don't *look*."

"Seriously, Mom, were you dying?"

Mary Ellen shrugged. "It was strange at first, but you just… get used to it. You start drawing, and all this stuff starts to, I don't know, fall away. Your hang-ups." She remembered it so clearly now: the grain of the paper, the charcoal smearing under her damp palm, the way the model's body had floated apart into ridges and knolls and hollows, each shape a landscape unto itself. The frustrating, invigorating debate between her eye and her hand as she groped around for the truth. It was only when she let go of her idea of a torso, her notion of a neck, that she really began to see. "I loved it," she said, running her hand along the back of one of the chairs.

Some students began trickling into the room, so Mary Ellen took the girls down the hall to see the painting studio, a printmaking shop, a small gallery of student work. The air was thick with linseed fumes and the chalky smell of gesso, and Mary Ellen found herself inhaling deeply, every breath alive with memories. Seeing through the skin of the world, curling up inside a fleeting moment, opening herself up to truth—she'd known how to do these things once, or had been learning to, anyway. How strange to live life as two different people, to shed your old self like a skin and emerge in another form altogether. Had it really been that easy?

"Mom, can we go see the gym?"

"Yes, of course, in a minute." Mary Ellen stood in front of an abstract pastel sketch pinned to the wall, studying its composition. Bold, widening beams of color slanted through vertical refractions, the whole thing overlaid with sweeps of bright pink. It was impossibly wild and yet so intelligent, so coherent, like a song about light. Like a magic trick. Mary Ellen never really had the magic the way some of the more talented kids in her classes had, but that hadn't bothered her, somehow. Art was play, it hadn't had a chance to turn serious, and she supposed that was why she'd left it behind so easily—the way she'd abandoned her Lite-Brites and her sticker collection and her ballerina-topped music box.

"Mom?"

But what if she hadn't? What if she'd given it a chance to turn serious—or if not serious, at least meaningful? Who would she be today?

"Yes?"

"Can we go?"

Mary Ellen inhaled deeply, one more time, then reached into her purse for a map of the campus. She had no idea where the gym was.

There were tablecloths at L'Auberge, but they were yellow, not white, and steak au poivre wasn't on the menu. Fortunately, Mary Ellen's gin martini was made right, bracingly cold and dry, so she got a second one while the girls fretted over what to order. She did remember the place, could even recall where she'd sat with her father— near the fireplace, under a large, hazy painting of some

French-looking cows. It was the kind of place her parents loved: quiet, old-fashioned, reassuringly expensive.

Her parents hadn't always gone to these sorts of restaurants. They'd both grown up in blue-collar families and worked their way to the top, the hard way (the *right* way)—her mother a successful rep for a medical device company, her father a partner in his law firm. They'd had Mary Ellen late in life, after being told it was hopeless, and even this miraculous event was understood to be a product of their striving: something to be savored, along with so many other accomplishments, over evening cocktails and little dishes of pistachios.

"Cheers," Mary Ellen said now, raising her nearly empty martini glass. "To your brilliant careers." Sydney and Shelby obligingly lowered their heads and slurped soda through their straws. "And to Gramps, who first brought me here, back when I was a naive sophomore." She tipped her drink back, blinking rapidly.

"This place was here back then?"

"Way back then?" Mary Ellen smiled ruefully. "Yes. Your grandfather brought me here to talk about my future. He wanted to make sure I got the most out of my education." The waiter brought their food, and Mary Ellen looked longingly at Sydney's risotto. "I should've ordered that. I don't know why I got the fish."

"And did you?" Shelby asked.

"What?"

"Get the most out of your education?"

"Well, sure," Mary Ellen said, wondering if her daughters understood that all of this—the college trip, the dinner, their entire way of life—was in some way or another the result of her choices while at UNC. "Once I switched over to marketing, anyway. Which, incidentally, was your grandfather's

31

idea." Mary Ellen took a bite of fish but found it hard to swallow. She had a sudden flashback to that meal, to the steak au poivre, which Daddy had ordered for her. She could remember the way her knife had parted the purplish meat like a scalpel, blood slipping around the edges of the thick, gray sauce and pooling under her green beans. She hated rare meat. She always had.

"Just try to remember," she said, wiping her lips, "that this is your time." She lowered the napkin to her lap and twisted it between her hands. "Don't rush it. And don't be so damn…obedient." The word caught in her throat.

The twins glanced at each other, then down and away.

"I mean, don't be too eager to please. Sometimes I feel like, if you're just trying to do what everybody expects of you, you miss out. Maybe you end up over here"—she jabbed her hand toward the fireplace—"when you would've been a lot happier out there." She pointed out at the patio. "I don't know."

"So you're saying we should let our freak flag fly?" Sydney said, licking her spoon.

"You do you?" Shelby contributed.

"Right. You do you." It occurred to Mary Ellen that this conversation was ridiculous; her daughters' generation considered self-expression and rugged individualism to be their God-given right. They didn't need to be told not to let someone else order their steak. As far as she could tell, they didn't need much of anything—from her, anyway.

"Excuse me, I have to…" She got up and found her way to the bathroom. There was a small love seat in an alcove beside the sinks; she sank down and rested her forehead on one hand. She was remembering more now, not just the bloody steak but the rest—the way Daddy had brought up the cost of tuition. The way he'd warned her against wastefulness. Time, money, connections in Philadelphia... They were all precious, and not hers to squander. "You can draw pictures any time. You don't need a college education for that," he'd said. "Put your creativity into something more useful."

Which was exactly what she'd done. Mary Ellen used her creativity every single day: convening focus groups to study the difference between the words *safety* and *trust*. Drafting a two-million-dollar budget for the point-of-sale rebrand. Assembling PowerPoints. Tallying travel expenses. Spinning tales about her emergence from childhood into this glorious grown-up life.

She leaned her head against the wall and tried to take some deep breaths. These kinds of thoughts had been coming to her more and more since her father's death, and they felt like a terrible betrayal. It was as if something inside her had been set loose, something blackhearted and selfish. If this was the way she grieved, she wanted no part of it.

Of course everyone had regrets; everyone wondered who they'd be if they'd taken the other job, married the other guy, boarded the next train. But there wasn't anything you could do about it—life traveled in one direction. If Daddy were here, he'd tell her to stop her navel-gazing and try taking up tennis. It was unconscionable to use his death as an excuse to wallow in self-pity.

She closed her eyes and pictured her parents in their inflatable easy chairs, spinning slowly across the pool in their modestly landscaped yard on the Main Line, fingers loosely intertwined, navels safely tucked away. If they ever complained about anything, it was swaddled in a thick blanket of tipsy humor. "It was so funny," her mother would chortle, "the way that radiologist was staring at my blouse. The last thing he needed was a new X-ray machine!" Mary Ellen grew up understanding that "so funny" was usually code for something unsavory, but the code protected them, insulating them from prickly revelations that might puncture those floating chairs.

And the truth was, Mary Ellen loved her parents' equanimity; it was something she'd cultivated in herself. Why make life harder than it already was, they'd always said, and they were right. When something had happened with her father's secretary—what, exactly, Mary Ellen would never know—there had been a few evenings without happy hour, when her mother had locked herself in her bedroom and refused to make dinner. But eventually, she'd pulled herself together, and to Daddy's and Mary Ellen's great relief, things quickly returned to normal. In fact, happy hour wasn't just reinstated; it began earlier and lasted longer.

Mary Ellen stood up and looked in the mirror, smoothing her hair and running her fingers lightly under her eyes. The secretary situation had happened during her freshman year of high school, which meant she was now the exact age her father had been at the time. The incident had never been spoken of and was never, as far as she knew, repeated. Always an enthusiastic collector of Audubon prints, Daddy had suddenly decided to take his hobby to a new level, traveling to auctions and visiting dealers every weekend, causing small wrinkles to appear between Mommy's eyebrows when she reviewed the checkbook register. "It's his stress relief," she would sigh, and it was only now that Mary Ellen recognized that some sort of silent bargain had been struck.

It seemed to work; they were happy together for many years. Then Mommy died of a heart attack in her sleep, leaving Daddy alone with his Audubon prints for nearly a decade. He'd seemed content; Mary Ellen had visited him several times a week at first, then on occasional weekends. Things had been so busy around the time of his accident that she hadn't been to the house in nearly a month. The neighbors had called the police when they noticed the newspapers piling up.

Mary Ellen shook her head and washed her hands thoroughly, with lots of soap, and held them under the dryer until her skin began to burn. Don't dwell on it, she told herself for the thousandth time. You'll ruin everything.

She returned to the table, where Sydney and Shelby were engrossed in their phones. She refrained from making a comment about devices at the table, knowing what the answer would be—what it always was. Muddy sneakers in the living room? "Dad lets us." Going to school in pajama pants? "Dad lets us." Oh sure, she'd taken a stand a few times, on the big issues (boys sleeping over, underage drinking), but on the whole, Matt made the rules while Mary Ellen was at the office.

"It's going to be strange when you're gone," she mused, resting her cheek on her fist. "Just me and Dad in that big, old house."

"Less laundry," Shelby pointed out.

"Dad's probably going to try to get you to take up squash or something, so he has someone to coach," said Sydney.

"Ha," Mary Ellen half laughed. "No chance." She picked up a butter knife and polished it with her napkin. "I've been thinking, actually, that I need to do something artistic. Seeing those studios today, I don't know. It brought back a lot of memories."

"Like painting?"

"Maybe." Mary Ellen frowned. "Or photography? There's a class at UArts I've been thinking about." She'd received

35

a brochure about the class a few weeks ago, and after a brief fantasy about becoming one of those artsy continuing education types, she'd tossed it into the recycling. Now, though, it occurred to her that it might be helpful to have a distraction—something tidier than painting, perhaps, but still creative. A chance to reconnect with that long-haired girl she hadn't thought of in so many years.

The twins nodded, then their eyes wandered back to their screens. Mary Ellen sat watching them—the way Shelby's eyebrows pinched together in a way that reminded her of her mother; the way Sydney's cheekbones were beginning to emerge from her face's girlish softness. They seemed so much older than she'd been at this age, so much more complete. Maybe they weren't the exact people she'd expected to end up with, but they were their own people, after all. The best thing she could do for them was to just stay out of their way.

"Will there be anything else?" asked the waiter. The girls looked up from their screens, faces blank. "Dessert?" They shook their heads.

"Thanks," Mary Ellen said, "but I think we're all done."

3

The graduation tassel, Ivy noticed, was hanging at a crazy angle from the rearview mirror, pointing toward the car's back window instead of the floor, like in one of those optical illusion rooms at the carnival. She wasn't sure how the car was managing to hang on to the side of the ravine at this angle, but she figured her only way out of this was to take her foot off the brake and stomp on the gas and hope like hell the car could pull itself back up onto the road.

Ivy sucked in her breath and lifted her foot, but before she could stomp on the gas, the car began to roll, fast, like she was being sucked down the throat of the forest, into its cracking, roaring guts. The back of the car caught on something, but the front insisted on continuing, turning the car across the slope, which, in gravity's view of things, was an inefficient way down. So with a groan, the car heaved onto its side, throwing Ivy onto the driver's side door, dollar-store cookies raining on top of her, and then the roof creased inward as something reached up out of the mountain and put a stop to the slide.

"FUUUCCCKKK." She was curled up on a bed of broken glass, the door handle digging into her hip, her head pushed forward by the bent-up roof. The car made no sense—windows where seats should be, the dashboard sideways, the steering wheel pressing into her thigh. Ivy turned her head slowly, experimentally, and saw red leaves and scraps of white sky through the passenger window. "Fuck," she whimpered, hiccupping with a sort of gasp-sob combination. She pulled her arm out of the glass crumbs and grabbed the steering wheel, hoisting herself into a crouch. The motor was still running, so she found the keys and switched it off. She reached up to the passenger door and pulled on the handle, but she was too far away to push the door up. Lowering one of the armrests in the middle of the seat and bracing her knee against it, she pushed herself upward against the door, which was as heavy as a drunk. She lowered her head and pushed with her upper back, unfolding her body as the door heaved upward into the sky.

Ivy swayed there like a jack-in-the-box for a moment, trying to sort up from down. The car was mashed against a large tree. She couldn't see the road at the top of the brambly slope. The only sound was the rushing water about ten yards below her. No sirens, no shouts, no dogs. Ivy crouched on the remains of the driver's side window and picked some cookies out of the mess, shoving them into her hoodie pocket under her jacket. She found her wallet between the driver's seat and the window. The soda bottle was behind the driver's seat, but she couldn't get her arm past the crumpled roof and couldn't move the seat because the lever was crushed against the door. She tried the passenger seat and managed to get it pushed forward enough to allow her to squeeze her arm into the back of the car and snag the bottle with her fingertips.

Pulling herself out of the car, she dropped to the ground

beside its weirdly upturned belly. She sidestepped down the slope to the creek, which was busying itself among some boulders, oblivious to Ivy's noisy arrival. The water was clear and fast moving; she wondered if it was okay to drink it. She cupped her hands and slurped a little. It didn't taste like mud, so she drank some more. The taste was sharp, metallic. It scraped the sugar from her mouth and chilled her insides. Ivy lifted handful after handful to her mouth until her stomach felt like a balloon. Then she emptied the orange soda bottle, rinsed it, and filled it with more water.

She looked up toward the dirt road, craning her neck to see some sort of break in the slope. It was so steep even the trees couldn't hang on; they were lying all over the place in various states of rot. In some spots, the ground wasn't even the ground. It was more of a wall, stripped free of ferns and leaves, like a freshly scraped knee, roots snaking out of the raw-looking dirt.

She couldn't see the road, but she knew it was up there somewhere, and that it was her only hope of finding her way out of these woods. She wasn't sure what she'd do once she got there, though. Hitchhike to a bus station? Steal another car? The gaping uncertainty—combined with the thought of climbing the steep, muddy slope—wore her out. She decided to walk along the creek until the way up became more obvious.

It wasn't easy; the creek kept eating away at the bank, forcing Ivy up the slope, her thin Converse useless against the sliding leaves and moss, the bottle of water throwing her off-balance. She considered ditching it, but she'd seen plenty of I Survived episodes about people lost in the wilderness after their car broke down or they took a wrong turn hiking. They always wished they had a bottle of water.

Climbing farther up and across the slope, she found a shallow stream sliding thinly, sluggishly toward the creek. She turned to follow the trickle upward, digging her feet into the softened banks. After she climbed for a while, her gaze caught on something silvery: the foil of a cigarette package half-buried in leaves. A little farther on, she found a matted shoelace, then a plastic grocery bag. Ivy stopped walking and looked up the slope. A colorful smear of beer bottles, soup cans, broken toys, batteries, and tampon boxes stretched up the mountainside to the edge of the dirt road. Here and there, trash bags slumped against tree trunks. A few yards from where she stood, facedown in the trickling stream, lay a bloated diaper scrawled with pastel-colored teddy bears, its edges tinged greenish-brown.

"Christ." Ivy gave her water bottle a disgusted look, then dropped it among the trash—happy to be relieved of its weight but not its comfort—and picked her way upstream. A raindrop struck her cheek and slid down, cooler and brighter than a tear; then, a few more tapped lightly on her hoodie. The forest began to tick like a clock, leaves nodding and trembling as water drops struck and rolled their way down.

Where the rise met the road, Ivy had to seek out thick-stemmed ferns and saplings to hoist herself onto the flat track. She lay there facedown in the dirt for a minute, breathing hard, the rain beginning to soak through her jeans. She could hear something ringing out in the distance. Dogs. She raised her head, then got to her knees, but she couldn't tell which direction the barks were coming from. They'd only be using dogs if they thought she was on foot, and they'd only know she was on foot if they'd found the car. If they'd already found the car, she was screwed—it wasn't that far behind. But the dogs sounded so distant she couldn't imagine they had anything to do with her. She wiped her hands on her jeans, got to her feet, and started to walk.

The barking was getting louder, but she couldn't tell if she was closing in on the dogs or the other way around. The dirt track had left the slope's edge to climb over the top of a rise and wind through some scrubby trees. Here and there, bright-red-and-yellow shotgun shells poked out from among the ferns.

She saw movement out of the corner of her eye, off in the tree shadows: something bigger and meatier than a falling leaf or a nodding branch. She stopped to stare into the trees, but the rain was dripping into her eyes, smudging her vision. She stood for a moment, licking water off her top lip, waiting for something more, but aside from the subtle jostling of leaves by the raindrops, the woods were still. She was seeing things.

Ivy hurried on, telling herself to stay cool. She couldn't understand this road, its lack of purpose, its aimless wandering, but one thing was sure—it was taking her closer to the dogs. The track wandered down off the rise, then hopped another small gully and bent around to the left. Ivy slowed at the sight of a rusted-out school bus parked in the trees. The barking was coming from behind it, loud and panicky. She moved to the far edge of the road and took a half step forward to see a house farther back in the trees, behind the bus. It was small, half covered in baby-blue siding, half in pink insulation, a door and two windows punched in its front wall without much ceremony. Two black dogs were springing off the chain-link sides of a pen, raising their chins to bark toward the sky, which rained down echoes over the whole mountain.

The scene reminded her of the half-invisible people living around the edges of Good Hope, where they burned trash in shed heaters and strung up deer hides in their yards like big skin sails. There was a wildness about them that made people nervous. Ma had always warned Ivy to stay away.

Ivy backed up, putting the house out of sight again behind the bus. Moving slowly, she edged into the woods and back down toward the creek, giving a wide berth to the bus and the dogs and the general feeling of redneck meanness hanging in the air.

She was about ten yards down the hill when she heard a man's shout, then the ring of a boot against chain link. The barking trailed off into whines. Ivy plunged straight down the hill, sliding through sodden mats of leaves and hopping over branches. When she got to the creek's mossy bank, she forced herself to turn and look up to the road, but there was nothing to see other than rain-darkened tree trunks and occasional leaves slapping wetly to the ground.

Ivy found a narrow spot in the creek and sidestepped the length of a fallen tree, then hopped over to a rock and a thatch of leaves, and finally just splashed the rest of the way across the creek bed. On the opposite bank, she started running, her jeans wet and heavy, her feet sinking into mud flats and wanting to leave her shoes behind. She was shivering wildly, which made her arms and legs all jerky, and she fell once, then again, her hands and knees sinking into the mush and a low howl escaping her clamped jaw. Then the bank shrank into the slope and she was forced upward once again, scrabbling along the wall of the ravine like a half-stepped-on cockroach.

Finally, she found a wider, more level area leading back to the creek side, and when she got down there, she saw flat rocks lined up in a sort of path. There were No Trespassing signs nailed to trees here and there, and the stones led to the slope and began marching upward in what was definitely a rough staircase. She climbed them slowly at first, then sped up, deciding she didn't care where they went, relieved to be walking on something hard, something regular, something that fought back against the forest's slippery mystery with some kind of good sense.

Above her head, a building loomed out of the hillside like a shoebox about to fall off a shelf. Ivy's eyes were streaming with rainwater, so she couldn't make much of it. When she finally got to the top step, her breath lunging out of her throat in thick, rasping clouds, she wiped the wetness from her face and took a good look.

It wasn't like any house she'd ever seen. It was made of huge boxes that looked like shipping containers, or Dumpsters, stacked on top of each other and wedged into the hillside. The boxes were made of rusted metal, with entire sides cut away and filled with glass. Two long boxes faced one way, and two shorter ones were set perpendicular, at the end, making an L. A wide deck of nearly black wood, no railings, stretched out from the base of the house, ending where the earth dropped away.

Ivy used the last strength in her trembling thighs to climb up onto the deck, then she slowly approached the glass wall of the lower story. Everything was dark and still. She cupped her hands around her face and pressed it against the cold glass. A hard-looking couch. Two armchairs. A row of low, glossy white cabinets covered with books. "What the fuck," she muttered. This house didn't seem to belong in these unruly, wet woods, but at least it didn't appear to be owned by a gun-toting meth addict. Was it empty? Could she steal a few dry, protected moments on that couch?

Ivy followed the deck around to the side, hopped off, and walked up the slope to the front of the upper box, which was bordered by a leveled-off lawn that bled back into the forest a little way from the building. At one end of the main box was a glass door crowned with a rusted metal awning. There was a dirt road off to the left, maybe a driveway, slicked over with wet leaves, a few spindly baby trees poking up here and there. Not much traffic, Ivy guessed. Not lately anyway.

She turned back to the house and tried the front door. Through the glass, she could see a raincoat hanging on a hook and a row of rubber boots and clogs. She shoved the door with her shoulder, knowing it was useless, just shoving out of frustration. The day was edging toward darkness. The awning kept the rain off, but not the gloom.

It didn't have the look of a year-round house. No grill on the deck, no chairs in the grass, no beer can set down and forgotten for a day or two. A settled feeling. Ivy felt around the top of the doorframe, checked the crannies where the awning met the wall. She found a big rock a few yards away and lifted it, pressed her fingers into the crawling dirt underneath. She thought for a moment about just heaving the rock through the glass door, then told herself to be cool, to use her brain. If it was a vacation house, there was probably a key hidden somewhere, right? You wouldn't want to drive all the way from the city and realize you'd forgotten your key.

Ivy focused on the stacked stone foundation, following it along the house to the far corner, where it widened as the ground dipped away. A canoe was tipped against the short side of the house, no paddles anywhere around. There was a gap in the foundation at the corner, where a downspout was pouring water like a faucet. She knelt down to look underneath, but it was too dark to see. She slowly stretched her hand into the darkness, biting her lip as she patted the ground behind the stones. Her hand met something smooth, plastic. A bottle. Vitamin B12. Something metallic rattled inside.

She took out the key and tucked the bottle back where she'd found it. She ran to the door, her hands fluttering, her whole body quaking with cold and hunger and a sudden surge of fear. More than the police, more than the dogs and the shouting mountain man, she felt chased by the darkness, which was bearing down fast.

Inside, she lunged for the light switch. Her breath filled the entryway with clouds of steam. She stripped off her jean jacket and put on the coat that was hanging by the door. Featherlight and plasticky, it didn't do much against the cold. She found a thermostat on the wall and set it to eighty; air started whistling through metal vents in the floor with a smell of burning dust.

The house was wide open and glassy, like a fish tank in the treetops. Some of the floor-to-ceiling windows were on tracks, like sliding doors, with thin, silvery cables stretched across to keep people from falling out. At one end of the L was the kitchen, all red, as slick and shiny as the maraschino cherries Agnes liked to eat out of the jar. Ivy started slamming through cabinets. Pots, pans, plates, glasses, some dried pasta, and a couple of cans. A jar with a picture of a knife spreading chocolate on a piece of white bread. Ivy opened the jar and scooped out some soft chocolate on her finger, then added a finger, digging out huge dollops of the stuff, filling her mouth with thick, sticky gobs. It was like peanut butter, only richer; it was like fur-lined mittens, swimming pools, and twenty-four-carat gold all mixed together. Ivy felt dizzy. She put the jar down and wiped her fingers on a stiff towel. She opened another cabinet and found a box of organic rice crackers, which she ripped open.

Mouth full of crackers, she went through the rest of the drawers and cabinets. There were some mini bottles of tonic, something called wheat beer, and three big bottles of fancy water. There were gadgets—blending things, chopping things, mixing things—like the place was some kind of restaurant. Heavy, rough–looking plates and bowls that didn't stack right, cups and glasses so light and thin you could crush them in one hand. The fridge stood open, dark and silent, a box of baking soda its only inhabitant.

A long, ash-gray wooden table divided the kitchen from the living room; low backless benches ran along the sides. The living room was just as bare, with matching leather couches, like the seats of an old car, facing each other over a plain glass coffee table.

It was weird: these people had money, but no clue how to spend it. If she had the cash, she'd buy the most deliciously fluffy couch she could find, maybe one of those sectionals with the long chair at the end. A couch you could disappear into for hours, wrapped in a thick blanket, watching movie after movie on your big flat-screen.

Ivy went downstairs and rummaged through a closet, where she found life jackets, paddles, and a pair of ugly sandals with nylon straps. No sleds, gloves, goggles, or shovels, though, and no coats either, besides the rain jacket she'd found by the front door. So it was a summer place. That was good. That gave her all kinds of time.

She found her way into one of the bedrooms. The bed faced a glass wall looking into the forest. The sky had gone dark purple behind the trees, turning them into black, feathery silhouettes. Ivy flicked on the light, and the trees disappeared. The room looked a little more lived-in than the other ones: silk flip-flops by the bed, a pearly gray bathrobe hanging on the back of the door. There was a stack of books on one of the night tables, and a long row of them across the top of the white cabinets, their spines stamped with big, one-word names: Duchamp. Twombly. Pistoletto.

She flicked on the light in the bathroom and blinked at her reflection in the mirror. Her pale cheeks and neck were tentacled with wet hair, her forehead streaked with mud, her thin shoulders lost in the black raincoat. She hardly looked like a brazen car thief; more like a drowned rat. Ivy wiped her face with a towel and let the coat drop to the floor. In the bedroom, she pulled open a drawer: plain T-shirts. Another drawer: thin pajama bottoms. She changed quickly, then shrugged on the gray bathrobe.

Still shivering, she pulled the robe tight and sat on the bed, running her hand over the comforter. Like everything else in this place, it was smooth and airy—not like the gritty, pilled blanket on her bed back home. She crawled under the comforter, turning toward the stripe of light coming through the bathroom door. The pillows cradled her head lightly; the blanket settled gracefully over her bones. For a brief moment, her mind flickered with worry, but then she closed her eyes and gave the worry away.

Sometime later, Ivy jolted awake, scrambling to put things together. Her cheek was sweaty against the pillow. She sat up and saw the shape of a person vaguely outlined in the glass wall—her reflection, she realized, after a gut punch of fear. What had woken her up? She wasn't sure if she'd heard a snapped branch or a growling dog, or both, but her pricked senses told her something was moving outside, that it was sniffing at the glass, that it was there for her.

The bathroom light was putting her at a disadvantage— she couldn't see anything outside, while she was on full display—but darkness didn't feel safe either. She sat frozen for a few more minutes, then reluctantly got out of bed and reached through the bathroom door to switch off the light. She crept to one corner of the window and pressed her face against the glass.

It wasn't shadowy darkness or starry darkness or movie-theater darkness out there; it was darkness she could only describe as the end of everything. Nothing and everything compressed over millions of years into a hard chunk of coal that turned itself inside out again and again until it was gone. Ivy got back in bed and hid there, blanket pulled up to her eyes, ears straining and raw. The heat whistling through the floor vents made a hollow, faraway sound. Somewhere upstairs, water dripped onto metal.

Ivy's nighttime fear was quiet, creeping, as shapeless as smoke. It didn't howl or leer or threaten; it didn't shoulder the front door or break bottles outside the window. There was nothing to yell at, nothing to scratch or kick or elbow in the nose. It had no name, no weight, and that made it so much worse than any other fear because it left her powerless and lost. If only she could hear Agnes breathing deeply in the bed next to her; if only Gran were down the hall. If she could just climb into bed next to Colin, tuck herself under his arm, and sway along with his deep, sleepy breathing until the fear went away.

She lay listening for what felt like hours, terror slowly congealing into boredom, then inching toward oblivion.

And then somehow, she was staring dreamily into the skinny pines, the carpet of ferns confettied with morning light. The bed was wide and warm, the room's soft colors slowly waking up along with her. Ivy stretched under the comforter, seeking out cool spots and unclenching her joints. What had she been so scared of? Look at everything that waited for her: a shower, clean clothes, food. She could brush her teeth, pee in a toilet. Nobody knew she was here. The idea that someone or something was lurking outside the glass was crazy; she just wasn't used to the peace and quiet of nature.

She hugged one of the pillows, a bubble of laughter rising in her throat. She'd done it. She was gone, free, nothing but a memory and a story. She imagined the buzz of excitement running through the school hallways: the *oh shits* and the *get the fuck outs*, the muffled laughter outside McFadden's office door. Ivy could always be depended on for entertainment—jumping naked into Brick Pond, flipping off the Southside girls—but this? This would become the stuff of legend. *Remember Ivy? She was bigger than this place. Other people are all talk, but Ivy was different. Crazy, sure, but you gotta hand it to her—the girl had guts.*

Ivy rolled onto her stomach and spread her arms wide, embracing the firm mattress. Beyond the shower and the food lay other possibilities. She'd stay here as long as she could, letting things blow over. Then she'd hitchhike to the nearest bus station and buy a ticket to the most westward point she could afford. The car had been useful, sure, but its New York plates had become a liability, and she had a better shot at disappearing without it. She was going to need money, obviously—$52 probably wouldn't even get her as far as Chicago. But she'd make stops along the way, working at gas stations or walking dogs or panhandling if she got desperate. She felt excitement sparking in her brain once again, the same jittery exhilaration that had come over her when she first roared out of Good Hope in McFadden's car, leaving behind all the sickness and despair, leaping toward the life she was meant for.

She rolled over. For now, she needed to get a handle on her current accommodations. "Stickin' your nose in," Gran would call it when she'd catch Ivy reading a note taped to a neighbor's car or listening out the window to an argument in the street. Ivy knew Gran hated her curiosity. "Keep to yourself and don't borrow trouble," she always said. But Ivy couldn't hear sirens without looking to see which way they were going; she couldn't sit on the bus without trying to figure out who was going to see their parole officer and who was going to family court. That tired-looking lady nodding off while a baby played with her hair—was that the ma, or the grandma? That guy sitting in a nest of empty soda bottles and plastic bags inside his car—was he living there, or just messy? And that girl with the busted-looking weave and stoned half smile—what the hell was she doing with a brand-new iPhone?

The bedroom drawers held shorts, T-shirts, and light-weight cargo pants in colors from beige to gray to off-white. Gap, Banana Republic—rich people's bumming-around clothes, as soft as baby blankets. There weren't any men's clothes to be found, or kids'. The bathroom was stocked with shampoos and soaps and lotions Ivy had never heard of: Aromatherapy Almond-Sage Rinse. Sea Salt–Orange Peel Scrub. Kelp Butter. There was a guitar in the downstairs sitting room, and a basket holding a tangle of cords and adapters for charging just about any device ever made. But as far as she could tell, there was no TV. Anywhere.

It was weird—not just the absence of a TV, but the lack of anything tied to an actual person with a beating heart. Newspapers, ashtrays, embroidered pillows, grocery lists, Hallmark cards, dried-up pens, commemorative shot glasses—none of it. The place was as bare as a rock.

Even the basement was empty, except for a cabinet holding paintbrushes and tubes of paint. Leaning against the wall, under a sheet, were some small and medium-size canvases. Ivy tipped a few of them forward, browsing the pile only long enough to decide that whoever had painted them had a sick sense of humor. It was the kind of stuff Asa would probably like—crazy modern art, not even trying to be good, just trying to be as ugly and in your face as possible. A colorful *fuck you* to the world. She shook her head, wondering what kind of person would be so hard-edged and reserved upstairs, and so pissed off down here in the basement.

She let the sheet drop back over the paintings, then went up to the kitchen. She took all the boxes and cans of food out of the cabinets and spread them on the counter. She pushed the packages around, grouping them, thinking them over. She could probably do okay for a month, getting by on pasta and beans and a couple of crackers a day, with a little of that chocolate spread to take the edge off. There were two granola bars per packet; she could eat half a bar for breakfast every other day, and they'd last her for twenty days. Just enough time for them to call off the search.

She walked along the windows, scanning the woods in all directions. No other houses to be seen; no roads either. She went downstairs and rummaged through the clothes, pulling out the warmest outfit she could find. Everything was too big, but she rolled up the pants and tucked the shirt in the waistband. She tugged on her hoodie, then her jean jacket, still damp, on top of that. Upstairs, she put on a pair of rain boots.

Outside, she tucked her hands under her armpits and circled the house, then walked into the woods for a bit, scanning for signs of neighbors. There weren't any other houses around, but No Trespassing signs seemed to form some kind of boundary around the house. After passing the signs, she caught sight of something square, wooden, and man-made through the hemlocks. It was some kind of platform with plywood walls, nailed into the crotch of a tree. Ivy wondered if it had been put there by kids living nearby, but when she climbed into the wooden box, she found crushed beer cans, an empty shotgun-shell box, and a jerk-off magazine. Hunters.

She jumped out of the tree house and went back the way she'd come. When she got to the Dumpster house, she headed up the driveway, which switched back and forth a few times up the steep hill—long detours that Ivy avoided by cutting straight up the slope. She stopped a few times to catch her breath, looking down toward the house, which was disappearing among the pines. After twenty or thirty minutes, as she was starting to wonder how long a driveway could be before you had to just call it a road, she heard what sounded like a car. She climbed some more, and soon she was sure of the sound: tires on asphalt.

The spot where the driveway joined the road was steep and hidden in the brush. A large tree off to one side was studded with red reflectors and a house number, 1465. Ivy stepped behind the tree and peeked out at the road, which had a narrow shoulder and only one middle line. As she stood there, two pickup trucks passed. Their breeze washed over her warm face, and she felt some of the worry lift from her shoulders. This was a road that was going somewhere. It led to dollar stores and soup kitchens, to gas stations and pay phones, to a place where she could get in touch with Asa, just to let him know she was okay and find out what everyone was saying.

Ivy ran her hand over the tree trunk. It was craggier than a pine tree, the bark deeply creviced and glazed with pale-green flakes. She looked up into its branches, which bowed sturdily over her head. She wasn't cold anymore. She reached around the trunk and grabbed a reflector, dug her fingertips under its edges, and pulled. It came out of the bark easily. She pulled the next one out, then the third, then pried away the four digits of the house number. She wound up like a pitcher, leaned back, and threw the numbers as hard as she could into the brush.

4

Mary Ellen returned to Philadelphia from UNC with a renewed passion for her work. Or if passion wasn't the right word, *determination*—to make the best of the lot life had handed her, at least until her retirement funds were vested.

After a few weeks of forced enthusiasm for a logo project she knew was nothing more than a year-end budget-hedging spree, Mary Ellen's determination began to wane. Getting out of bed in the morning felt like pulling herself out of a tar pit. She found herself putting off projects until the last minute, which was completely unlike her. On her way to her office, she would rush past her team's cubicles, avoiding eye contact, pretending to be too busy to stop and talk. When her assistant brought her a mug of tea without being asked and awkwardly reached out to pat her hand, Mary Ellen knew something had to change.

"You need a hobby" would have been her father's advice, so she decided to look into evening classes. The University of the Arts Continuing Ed program offered a number of photography courses, but by the time she got around to registering, there was only one class with any seats left: Agency and Intentionality in a Post-Representational World.

The class was mostly theory, with a long and intimidating reading list, but this suited Mary Ellen's needs perfectly. She bought a pack of colorful highlighters and used them to illuminate her texts. She came to class prepared with lists of questions and did her best to apply the theory to her weekly photography assignments. Whenever the teacher mentioned an art show she liked, Mary Ellen would make a point of going to see it over the weekend.

She also bought a journal—something she hadn't done in years. In college, Mary Ellen had bought and filled dozens of the little books, her mind spilling over with ideas and musings. But after graduation, when she started her job, keeping a journal began feeling like a chore, so she'd stopped. Now it felt strange, writing to herself. She barely recognized her own voice on the page. But as the reading assignments in her photography class became more challenging, Mary Ellen found it helpful to take her swirl of thoughts and press them between the pages of the little leather-bound book, where they became more manageable.

The teacher of the course was a fiftysomething woman named Justine who mesmerized Mary Ellen with her effortless aura of cool. She would come to class wearing crumpled suede boots and drapey greige sweaters and uncompromising black-framed glasses. She'd throw down her worn leather satchel, sit on the edge of a desk, and launch into wearily bemused stories of art-world squabbles, scandals, and multimillion-dollar deals. She knew everyone, read everything; she was constantly attending unadvertised art "happenings" in abandoned subway stations and electrical plants.

Mary Ellen would sit in the front row, puzzling over the frayed hem of Justine's sweater, the almost invisible edge of gray in her part, the Chanel logo on her glasses. She wondered if Justine ate dinner before or after class, out or in, with wine or beer, or a cocktail first and then wine. She'd mentioned she was divorced, so did she go to all those gallery openings alone, with friends, on a date? Mary Ellen tried to imagine Justine running a mundane errand, like getting her driver's license renewed. Would she leave the house in yoga pants? Did she own yoga pants?

Mary Ellen studied Justine as carefully as she studied the books and articles on the class syllabus. Justine, on the other hand, paid Mary Ellen scant attention, only occasionally offering individual critiques in which she encouraged Mary Ellen to crop, overexpose, and blur her pictures into abstraction. Mary Ellen took this advice, not always understanding it, but determined to ace the class—at least metaphorically, since there were no actual grades given out.

She noticed that Justine responded most to pictures that Mary Ellen could only describe as ugly or disturbing, so she would spend her weekends and lunch hours searching the city for the right sort of subject matter: broken glass, cigarette butts, a pigeon flattened in the middle of the street. She would import the pictures into Photoshop and make them even uglier, tinting them yellow-green, for example, or stripping out the color altogether. Sometimes she would zoom in on an arbitrary corner of the photo, reducing it to nothing more than a few abstract pixels, which she would name after the original picture: "Pigeon, Market Street."

It wasn't until the end-of-semester student show that Mary Ellen actually seemed to register on Justine's radar. A woman who introduced herself as Birgit Paulson, owner of a small gallery, stood for a long time in front of Mary Ellen's three photographs—colorless, heavily manipulated compositions—and began asking Mary Ellen questions about her process and her portfolio. Justine hurried over and volunteered that Mary Ellen's portfolio was actually "very interesting," and that Mary Ellen would be happy to show it to her any time.

"She's major," Justine breathed in Mary Ellen's ear after Birgit walked away. "A very connected gallery in Fishtown. This could be really good for you."

"But I don't have a portfolio."

"You will. We just need to buy some time."

Justine's way of buying time, it turned out, involved introducing Mary Ellen to everyone she knew—a blitzkrieg of buzz generation. Justine explained that while word was filtering back to Birgit that Mary Ellen was making the rounds, Justine would suddenly become too busy to arrange an actual meeting. "Trust me," she told Mary Ellen, "by the time you have some work ready, she'll be throwing herself at us."

Mary Ellen considered the whole thing laughably far-fetched, but she was enjoying Justine's attention, and she felt privileged to gain entry to her world—a place where people talked about things other than sports and real estate, and where important business was conducted at midweek parties in fringy neighborhoods.

The party where she found herself one unseasonably warm November evening was being thrown by Justine's friend Peter, a filmmaker and naturalist, and was billed as the perfect opportunity for Mary Ellen to meet all the right people who knew people who probably knew Birgit. Peter lived in a trinity—one of those tiny Philadelphia row homes with one room on each floor, from basement kitchen to roof deck, strung together by a treacherously steep winding staircase. Perfectly fine for a single man, Mary Ellen thought as she squeezed through the front door behind Justine, but not great for a crowd; a firetrap, really. She craned her neck to see if there was a rear exit, but the lighting was dim and Justine was pulling her impatiently through the mass of bodies.

Justine stopped in front of a generously bearded man. "This is Mary Ellen," she shouted to be heard over the other people in the room, who were also shouting. "My latest project. She's a photographer. Mary Ellen, this is Peter."

"Hey," said Peter, taking Mary Ellen's hand and holding it for a beat longer than was comfortable. "I love a good project, especially coming from Justine. You must be one to watch."

"Oh, she's just being nice," Mary Ellen said with an embarrassed laugh that stopped when she caught Justine's eye.

"Justine never does anything just to be nice," Peter said, fondly bumping his shoulder against Justine's forearm. "Help yourselves to drinks. They're in the kitchen, down those stairs."

No, of course, Mary Ellen thought, following Justine toward the stairway in the corner. Justine was anything but "nice." Selectively generous with her time and opinions. Aggressively sociable under the right circumstances. But nice?

In fact, it was Justine's not-just-being-nice intensity—her *rigor*—that had jolted Mary Ellen out of her post-college-visit malaise. Taking Justine's class had made her feel challenged and stimulated in a way she'd only felt in college, or perhaps in the early days of her career, when she was still trying to prove herself. Her mind buzzed with movements, theory, vocabulary; she found herself questioning everything she'd always thought about art, architecture, literature, even music. It was thrilling, and a little scary, like riding in a car that someone else was driving much too fast.

When they got to the kitchen, Justine became absorbed in

an urgent conversation about tenure politics, so Mary Ellen headed for the bar, where she was grateful to find a bottle of decent gin among the warm Pinot Grigios and Chardonnays. She took her time plucking softening ice cubes from the sweating bucket, squeezing a lemon wedge over them, pouring the gin, relishing the bottle's familiar heft, wishing there was a real glass instead of the sharp-edged plastic cup.

She shook the cup, lapping the gin over and around the ice cubes for a moment, then drank. Sweet and bitter, the first sip always burned a little, alcohol rising like campfire smoke into her head while the liquid plunged into an icy pool at the bottom of her empty stomach. She stood facing the bar for a moment, pretending to examine a wine bottle. The whole idea of interacting with strangers at a party seemed like an unnecessary exertion for someone her age— like running, which she'd taken up a few years ago, when she turned forty-five, and which had resulted in severely strained Achilles tendons.

When she was in college, she'd been more supple, more motivated. She'd pushed her way boldly through crowded rooms, cheerfully accepting the keg-pumping services of whatever young man was ready to fill her red cup, smiling easily, sometimes even dancing. But parts of her had stiffened over the years, including her smile, which, when she posed for pictures, felt like a forced cracking open of her face.

She turned around; Justine was gone. The kitchen was crowded with clusters of laughing people. She studied some postcards stuck to the stainless-steel refrigerator door with tape.

"Sorry…" Peter had materialized next to her, struggling to hold three six-packs of beer in his arms. "Can you open that for me?"

"Oh. Sure." She held the door while Peter rearranged

bottles in the fridge. "So how do you know Justine?" she asked, averting her eyes from the crusty assortment of condiments inside the fridge door.

"I met her at Starbucks, which is funny, because neither of us ever goes there, but we were both waiting for the bathroom." Peter pulled out some Tupperware containers, peered through their sides, set them on the floor. "She started interrogating me about my life. I think we talked for thirty minutes before we realized there wasn't anybody in the john."

"Oh, I hate that," Mary Ellen said. "When there's a line for the bathroom, and everyone thinks there's someone inside, but then someone walks up and pulls extra hard on the door, and you realize you've all been believing in something that isn't there."

"Organized religion!" Peter said. "Okay, these have to go." He stood up with the Tupperwares in his hands, looking hassled. "I don't have time to empty these." He went to the trash and stomped on the pedal to open the lid.

"Wait!" Mary Ellen said. "Don't throw away all your containers. Let me empty them for you."

"Really?"

She swallowed the rest of her gin, set down her cup, and reached for the containers. Peter shrugged and handed them to her. "Thanks, dear."

Mary Ellen found a spoon and began scraping the food into the trash. It felt strangely intimate, interacting with the graying remains of what she supposed had been dinners for one, perhaps eaten in the glow of the television, or on the counter with a magazine held open by the edge of the plate: half a chicken breast with a few limp spears of asparagus; a sticky, congealed bean salad; some lumps of meat in a rubbery sauce that smelled like death. She threw herself busily into the task.

"What are you doing?" hissed Justine, who had reappeared.

"Helping Peter clean out his fridge."

"No. Stop. Come with me. You need to meet people."

"Let me just wash these—"

"No." Justine took the containers and threw them into the sink.

"I need another drink then."

Once Mary Ellen had resupplied herself with gin, she and Justine carefully wound their way back up to the living room. The crowd had swelled, making it even more difficult to maneuver. "Richard!" Justine called, leading Mary Ellen toward a tall man who seemed to be draining a beer bottle in a single swallow. "Richard, I want you to meet someone. Mary Ellen is a photographer."

Richard lowered the bottle and wiped his mouth with the back of his hand. "Hi. What kind of work?" he asked.

"Um," Mary Ellen said, looking at Justine.

"Representative abstraction," Justine said. "Very Siskind-esque."

"Ah," Richard said, nodding. "Did you know there's a really good Siskind in that group show at Strike Collective?"

"I've been meaning to go," said Justine. "Doesn't Alexandra have a piece there?"

"Yes, that big collage she was working on for so long. It's good—a real takedown of all that faux Arte Povera stuff that's been going around."

"Oh, I know—did you see that Dominetti show—"

"In Barcelona? Shameless."

Mary Ellen did her best to follow the conversation, making mental notes of names to Google later. She wondered what it was like, being an art person, understanding the references encoded into every piece of work, having well-informed opinions about what was good and what was bad. Since starting Justine's class, she'd come to realize how shaky her own frame of reference was. Whether she "liked" something, whether she found it pretty or skillful or pleasing in some way, turned out to be completely beside the point.

Richard was poking Justine's shoulder. "By the way, I heard something juicy about you," he said.

"Oh God. What?"

"Lina Burns saw you at Blick. Buying *paint*."

"Not true."

"Come on," Richard growled. "Oils, for Chrissake. What's going on?"

"Lina Burns doesn't know what the fuck she's talking about," Justine said, crossing her arms.

"Well, I hope it's true. I asked what colors you bought, but she couldn't tell."

"That's because Lina is color-blind."

"Don't be mean."

"I'm not painting, and if I were, I wouldn't tell you."

"So you *are* painting."

"Hey, is that Erica?" Justine waved at a woman across the room and rushed off, leaving Mary Ellen and Richard alone together.

"So." Mary Ellen swirled the melting ice in her cup. "How do you know Justine?"

"I taught with her at Tyler," Richard said, holding his bottle up to the light. "Before she was let go. I'm going to get another beer. Do you want one?"

"I'm okay, thanks."

Having lost sight of Justine, and needing to look purposeful,

Mary Ellen moved toward the stairs. As she picked her way up the spiral to the second floor, her mind coiled around the conversation she'd just heard. Was Justine a secret painter? What sort of art? Hadn't she said that artists and teachers never intersect? Could someone like Justine—someone who knew so much—ever be satisfied with her own work? Did she really get fired from Tyler?

Mary Ellen found a table of drinks in Peter's study on the second floor. The gin was making her thoughts loose and uncoordinated, but she was actually enjoying the exotic whirl of uncertainty, and she celebrated by pouring heavily this time. She turned around and found herself standing at the edge of a small clump of people. She shifted slightly to the left in order to position herself in front of an opening, and like magic, they parted, enlarging their circle, smiling and asking what she thought about GMOs.

It was starting to feel kind of good—being at a party, meeting new people, standing in a room with red walls and a handsome oak desk, with terrariums on the windowsill and books stacked both upright and sideways on the jumbled shelves. Justine was like her fairy godmother; she'd pulled her from the ashes of middle age and brought her to the ball.

Not that she and Matt never went to parties—of course they did. But usually they were out on the Main Line, where so many of their friends had decamped after having their kids and making their money. Outdoor sofas and crab canapés. Wine that sparkled and conversation that didn't. They would drive home feeling groggy and satisfied, the way you do after Thanksgiving dinner. That was nice, they'd say. Harry seemed happy; has he lost weight? Amy sure is obsessed with mulch. I wonder where Caroline was; did someone say she's in Sedona? Maybe we should go to Sedona.

Now Mary Ellen was chatting with someone she'd never met before about hydrofracking. A girl in braids was organizing a march on Harrisburg; the crowd was going to lie down and play dead on Commonwealth Avenue. Mary Ellen promised to join them, knowing full well it was happening on a day she had to go to Cleveland for focus groups. But tonight anything seemed possible—even being in two places, or being two people, at once.

She decided to see what was on the third floor. She excused herself and refilled her glass, then wound upward, her hand on the wall, uncomfortably aware of the way the steps were vanishing down the center of the spiral behind her. The stairs delivered her to Peter's bedroom, where three people were lying on his bed smoking, and others were leaning against the floridly papered walls. Up here, everybody seemed limp, slumped, in need of support. A purple satin dressing gown hung from a black iron hook. The windows were slathered in velvet.

Mary Ellen sat for a moment on the end of the bed, careful not to touch the bare feet of the people lying behind her. She felt hungry, but the food was all the way down in the basement, underground, as far as possible from this lush aerie. The people on the bed were murmuring and laughing softly. Did they want privacy? Mary Ellen began mustering the strength required to stand back up, but then a man sat next to her, causing the end of the bed to dip alarmingly.

"Hello."

"Hello."

He was handsome, and he was looking her square in the face. Mary Ellen felt heat gather in the top of her head. Had she invited this? What was happening? The man kept looking at her, his expression unchanging; he seemed to be waiting for her to take off her blouse. Smoke billowed around her face, stinging her eyes. She waved it away "So how do you know Peter?" she asked.

"Who's Peter?"

"The person whose bed we're sitting on."

The man put his hand on the mattress and leaned on his arm. The arm was remarkably hairy. "I think he's friends with my wife."

"Oh." Mary Ellen looked around to see if there was an angry woman glaring at her. "Is she here?"

"Why do you ask?"

"Um…" Mary Ellen drained her cup. The man was wearing cologne, indicating that he was either foreign or from South Philadelphia. Mary Ellen was reminded that she liked men who wore cologne. Cologne was aggressive; it stuck to you, like a flag that had been planted in your soil.

The man pulled out a pack of cigarettes. "Would you like one?"

"No thank you." Mary Ellen hadn't seen this many people smoking since the eighties. And in bed, no less! Matt was going to be horrified by the smell. Not just of cigarettes, but of this man's assertive aroma, which seemed to be extending its long fingers into her clothes and her hair. What was she doing?

She should have invited Matt, even though he would've hated this party. Matt didn't wear cologne. He showered often, though—sometimes more than once a day—so he always smelled like Ivory soap. There had been a time, before the girls came along, when Mary Ellen and Matt had taken a lot of those showers together. Twin babies had put a stop to that a long time ago. Just the thought of all that slippery nakedness was laughable to Mary Ellen now, especially with all the sagging and wrinkling that had happened under her thick terry bathrobe. Mary Ellen's modesty, she'd long decided, was her contribution to their marital equilibrium.

On the far side of the room, a small door opened, and a blur of bodies streamed into the bedroom. The door appeared to lead to a balcony, but the number of people coming through it seemed wildly out of proportion with the size of any balcony she'd ever seen. "I think I need some air," she said. "Nice to meet you." The man shrugged.

The balcony turned out to hold a spiral staircase, which led to a roof deck. Mary Ellen contemplated the twirling open ironwork and wondered if it was up to code. Up above, she could hear music and laughter, so curiosity got the better of her and she slowly, bravely made her way to the roof.

At the top, Mary Ellen hugged herself against the chill and tried to get her bearings in the sudden soaring openness. Peter's house was in the middle of a long line of row houses, with another row backing up to it, and every house was topped with a roof deck, and every deck, it seemed, was having a party. Strings of glowing bulbs stretched from roof to roof, gathering everyone in a warm net of light as a shared soundtrack thumped from speakers two or three doors down. Beyond the rooftops, to the southwest, the towers of Center City pronged brightly into the sky, shrunk by distance to the same height as Peter's neighborhood. A man in a flannel shirt poured something dark into Mary Ellen's empty cup. She sipped. Bourbon. Well, why not.

Conversations were flowing all around her. Mary Ellen found herself slipping easily into one, and then another, even managing to say funny things, relevant things, to actually *contribute* to the muscular give-and-take. At the same time, she was becoming aware of a sluggishness in the mechanics of her eyes, requiring a concentrated effort to crank each face into focus as she turned from person to person, although she was pretty sure it wasn't noticeable to anyone but herself. She formed her words with care, coordinating her lips and tongue with precision—or if not precision, composure. She found herself talking a lot about her photography ("I'm inspired by the work of Siskind"), and this spun off into declarations about the aesthetics of film, and the rigor of delayed gratification, and the degradation of photography as an art.

"Are you saying digital technology is killing the art form?" This was from a girl with long bangs wearing high-waisted pants and a batwing-sleeved sweater. She was too young to be dressing this way out of nostalgia, but the outfit was definitely bringing back a lot of memories for Mary Ellen, who suddenly longed for her favorite pair of fold-over-waist jeans.

"I'm just saying there's so much faux seriousness out there these days, with the filters and the automatic selective focus and all that," Mary Ellen replied. "It's cheapening photography."

"Well," said the girl, "I'm not saying art history is irrelevant. I mean, yeah, studying the masters helps you situate your point of view." She tossed her bangs out of her eyes. "But to me, the democratization of technology has radically energized the art of photography. It's the institutions who are so heavily invested in outdated taxonomies and disciplinary structures—the galleries and museums profiting from a…a… *freeze-dried* conception of the photographic canon—who've been cheapened."

Mary Ellen folded one arm against her stomach, using it to support the arm holding her cup aloft. She squinted at the girl, trying to sort the words she'd just heard into their proper order so she could figure out how to respond to them. Did she say taxidermy? "I thought you said taxidermy," Mary Ellen exclaimed, laughing. "Did you say taxidermy?"

"No."

Someone cranked the music up then, and a tidal wave of bass surged across the roof decks. Mary Ellen could feel it hit her chest; she felt it curl around her hips. The flannel-shirt-wearing, bourbon-pouring guy started bobbing in front of her, nodding his head to one side, then the other, shoulders slumped, hands limp. Mary Ellen bobbed along with him, enjoying this low-commitment style of dance. They were just letting the music flow through them, sharing a rhythmic urge, being in the moment, no pretense, no irony. Mary Ellen closed her eyes and swayed her hips, but this made her dizzy. She opened them, stumbled a little, laughed. Other people were dancing now; nobody was looking at her. The music was dark and nasty, full of strange vocals and dirty hooks.

Mary Ellen's shoulders started getting into it; her arms began pulsing at her sides. When was the last time she'd danced? Her niece's wedding? That hadn't felt like this; this was different. This moment—the music, the net of light, the sky, the freedom to move however she wanted—was transformative. It was as though she'd split down the sides and wriggled out of herself, the real Mary Ellen finally set loose on the world.

Suddenly, she found herself dancing in front of Justine. Where had she come from? "Where did you come from?"

"Over there. Having fun?"

"Are you kidding? Look at me. I'm dancing!"

"Yes, you are."

"Thank you." Mary Ellen paused her dancing and brushed her hair from her forehead. "For bringing me. And everything else. Teaching me all that stuff, helping me with Birgit." She took a drink. "I just wish I had more time for taking pictures, you know? Work—" She flapped her hand in the direction of Center City. "Ugh."

"Forget work." Justine pointed a finger at Mary Ellen's chest. "It's time to start shooting. You need to *produce.*"

"I know. It's just such a crazy time of year—"

"Aaahhh." Justine waved her hand impatiently. "I hate when people say that. It's always a crazy time of year. Take a sabbatical!"

"A sabbatical? Lord, they would kill me. We're launching this new positioning platform. You have no idea what a big deal it is. We're shifting from the word 'safety' to the word 'trust.'" Mary Ellen peered down into her cup, shaking her head, then suddenly looked up and laughed. "Oh my God, is that the stupidest thing you ever heard?"

"Well, you can't get anything meaningful done in your spare time. You'll never get the momentum you need. I think you should take some time off…at least a week or two."

"I don't know," Mary Ellen said. "I've never done anything like that." Justine's determination was making her nervous. She seemed to think she could conjure a serious photographer out of thin air with nothing but the power of her will. "Can I ask you something?"

Justine leaned against the deck railing and raised her eyebrows.

"I guess I don't…I don't really get how the gallery business works. The commission part of it. Are you…?"

"What?"

"What's your… I mean, what's in it for you?"

"I'm not getting a cut or anything. Don't worry." Justine pulled her hair into a ponytail and let it go. "I did really well in my divorce. I just teach to keep from going crazy. And sometimes I see someone who could use a little mentoring, a leg up."

"Oh. Well, thank you."

"And to tell you the truth…" Justine turned and looked

over the railing to the street below. Then she turned back to Mary Ellen. "Some people in this town have been acting like I've been put out to pasture or something, and that's bullshit. I hated teaching at Tyler. I was so glad to get out of there. Tyler was not the reason my students did well. *I* was the reason."

"I'm sure—"

"Put me anywhere. Put me at UArts, put me at the fucking Art Institutes, I don't care. I can still find opportunities. Women, minorities—" She extended a hand toward Mary Ellen. "People in different...age brackets. I can find the voices nobody is listening to. I can help them be heard. I don't need to be part of the elite art school establishment to do that."

Mary Ellen smiled uncertainly, absorbing this new information. Was she a minority? Was Justine insecure? "I can't believe anyone would doubt you," she said. "That's—"

"I know. So listen." Justine pushed herself away from the railing. "I have a place you could use. For a week or two, whatever you can manage."

"Really?"

"It's a pretty great mountain house. I got it in the divorce. It's north of the Poconos, at the top of a ravine overlooking a creek. There's no TV, no internet, no cell service. It's just you and the woods. I think it would be the perfect place to hunker down and work on your ideas."

Mary Ellen looked around. The thread of the beat was still weaving itself through her chest, stitching her to the other dancers, pulsing through them all like the tides, like the dawns, like the impatient swell and collapse of life itself. She didn't want it to end, and Justine seemed to be telling her it didn't have to. "Did you say there's no cell service? Is there a land line?"

"No. Nothing. I'm telling you, a lot of people would kill for the chance to stay there. I usually don't invite anyone."

"Well, in that case!" said Mary Ellen with a laugh. She took a drink, wondering if this was all too good to be true. It probably was.

"So you'll go?"

"I don't know. Fine, yes. Why not!" Mary Ellen laughed again, feeling the urge to dance some more.

"Great. This is good." Justine tapped her upper lip with her index finger. "Just make sure you stay in the same abstract, textural zone, okay? You'll want to try to develop a visual vocabulary, which will be easier in a limited environment. In the meantime, I'll work on finding a large-format printer. We need to print everything *huge*...the bigger the better."

"Okay." Mary Ellen started bobbing up and down again, but Justine beckoned her toward the iron staircase. Mary Ellen sighed and followed her. At the top of the stairs, she paused, holding on to the railing with both hands, hesitating to lower herself onto the first step, which seemed to be miles away. A group of people was lining up behind her, like kids at the top of a water slide, so she had no choice but to proceed. As she went down, her heels kept getting caught in the ironwork, which was pierced with heel-size slits. She tried not to put any weight on her heels but kept forgetting, so she had to jerk her feet upward to free them each time they got caught. The stepping-down and jerking-up combination was confusing.

They finally made it to the balcony, then through the door to the bedroom. Justine took Mary Ellen's hand and brought her through a crowd of people standing at the foot of the bed, then led her to the stairs. Mary Ellen ran her hand along the wavy plaster wall to steady herself as she followed

Justine to the second floor. "I've decided it's time to make some changes," she said to Justine's back. "I've known that for a while, but tonight things kind of came into focus for me, you know?" On the second floor, people were crowded around one of those tall Middle Eastern pipe things, sucking smoke from a long hose. Mary Ellen paused and stared, swaying a little, then hurried after Justine, who was winding her way down the next set of stairs.

"My daughters don't need me anymore, my job feels pointless, and I don't know... I think I ended up on the wrong path somehow." She was feeling tired, suddenly. These stairs were exhausting, with their triangular treads, which required you to aim so precisely with your foot, lest you land on the narrow part with your big, not-so-narrow foot and plunge over the edge. The thought made Mary Ellen dizzy. She paused and leaned against the wall, trying to stop the spinning, but even though she was very still, the stairway continued to rotate around her, a little wobbly on its axis, like a bent bike wheel. "Justine?" Mary Ellen carefully lowered her right foot to the next step, but despite her best effort, it ended up on the narrow part of the triangle and skidded out from under her, and she slid down the next three or four steps, her calves like skis.

"Whoa!" said a man who was coming up the stairs as Mary Ellen came to a stop on her bottom, bourbon fumes rising off her chest, which felt wet. She set her empty cup on the step and realized the person talking to her was the cologne-wearing man from the bedroom. He held out his hand. "Can I help?"

"I'm fine."

But he'd already taken her by the arm and was helping her down the rest of the stairs, gently guiding her as if she were elderly or recovering from surgery. "I'm fine," she repeated, when they reached the ground floor. She pulled her arm away and looked around for Justine. "I've got to get going."

"You're sure you're all right?"

"Of course I am," Mary Ellen said impatiently, heading for the front door. "I'm just going to call my husband." She paused and looked back at the man, whose thick, black eyebrows were drawn together. "My *husband*," she repeated. "I'm married."

"Yes, ma'am," said the man, and he raised his first two fingers to his forehead, giving her a salute. Under normal circumstances, this would seem like a friendly, slightly goofy send-off, but through her drunken haze, Mary Ellen understood that she was being made fun of. She whirled around, lost her balance, and grabbed on to a girl standing by the door.

"Sorry. Sorry." Mary Ellen managed to get herself out the door and onto the front sidewalk, where she found Justine.

"Everything okay?"

"I'm fine," Mary Ellen said, fumbling with her phone. "I just feel kind of mixed up. I don't think I belong here."

"Sure you do." Justine took out a cigarette and lit it. "You just need to go home and sleep it off. Do you want me to call you a cab?"

"No thanks," Mary Ellen said, sinking onto the stoop. "Matt'll come get me." Her uncomplaining chauffeur, her tether to the real world. She suddenly longed to see his face.

"Okay, well, we'll talk," Justine said. "Let me know what dates you want the house, and I'll make sure someone comes to plow the driveway."

Mary Ellen nodded. "CALL MATT," she barked at her phone.

"Calling Matt," the phone answered equanimously.

When she looked up, Justine was halfway down the block, nothing but a tall, thin shadow punctuated by a languidly moving, bright-orange speck of fire.

5

Ivy took one of the backpacks out of the closet and put a bottle of water in there, along with some clean clothes, a half-gone bar of grapefruit-scented soap, her shoes, and a map she'd found in the kitchen drawer. She took down the flying deer newspaper clipping, which she'd taped above her bed, and slid it back into her wallet. She layered a couple of shirts under and over her hoodie and jean jacket, pulled the rubber boots over three pairs of socks, pulled another pair of socks over her hands, and headed up the frost-bleached driveway to the road.

She hadn't come close to waiting the twenty days she'd originally decided on, but it turned out she sucked at rationing food. She also sucked at keeping her thoughts under control. She'd started obsessing over the scene back home—what people were saying at school, what everyone thought about her wild lunge at freedom. Were people laughing at McFadden? Were rumors flying about Ivy—where she was, what she was doing? Did people finally understand what she was made of? It was like a bad rash, the itch to know, and the more she scratched at it, the more it drove her crazy.

Behind those thoughts were other, sneakier thoughts—that

maybe, if people back in Good Hope had a newfound appreciation for her, it wouldn't be so terrible to go back and start fresh. Sure, she'd get in trouble, but if she turned herself in, it wouldn't be so bad. It couldn't be worse than this—being stuck all alone in a glass box for days on end, trying not to eat all the food but lacking anything else to occupy her brain. If she had someone else around to talk to, maybe it wouldn't be so hard. But as it was, she was getting pretty damn tired of listening to nothing but her own thoughts day in and day out.

She'd looked at the map and decided to head for a town called Eaton, southeast of Forks and a few miles from 84. It looked big enough to have a bus station. She'd buy a little food, see how much she had left for bus fare, then call Asa to find out what was going on.

She got up to the road and went left, which seemed like the right way, based on her guesswork with the map. She crossed to the other side, and when she heard a car coming up from behind, she stripped a sock off one hand and held out her thumb, walking backward, trying to look friendly but not stupid. "Come on," she muttered as the car slowed and a middle-aged woman peered curiously at her. After meeting Ivy's eye, the woman jerked her eyes back to the road and sped off. Another car did the same, then a pickup truck. Ivy knew how she looked, with all the layers and no coat, oversize rubber boots, a sock on one hand. Not like a local high school girl headed to her boyfriend's house, someone you could chat with about Friday's game, then say, "Tell your momma I said hi," and "Call me if you want a ride back home." The only person who was going to pick Ivy up was somebody who liked what he saw: a skinny runaway expected by no one, teeth clenched against the cold, in no position to bargain.

She walked a while without putting her thumb out, keeping her eyes on the cellophane, straws, and plastic bottles that fluttered and rolled every time a car went by. Ivy knew how close she was to becoming a piece of that litter, blowing into the dark corners of towns where no one would want her. Exactly $52.89 stood between her and those matted, directionless kids, *Please help* scrawled on ripped cardboard, flea-bitten dog at the end of a piece of frayed rope. $52.89 and a sense of purpose.

A beat-up Honda pulled onto the shoulder just ahead of her. Ivy approached the driver's window. An old man in a camouflage jacket and hat turned his head but didn't look directly at her. One of his eyes was clouded over.

"Need a ride?"

Ivy peered into the car. Hanging from the rearview mirror was a delicate silver chain that ended in a crystal sphere, which caught the morning light and bounced tiny shards of it around the grimy car. "Sure."

The man grunted and rolled up the window, and Ivy went around to the passenger door. The car smelled like cigarette smoke and grease; there was trash everywhere. Ivy had no choice but to put her feet on a pile of newspapers and McDonald's bags.

"Where to?" The man coughed. The heat was blasting out of the vents, and sweat shone on his forehead.

"Eaton?"

"I'm going as far as Agloe. Eaton's another thirty miles."

"Agloe then." The man didn't look at her, just started driving. Ivy pulled the socks off her hands and stuffed them in her jacket pockets. "Is there a bus station in Agloe?"

"Nope." He dug in his pocket, pulled out a handkerchief, and wiped his face.

So she'd get some food and call Asa before figuring out the bus situation. She watched the crystal sway from the rearview mirror. It was a gift to Ivy's tired mind, that kind of weird detail. She started chewing it over: maybe the necklace belonged to the guy's granddaughter, a little girl who loved him more than anybody, who didn't care about his cloudy eye. She gave it to him to remember her by when her parents split up and her dad took her to live with relatives in Mississippi. "Come see me, Grandpa," she'd said when she dropped it into his calloused hand. "Come down to Mississippi." And every day he worked hard and saved his paycheck for gas money so he could do just that.

Or maybe this was his sister's car, and he was borrowing it while his truck was in the shop, and she was going to kill him when she saw how dirty it had gotten. Ivy mulled over the possibilities for a while, watching the trees rush by, until finally sidewalks appeared, and then driveways and houses.

"I can let you off at the Price Chopper, unless you need to go somewhere else."

"No, that's fine."

They pulled into the parking lot, and Ivy began to prickle all over at the thought of buying food. "Thanks a lot," she said, getting out. She thought about asking the old man about the crystal, but he didn't look like he was in the mood for conversation.

Inside, there were Christmas decorations dangling from the ceiling and bins of plastic candy canes. Ivy took a basket and wove haltingly through the aisles, looking at prices and trying to figure out how to spend the least amount of money on the largest amount of food. She picked up a box of Pop-Tarts, frosted apple caramel, and stood transfixed for a moment by the picture on the box. Crystals of sugar sparkled on top of a coffee-colored caramel shell. She put it in her basket.

She found her way to the produce section, where there were orange slices sitting in a plastic sample bin. Ivy took one and tore the bursting flesh from its peel with her teeth. The sudden acidity burned her mouth, but then it turned sweet. She took another one, then another. After the fourth one, she looked up and saw the man with the cloudy eye watching her.

Ivy lowered her head, wiped some juice from her chin with the back of her hand. She dropped the orange peel into the bin on the floor, then took some bananas and went to the register. Her total came to $6.56. She asked the cashier to change another dollar into quarters.

When she got outside, the air bit at her cheeks and small, hard snowflakes were falling. She found a pay phone right outside the door, and it worked, crazily enough. Ivy dialed Asa's cell, realizing that she didn't even know what day of the week it was. He was probably at school, with his phone turned off. But it didn't go straight to voicemail, and after a few rings, he picked up.

"Asa, it's me."

"Oh my God, Ivy, you crazy bitch!"

"Hi." A dumb smile burbled through her lips at the sound of his voice. She pictured him sitting in his Honda during lunch, joint pinched between his fat fingers, bag of burgers beside him on the passenger seat. "Miss me?"

"Where are you?"

"Montana."

"No fucking way!"

"Not really. But I'm headed there. I think I am, anyway."

"Did you really steal Mrs. McFadden's car?"

"Maybe."

"You crazy bitch. Oh my God."

"Asa, what's everybody saying?"

"About what?"

"You know…about me. What I did."

She heard him inhale deeply, hold it for a moment. Then his words came out in a hoarse whisper. "I don't know. You know."

"What?"

"That it's too bad."

Ivy flicked the coin return flap in and out. "What's too bad?"

"When are you coming home?"

"Why are they saying it's too bad? What does that mean?"

"You know, that you fucked up like that."

"I did not *fuck up.*"

"Well."

"No, Asa. I fucked McFadden over. I did not fuck up. I'm getting out, unlike the rest of you losers." She squeezed her eyes shut. "Sorry. Not you."

"Okay, okay, God. I just think everybody's kind of bummed that you, of all people, hadda go that route. I mean, they're going to haul you in. You know that."

"No they are not, Asa. I'm not getting caught, okay? I'm out of there. I'm gone. I'm not the kind of person who can stay in a place like that and take care of sick people for the rest of my life. Okay? I'm not that…that kind of person."

"Aww, come on. You're—"

"No, Asa, stop. Jesus." Ivy tucked the phone between her shoulder and her ear and tore into a packet of Pop-Tarts, her hands stiff with cold. The crystals of sugar weren't nearly as big or sparkly as they looked in the picture, but she broke off a piece and shoved it into her mouth, chewing furiously. "Have you talked to Agnes or Colin?"

"Colin came over here looking for you. That was before the cops called and said you were in Pennsylvania."

"What did you tell him?"

"I…" More inhaling. "I said I didn't know where you were, and I was really sorry."

"Sorry? Asa, don't be *sorry*. You should be happy for me!"

"Well, I am sorry. I'm sorry you're a car thief now and that you're gonna go to juvie and have a record and everything's going to be harder for you now."

"Oh, please." Ivy pulled the socks out of her pocket and shoved her hands into them. "I told you I'm not getting caught."

"Everyone always said you were the smart one. The one who could actually get out and do something with your life."

"That's what I'm doing, Asa. Jesus."

"No, like going to college and stuff."

Ivy held the phone out, tilted her head back, and shouted at the sky. "Oh my gawwwd."

"C'mon, Ivy, we're all just worried about you."

"Worried?" She coughed out a hard laugh. "That's great. How come you weren't worried about me back in Good Hope? Don't you know what was going to happen to me there? College or no college, I was going to end up stuck at home for the rest of my life, broke as hell, working some crap minimum-wage job, taking care of my ma and gran, changing their diapers, and by the time they died, my life would be over too. Don't worry about me *now*, goddamn it! Be happy for me!"

"But, Ivy, they're your family. Are you at least gonna tell them where you are?"

Ivy shook her head, feeling the familiar blackness crowd her chest. "I'm done," she said. "It's eat or be eaten, Asa, and I was about to be eaten alive. This is how I am, okay?"

"No it's not."

"Yes it *is*, Asa, *fuck*. Why can't anyone just accept me the way I am? Jesus fucking Christ."

Some girls who were coming out of the store, the very picture of slutty Southside girls, widened their eyes at Ivy's cursing. One of them noticed the socks on her hands and nudged her friend, and they laughed. "Think this is funny, bitch?" Ivy yelled, but the girls didn't realize this was directed at them. They laughed some more.

"Ivy?" Asa said.

"This? This is funny?" She held up one sock-covered hand, now balled up into a fist, feeling a delicious, comforting rush of adrenaline gallop through her veins. "Bitch? *Fuck* you. Yes, you. You too."

"Ivy!" Asa said, louder this time. "Who're you talking to?"

"These bitches! And you too, Asa!" she yelled, slamming down the phone, throwing down the grocery bag, and advancing on the girls with her fist slung back. The girls screamed and backed away, one of them frantically scrabbling in her bag and pulling out a phone. "I'll fuck up your face with this, then see how funny it is, you basic bitch," Ivy cried.

"Call the cops!" the other girl yelled, cowering behind her friend, who was fumbling with her phone.

"I'm trying to!" the girl with the phone whined.

Ivy lunged forward and slammed her fist into the phone, sending it flying onto the pavement. She pulled her fist back again, and something caught hold of it from behind. She whipped her head around to find the man with the cloudy eye gripping her wrist, hard. He tipped his head in the direction of his car. "Let's go."

"You're going to pay for that!" the girl screamed, diving after her phone.

The man swung his grocery bags into the back seat of his car, and Ivy tore off her backpack and got in the passenger seat. "Take me to Eaton," she begged. "Please."

"Can't," the man said. "It's an hour out of my way, and a storm's coming. Plus, I think I got the flu."

"Shit." Ivy covered her face with her hands.

"I can take you back the way you came."

"I don't want to go back the way I came."

"I can drop you at the edge of town, but it's a big storm. Gonna snow all night." He coughed wheezily, sounding like Ma.

"Shit."

"Don't you have a place to stay?"

"I have a place to stay. I just really don't want to go back there."

The man pulled out onto the road. "Well, maybe you oughta go back there, least till the storm's over."

The crystal swung from the rearview mirror, but the sun had gone behind the low, gray clouds so there wasn't much light for it to toss around. Sirens moaned in the distance, and Ivy scrunched low in her seat. "Okay."

She waited until he'd gone a little past the big tree at the turnoff before telling him to stop. "I can walk the rest of the way," she said, looking around her feet. She groaned. "My Pop-Tarts! Oh my God. I left my food back there. I'm such a *dumbass*." She banged her forehead against the window.

The man reached into the back seat and rustled through his grocery bags, then brought one of them up front. "I was gonna give you this anyway. Seemed like you could use it."

Ivy looked inside the bag, then wound the handle around her hand, embarrassed. "You didn't have to—"

"It's okay. I gotta go."

"Thank you."

She waited until his car had disappeared around the bend, then backtracked to the turnoff. It was snowing hard now. She should've asked him what day it was. Was it Christmas yet? She should've asked him for some money. She should've asked him what happened to his eye, and why he had that crystal hanging in his car.

Back in the house, she opened the Price Chopper bag and spread its contents out on the counter. Most of the food was from the deli: Egg salad. Pasta salad. A loaf of bread, some slices of ham and cheese. There was a bag of chips and a bottle of store-brand soda. Looking at it all sitting there should've made Ivy happy, but instead, it made her heavy with some kind of sadness she didn't understand. Nobody had ever done anything like that for her before. That man had a heart different from what you'd find in Good Hope: something that took light and threw it back at the world.

Ivy wiped her eyes, then took a spoon and began shoveling egg salad into her mouth. She peeled some slices of ham off the butcher paper and shoved them in too. People back in Good Hope were too caught up in their own problems to help anyone out. And if they did try to help, like McFadden supposedly did, it was only to make themselves look good. "Everyone's got an angle," Gran always said, and she was including herself in that. When Ivy's dad died in the plant explosion down in Big Flats, Gran moved in to help with Agnes and Colin and, three months later, baby Ivy. But she made it clear she was only doing it for the free room and board, her own husband having died of cancer a year earlier, leaving her nothing but medical bills and a scabbed-over gash of grief.

Ivy took after Gran; that's what everyone had always said,

and it was true. In old pictures, Gran was the spitting image of Ivy, pale and thin with stringy blond hair, her squinty eyed smile held close like a secret.

Ivy was nine or ten when she overheard Ma telling Gran she had a black heart. They'd been fighting about money, as usual, and the money fight had turned into a fight about Ivy's dad. Gran said, as she often did, that it was Ma's fault he'd died, because she was the one who'd made him take that factory job.

"You have a black heart," Ma had answered, her voice low and shaky and full of truth.

It had stuck with Ivy—the image of Gran's heart like a rotten piece of fruit, oozing sticky juice, a haze of fruit flies all around it. And it was true that Gran never went out of her way to be nice to anybody, that she was tough and mean, her anger like a bird trapped in the house, hurling itself against windows and flying straight at your face if you were in the wrong place at the wrong time. Ivy had inherited it all—the temper, the blackness.

She cracked open the soda cap and chugged half the bottle. She crossed over to the couch and lay down, curling up on her side, watching the snow through the giant window. It didn't fall so much as it swirled, like smoke, gusting sideways and upward and around in circles.

Ivy had started really understanding the nature of her heart soon after Ma's sickness got bad. An ugly mood would come over her every time Ma asked her to carry the laundry basket or get the cast-iron pan up onto the stove. Guilt would come next, and then the blame. If Ma would just get better, things could go back to normal. It wasn't long before the whole uncomfortable swirl of feelings gathered itself into a wicked tornado. She hated Ma for moving so slow; she hated her for hacking up stuff in the bathroom every morning. She hated her for forgetting to ask about Ivy's math test, and for falling asleep in front of the TV without coming to say good night. Most of all, she hated Ma for making her feel this way, for forcing her to see her black heart, even though seeing it—*embracing* it—was what had finally made it possible for Ivy to break away.

Ivy closed her eyes, letting her tears pool between her cheek and the couch leather. It was time to get serious. She had to make herself a promise and never, ever break it, no matter what happened. She'd never go back. She wouldn't even *look* back. No more calling home. No more wishing and wondering. From this point on, it was just Ivy and her dream. That was all she needed. It was all anybody needed, really, to get by in this world.

6

"Do you have any Numbitol on you?"

"Yes. I already took some."

"You should drink a lot of water too, before you go to bed."

"I know. I will." Mary Ellen cooled her forehead against the car window, trying to calm her dizziness as the lights of Girard Avenue raced by. The backs of her legs hurt. Matt seemed edgy, his jaw tight, his foot heavy on the gas and the brake.

"I still don't understand why you went to this thing," he said. "Who were all those people? Did you know any of them?"

"They're Justine's friends. She wanted me to meet some new people."

"Don't you have enough friends? I mean, we're already in dinner party debt to, like, thirty people."

"I know." Mary Ellen closed her eyes. She longed to go home and go to sleep, but at the same time, she dreaded waking up the next morning for the inevitable headachy reckoning. She was sure she'd embarrassed herself in ways she wasn't even aware of yet. It would only come to her in the cold light of morning. "I don't think I'm going to be friends with any of those people."

"You smell like smoke." Matt stopped too abruptly at a

stop sign, and Mary Ellen winced as her forehead knocked against the window. "And that woman, Justine... I don't understand what's so great about her. She seems so full of herself." Matt had met Justine once—*once*—after picking Mary Ellen up from class one night.

"She's smart."

"And proud of it."

"Well, anyway, I think she's interesting, and she knows interesting people. But yeah, I was a little out of my element. And I drank too much. God." She laughed, fogging the window. "I even told Justine I'd go stay in her mountain house for a little while...for an 'artist retreat.'" That conversation, barely an hour old, felt as though it had happened years ago, back when she was young and stupid enough to think she could actually leap from one life into another.

"What?"

"I mean, I'm not going to do it."

"Oh. Good." He drove silently for a moment. "Considering how busy things are for you at work—"

"Don't worry." Mary Ellen knew Matt would be alarmed by the idea of her running off to the woods by herself. He hated any change in behavior or routine; he was at his happiest when everyone was playing their assigned position.

"Go on up to bed," he said when they got home. "I'll bring your water upstairs."

"Okay," Mary Ellen said, steadying herself on the newel post. "Sorry about all this. Thanks for coming to get me." Matt slung his hands in the pockets of his sweatshirt and gave her a half smile. She took this as a sign that he was no longer annoyed and smiled back, a smile that she hoped held reassurance and gratitude and a measure of her own forgiveness. Then she turned and went up to bed.

The next day, she worked from home. Propped against the end of the den sofa, she arranged her cashmere napping blanket over her legs, balanced her laptop on a cushion, and slipped her phone into the pocket of her terry-cloth robe. She logged into her Gallard account and sighed deeply as a flood of emails washed over her. She started by flagging memos and reports to read later, then went over the Global Influencer deck that had just come in from one of their consultants. She copy-pasted some of the findings into her positioning platform presentation, mapping the share trends by physician specialty and reordering the competitive analysis bullet points.

It was the kind of work that would normally lull her into a comfortable trance, but she was too distracted by her headache to lose herself completely. Her eyes kept wandering to the built-in bookshelves, which, she couldn't help noticing, were a little too neatly arranged, sections of books alternating with meaningless knickknacks. They were nothing like Peter's shelves, which had been piled with well-thumbed books that he actually seemed to have read and interesting objects from what appeared to be extensive travels to third-world countries.

In the center of her den shelves hung a family portrait: Mary Ellen, Matt, and the girls on the beach in matching white linen shirts, their faces glowing healthily in the rosy sunset light. It was the same sort of photo all of her friends had in their dens. Until now, she'd never thought twice about it, but today she found it irritating. What family ever walked around in matching outfits, except when taking one of these stupid pictures? Who were they creating this illusion for—their friends, who had all done the same thing? Was it for themselves—a comforting fiction that this perfect moment had actually happened?

Mary Ellen realized that instead of feelings of affection

or nostalgia, the picture had only ever inspired a sense of accomplishment: at having booked the best photographer in Avalon; at having found four white linen shirts in the right sizes the day before the shoot; at having sprung for the larger mat and UV glass for the frame. It was a job well done.

She turned back to her laptop and tried to focus on her work, but that was also irritating. The ad agency had sent over images for the upcoming focus groups: a woman putting on a bike helmet. A doctor counseling a smiling patient. The people in the focus groups—people who relished their job as professional opinion-havers—would not, she knew, experience any actual feelings of "safety" or "trust" upon seeing these photographs. But they would point to the bike helmet and say the word, and the moderator would record this event in a lengthy and expensive report, and everyone would fly home to present the findings to their teams and move on to "next steps." A job well done.

It was happening again, the swell of dissatisfaction that had been tormenting her for the past year, like a case of bursitis. The fact that it seemed to have been brought on by the death of her father continued to nag at her. Guilt made everything so much worse.

A howl came from the kitchen. Matt had been directing loud complaints at the television all morning; apparently, people in some other time zone were playing soccer. Mary Ellen clutched her forehead and called his name, but he didn't answer. She set her laptop aside, wormed her feet into her slippers, and went down the hall.

"What are you doing today?"

He was sitting at the counter, cereal untouched, staring red-faced at the TV. "I can't believe Iniesta blew that shot. *I* could've made that shot."

"Matt."

"What?"

"I was thinking. Let's go to ICA today."

"To what?"

"The Institute of Contemporary Art. There's a show I want to see."

He grimaced and laughed at the same time.

"Come on. You need to get out of the house. I do too."

"I don't need—"

"We can have lunch. There's that sushi place."

"I thought you had to work."

"I only have a conference call at two. I can play hooky the rest of the day."

Matt wiped a hand down his face. "Can't you go this weekend? Take the girls. They'll be more—"

"When's the last time we did something, just the two of us?"

Matt stared at the TV.

"It'll be fun," she said brightly. "I just need to take a shower first. I'll be right back."

She knew Matt was going to hate everything about ICA—the blurry video installations, the rigorously sparse galleries, the pious hush. It made her uncomfortable too, but it was a good discomfort, an *interesting* discomfort, and she thought she might be able to get him to see it that way. Matt had been trundling along in a well-worn rut just as long as she had. Maybe he would enjoy being pulled out of it for an afternoon.

The show was called *Transubstantiation*; Justine had called it a feminist comment on constructivism. Mary Ellen had relayed this information to Matt in the car on the way to the show, but she wasn't sure he'd been listening. Now he was leaned forward, scrutinizing the label next to a dress hanging inside a dry cleaning bag on a gallery wall. "Constructivism started in Russia," she explained. "It began during the Bolshevik revolution—"

"This one is called 'Number 7,485,'" Matt said, straightening up. "Do you think she really made seven thousand of these?"

"Maybe it's a comment on the commodification of art."

"Would you wear it?"

Mary Ellen snorted. "That's not the point, Matt." She looked at the dress, which had a photograph of a factory building printed on it. "Or I don't know, maybe it is. It's a photograph, hanging on the wall in a gallery, but it's also a piece of clothing. I read about this. I think it's called…" She snapped her fingers. "Productivism!" She beamed at him.

Matt sighed and put his hands in his pockets. "Does that mean it's good?"

"Well, it's interesting."

"How much do you think it is? You could buy it and hang it in your closet with all that other stuff you never wear." He gave his baseball cap a waggish tug, then retreated to a bench while Mary Ellen finished her round of the gallery. She felt pleased at having remembered productivism; she was definitely going to have to slip that into a conversation with Justine. She inspected the rest of the pieces, ticking through the movements in her head: relational aesthetics… postexpressionism…appropriation… It was all there, a trail of bread crumbs for the initiated.

"So what do you think?" she asked Matt, sitting beside him on the bench.

"Me?" He rocked his head side to side. "I don't know. Not really my thing."

"But doesn't it make you curious? To know what this is all about, what it's trying to say?"

"I'll be honest, Mary. I think most of it is hideous. I wouldn't want it hanging over my couch."

"Okay, but that's the thing. You're not supposed to *like* it." Mary Ellen put a hand on his arm. This was the most important thing Justine had taught her, the most seductively counterintuitive bit of wisdom that was now lighting her path through this new world. "Beauty, pleasure, gut reaction— that's all irrelevant." She pressed her lips together and canted her head back, filled with the power of this proclamation. "It's about *criticality*."

"That's not a word."

"It's about locating ideas within a cultural framework—"

Matt pulled out his phone and checked the time. "Oh look, it's sushi o'clock."

Mary Ellen sighed. "Don't you ever feel like learning something new? I mean, besides how to replace the InSinkErator."

"I read biographies."

"I mean learning something that changes you. That changes the way you see things."

"No."

"Matt."

"Seriously, Mary, no. I like the way I see things. And I don't understand all of...this." He lifted his chin toward the wall. "I don't get why you worship that teacher of yours, why you've started speaking in some kind of...code. I don't get it." He turned off his phone and shoved it back into his pocket. "It's like you're trying on a costume. Which is fine; it's fine to try stuff out, but you don't have to take it so seriously."

Mary Ellen drew herself up. "I take it seriously because it's serious. Art is serious, or at least it should be. And I don't *worship* Justine. I admire her."

"Okay. Sorry. Can we go eat?"

Mary Ellen felt her headache begin to swell again. She searched her bag for her bottle of Numbitol. "There's another room we haven't seen. But if you want to leave, I can meet you at the restaurant."

Matt stayed with her, though, or at least near her. As she perused the next room, he sat on a bench and scrolled through his phone. Mary Ellen tried to focus on the art, but her enthusiasm had drained away and she found herself standing too long in front of an abstract black-and-white photo, staring blankly at the grainy pattern.

Was this what it was going to be like when the girls went away to school? Would she and Matt drift about, doing their respective "things," intersecting only over occasional meals? Mary Ellen turned and looked at her husband, who was flicking at his phone with his thumb, his lower jaw thrust forward, exploring the inside of his upper lip with his tongue the way he always did. He was dressed in his usual outfit of sweatshirt and shorts (even though it was the first day of December, with snow in the forecast), nothing to distinguish him from the unemployed college graduate she'd fallen in love with twenty years ago, other than a gentle softening around his waist and jaw and two strokes of worry between the brows. Mary Ellen sighed and turned back to the photo.

They still had another year with the girls, but the Breckenridge trip was right around the corner. The twins would be spending half of January in Colorado with the Penn Charter ski team, giving Matt and Mary Ellen a two-week-long preview of life in the empty nest. Mary Ellen already had misgivings about the trip; the ski coach was known to turn a blind eye to after-hours partying. But more than that, she realized she was dreading coming home every day in the dark of January to find Matt, stripped of his entire raison d'être, still in his pajamas, watching ESPN, his head burnishing the sofa arm to an ever-brighter sheen. As if January weren't depressing enough already.

"Come on, Mary. Let's go to lunch. You need to be home in time for your conference call."

"Matt, you'll be home the whole time the girls are in Breckenridge, right?"

"Where else would I be?"

Mary Ellen sat next to him on the bench. "I think I'm going to take Justine up on her offer. I'm going to spend a week in her mountain house right after Christmas, while the girls are gone." As she said this, Mary Ellen felt a nervous quiver in her stomach that may or may not have been hangover related.

"What? Why then?"

"Justine wanted me to go during the winter, and—"

"No, I mean, why go when the girls are gone? What am I supposed to do, all alone in the house?"

"It's only a week, Matt. Maybe it'll be good for you. The change."

"I still don't understand why—"

"They're leaving in a year. I don't want to miss any time with them. But since they'll be away anyway…" As she was saying it, this reason struck Mary Ellen as perfectly valid.

"What about work?"

Mary Ellen leaned her head against his shoulder. There was something German shepherd–like about the way Matt worked to keep everyone together in their proper places, nobody straying from the herd. Which was understandable. He'd been so *comfortable*. "I'm quitting my job."

Matt jerked back, causing Mary Ellen's head to bounce, setting off sparks of pain behind her eyes.

"I'm kidding, Matt. Geez."

"Don't do that to me."

"Relax." Mary Ellen squinted at him. "But what if I did? You'd be all right, wouldn't you? You could go back to freelancing."

"I could never make what you make, Mary. You know that. Anyway, I thought you loved your job."

"Of course," she said, pressing her thumb and forefinger against the bridge of her nose. "Don't worry. I'm only going away for a week. Nothing's going to change."

"Promise?"

Mary Ellen gazed around the room at the mysterious jumble of objects reverently pinned to the dove-gray wall. She knew what her father would have said about them, what a laugh he and Matt would've had together. But would she even have come here if her father were still alive? Would she have accepted Justine's invitation, or would she have politely turned it down, explaining that her brand's positioning platform was far too important to leave to her underlings?

"Nothing will change," she said again, even though she was starting to realize, deep down, that something already had.

7

The pain in Ivy's head bloomed like a cabbage rose, a hot fist of petals unfolding against the walls of her skull. The pain jerked and pulsed and pressed, bloodred, against her eyes, and spread its tendrils into her ears and down her throat. Coughing pushed the pain into farther, darker corners, but she couldn't stop; she coughed and coughed like her lungs were trying to claw their way out of her chest; she coughed so hard she retched everything in her stomach onto the bed.

Such a waste, she thought, bundling up the bedding, trying to remember if there was any bread left in the kitchen, too tired to go up the stairs to check. How long had it been since she'd gotten the bag of groceries from the man with the cloudy eye? Time had been stretching and shrinking in unpredictable ways since she got sick, but she had a feeling it had been more than one week, less than three, but who could really say. Long enough to eat most of a loaf of bread and a pound of egg salad.

Ivy got a little confused looking for the laundry room. She was sure it was at the end of the hall, but now it was a bedroom, and she looked in all the cabinets but couldn't find the washer so she just stuffed the sheets into a drawer and hoped for the best. At least this bed was made up with fresh sheets. She climbed in and rode the waves of pain all the way out to the open sea.

She dreamed and dreamed, her dreams whizzing in manic circles like a roulette wheel, never wanting to settle into one story line, always circling back. She dreamed that Gran was in the closet drinking beer, and Ivy brought her a sandwich, but when she opened the closet door a bird flew out, and then she was calling Asa, asking him to bring her the homework she'd missed. Asa brought it, and it was all geometry, and she couldn't remember the Pythagorean theorem so she went to ask Mrs. Jacobson, the math teacher, who was in the closet drinking beer, and the bird flew out and hit the wall and slid to the floor, painting a bloody streak the whole way down.

When Ivy woke up, she was shivering violently and the sheets were damp. Outside the window, the world was coated in white flowers, and someone on the second floor was throwing fistfuls of petals into the air. Ivy decided to go see who was doing this, and also find something to eat because that would surely help her feel better. Getting out of bed was hard. The bed was fighting her, trying to pull her back. Her bones were all bruised, and it seemed like gravity was stronger than usual, like the earth had grown to the size of Jupiter. It occurred to Ivy that she was pretty sick, but any other thoughts about this kept flitting beyond reach and she couldn't seem to gain on any of them.

It took a while to get up the stairs; she had to keep sitting down to catch her breath. Finally, she emerged into the living room, and all the open space made her feel dizzy, so she sat for a moment at the big table, resting her cheek on the cool surface. A frail whimper leaked out of her mouth. She thought she'd been lonely before, but this kind of loneliness put every other kind to shame. She just wanted someone to put their hand to her forehead, pour her a glass of Coke, put a box of tissues by her bed. Gran had been the one to do it whenever Ivy was sick back home, although it usually took her a few days to be convinced Ivy wasn't faking. Gran was a terrible nurse—she would forget to make Ivy lunch half the time, and she was stingy with sympathy—but she was a warm body in the house and could be counted on not to let Ivy die.

Why had she come up here? Food. Ivy pushed herself off the bench and went into the kitchen. She surveyed the counter, which was covered with dirty dishes and empty deli containers. The good stuff was long gone, but there was still a loaf of bread somewhere. She'd been eating it for the past couple of days, a couple of slices a day, but she couldn't remember where she'd left the bag.

She pawed through the dishes and the trash, then opened the fridge and found it in there, a limp plastic bag with two slices of bread inside. Or rather, one slice of bread and one heel, just a shaving of crust. Ivy folded the heel in half and shoved it in her mouth, which was dry and full of sores. She poured a glass of water and did her best to work the bread down her throat. Then she picked up the last piece, which looked comparatively fluffy and sweet, like a slice of cake, and thought about what was next.

That slice of bread was the last of the food. This thought, at least, was coming through the fog like a pair of fast-moving headlights. It was the last of the food, and she was too sick to walk up the hill, and that white stuff wasn't flower petals, it was snow. Even without the snow, even if it were sunny and seventy-five, she knew she'd never be able to make it up that endless driveway to the road. She could barely make it up a flight of stairs.

Ivy pinched one corner of the bread slice, feeling the fluffiness turn hard, then ripped it away and laid it on her tongue. It didn't taste sweet; it tasted like everything else these days, like the side of a metal watering can. But it was pulling saliva into her mouth and waking up her brain. She took a big bite from the center of the slice, no crust, and it was like biting a cloud—one minute it was there; the next minute it was gone. She considered the remains of the slice. If she didn't eat it now, she'd just eat it the next day, so why the hell should she wait? She was going to get better eventually—tomorrow, maybe, or the day after—and then she'd be able to walk to town.

She shoved the whole thing into her mouth and chewed, wishing it really did taste like cake, wishing she could be wrong about the food situation, wishing there was actually a whole loaf of bread and some packages of ham and cheese lost somewhere in the kitchen mess. What did Gran always say? If wishes were horses, something something something. If wishes were horses, she'd kill one and eat it. If wishes were horses, this house would be a hell of a lot messier than it already was. If wishes were horses, she'd race them in the Kentucky Derby and win all that money because Ivy's wishes were bigger and stronger than anyone else's, and maybe nobody else would bet on them, but the person who did was going to be in for one hell of a sweet surprise.

8

M ary Ellen headed north along the Schuylkill River, skirting the Main Line, then emerged from a tangle of interstates onto the straight and orderly Blue Route. Traffic was light; she passed Allentown going about eighty miles per hour. The road was pressed into the earth, land bulging up on either side of it, obscuring her view of what was beyond. There was a dusting of snow on the ground, just enough to give the dead grass a white sheen. She rounded a bend and saw, straight ahead, a mountain stretched across the turnpike. It wasn't humped or tri-angular, the way she usually imagined mountains; it was more like a long wall—brown on the bottom and white on top—cutting across the landscape in a perfectly straight line as far as she could see.

Justine's place was somewhere on the other side of that wall, in what sounded like an odd location for a vacation house: just past coal country, between the Poconos and the Catskills in an economically depressed region called the Endless Mountains. There was no tourism to speak of, which was exactly what Justine liked about it. "No Starbucks, no Holiday Inn, no water parks. Just you and the

endless mountains and the woods," she'd told Mary Ellen.
Then she'd shaken her head. "Those poor woods."

"What?"

"The hemlocks. They're being eaten by a bug from Asia.
So the entire forest is in a state of decay. A tree fell on my
house last year—cost me a fortune to replace the glass. But
you know, the trees deserve to strike back. We fucked them
over with globalization."

"Oh."

"Anyway, it's moody and interesting. I think you'll like it.
And you're so far from everything, there's nothing to do but
work. You'll be able to really dig in."

Hard work was what Mary Ellen had come prepared for,
the trunk of the Mini crammed with books and back issues
of *Artforum* and of course, her journal—emergency supplies
to prevent mental starvation during the long, dark January
evenings. It would be strange, a whole week without elec-
tronic media, but she liked the challenge of it, like those juice
cleanses her friends were always talking her into. Maybe she'd
even enjoy it. Justine had told her the invitation was open-
ended; she could stay longer than a week if she wanted to.

She noticed that the oil-change reminder sticker in the
corner of the windshield said March 28. Matt must have
taken the car in. The wipers looked new too, and the floor
mats still had vacuum marks on them. It touched her, this
silent undertaking of marital duties. This was what it was
all about, after all—once the thrill of sex and the novelty of
babies and the complexity of raising adolescents had all flared
into life, then flickered out: the knowledge that when you
go on a trip your husband doesn't necessarily understand or
appreciate, he will nonetheless make sure you have enough
transmission fluid for the drive.

Food too. Matt had filled the back seat with grocery bags, enough supplies to last her the rest of the winter. "Are you expecting the apocalypse?" she'd asked, peering into a bag stacked with cartons of soup.

"I don't know. It snows a lot up there; they say there might be a big storm at the end of the week. If you're not going to take the big car, at least you'll be prepared to sit and wait for someone to rescue you."

"Justine has a snowplow service. But thank you, and please don't spend the whole time worrying." It was typical of Matt to over-prepare. He did a big shop every time snow was in the forecast, even though they lived two blocks from a perfectly good deli.

She was drawing near the long mountain, and now she could see a pair of tunnels punched into the base of it: one round and one square, with a dull cement surround that read LEHIGH TUNNEL. She plunged into the square hole and found herself in a tiled, fluorescent-lit tube reminiscent of a public bathroom. She'd never liked tunnels, and this one, in particular, was giving her that squeezed, helpless feeling of having one's options suddenly wrenched away. Driving became falling as she sped toward a slowly widening square at the end, just like the swimming pool under a high dive, only in this case her eyes were open, and instead of a crash of water, she was met with a crash of light.

On the other side of the mountain, the landscape was completely white, no patches of dirt or grass showing. The land began to rise and fall on either side of the steady road, small ripples occasionally swelling into waves. Mary Ellen was already starting to feel the solitude—different from the brief moments she would enjoy in her parked car after a long meeting, or sitting quietly at the kitchen table before

Matt and the girls got home. This was a weightless, tumbling feeling, with no horizon to fix on. The isolation would be frightening, she knew, if she thought about it too much or tried to resist. It would invite painful thoughts to take hold, thoughts she had no interest in entertaining. Her father's accident had happened more than a year ago. It was time to move on.

Justine, of course, had insisted that the isolation would be good for her. "Artists need to quarantine themselves," she'd said. "It's the only way you can strip away all the bullshit and access your purest ideas." Mary Ellen had no idea where to find her purest ideas, or how she would even know once she did locate them, but this trip was going to force her to figure it out.

Her family had been less enthusiastic about the idea of a week without internet or cell phone service. Sydney and Shelby had physically recoiled at her description of the house, and Matt had protested that it was dangerous.

"I'll be fine," Mary Ellen said. "People survived before cell phones, you know."

"But, Mom," Shelby had said, nervously fingering the zipper on her puffer vest. "No internet? I feel like you're going to prison. Are you going to be all right?"

Mary Ellen started to wonder if she shouldn't do this more often. Apparently, it was her steadfast reliability that had earned her family's collective indifference. Now she had them worried and confused, which felt comforting. She remembered the way Shelby and Sydney had clung to her when they were toddlers, clamped onto each side of her torso with such strength that she didn't even need to hold them up. Whenever Matt tried to carry one of them, the unlucky child would moan and cantilever her body into space, stretching her arms toward Mary Ellen like a flying squirrel about to take off.

She hadn't minded the clinginess; she'd actually relished it, all those years before puberty and sports took hold. On the weekends, she would dress the girls in matching tutus and take them to dance class, or accompany them to Build-A-Bear birthday parties. Work was less intense in those days; she'd been able to take afternoons off when the preschool needed a parent chaperone for a trip to the zoo. Some days she'd pick them up at lunchtime and take them to tea at the Rittenhouse Hotel, or hair-bow shopping at the Spruce Street Bowtique. They were beautiful girls; Mary Ellen loved dressing them in elaborately accessorized outfits and French braiding their hair, and the twins blossomed in the light of her attention.

The GPS ordered her onto I-81; billboards and gas stations sprouted thickly along the roadside as she passed through Wilkes-Barre and Scranton. After a few miles, she turned onto a smaller road and found herself rolling past one-story ranch houses with long driveways and elaborate inflated Christmas decorations. The road began winding, climbing and plunging, as the houses thinned out and the scenery grew more bucolic. The area actually reminded Mary Ellen of parts of Vermont, in a slightly scruffier, less whitewashed way. She hummed along to the radio, feeling her mood lift as the car wound its way up a boulder-studded mountain.

The GPS said she'd arrived, but she didn't see anything. She was supposed to look for a large tree with reflectors and a house number nailed to the trunk. Mary Ellen drove slowly, scanning the trees, but they were skinny, not large, and bare of house numbers. She found a wide spot in the road and turned around. Justine had given her the exact GPS coordinates, so this had to be the place. She noticed a gap in the forest, so she stopped the car and got out to peer into the woods. There it was: a narrow dirt road, which she assumed was the driveway, zigzagging down the hill.

As she inched the Mini down the snowy slope, Mary Ellen wondered if Justine had called the snowplow company as promised. She might have forgotten; after all, Justine never came here in the winter, preferring to spend time at her cottage on Sanibel Island—one of the many spoils of her divorce. Maybe, Mary Ellen thought ruefully, Justine would offer her the beach place in August, when it was one hundred degrees and humid, or in October, during hurricane season.

The car was actually doing fine; it had decent tires, and the snow wasn't that deep. She eased it around the final switchback and came to a stop in front of the house.

The place was pure Justine: a sophisticated sculpture of a house, clad in artfully rusted metal and vast swaths of glass. It was all edge and plane, unsentimentally intruding on the mountain's rough form, the snow's mounded softness, the trees' feathery boughs.

Glancing at the paper where Justine had written her instructions, Mary Ellen walked to the far left corner of the house and gingerly felt around behind the foundation. She pulled out a vitamin B12 bottle. It was empty. She shook it, stupidly, as if this would make the key magically materialize.

Mary Ellen felt her sense of adventure curdle into annoyance. She did not want to get back in the car and drive back to Philadelphia. Nor did she feel like searching for a locksmith in the middle of nowhere. *Damn it, Justine.* The whole free-spirited bohemian thing was great until it was time to remember things like getting the driveway plowed and leaving the house key in its designated spot.

Mary Ellen sighed and returned the bottle to its hiding place. She straightened and crossed her arms, considering the riveted expanse of metal. Stepping over a drift of snow that had gathered on the front stoop, she tried the door handle. It opened. Mary Ellen knocked her boots against the edge of the door, then entered the house and felt a gust of warm air. The kitchen counter, at the far end of the room, looked cluttered. She drew nearer, her boots squeaking on the bamboo floor. Then her breath caught in her throat. Open cans, dirty dishes, and empty soda bottles were piled on every surface, with what appeared to be shirts and socks wadded among them. Mud and forest debris streaked the floor, and the stainless-steel restaurant-style refrigerator was dull with greasy handprints.

Mary Ellen turned slowly toward the large main room. Art books were scattered across the floor, their jackets tossed aside, and a bath towel slumped over one side of the dining table.

She backed slowly away, pulling her phone out of her coat pocket. No signal. She'd have to drive toward town until she got to the spot with cell reception, then call Justine and deliver the news that—what? A squatter was living in her country house? There was no car outside; no recent footprints that Mary Ellen had seen. Could it be that the person was long gone?

"Hello?" Mary Ellen went back to the kitchen and looked more closely at the cans. They were scraped dry; so was the spoon. A piece of deli paper was tinged blue-green with mold. She went to the long, glass wall and looked down onto the deck. The snow, fluted along the grooves of the deck boards, was uninterrupted by footprints.

Mary Ellen picked up the towel on the dining room table

and held it to her cheek. Dry. Balls of tissues spilled across the sofa and onto the floor; more deli containers were stacked on the floor against one window. She heard a sound from downstairs: the sucking slide of a patio door. She went to the window and saw a girl, all flying hair and flapping shirttails, run stumblingly across the deck and into the woods.

Mary Ellen went downstairs. The den was strewn with clothes; an empty soda bottle lay on the floor. She looked out the sliding glass door at the footprints running across the deck. The girl hadn't been wearing a coat. And—was this even possible? Mary Ellen could have sworn she wasn't wearing any shoes.

9

The snow was fighting her, pulling down her pants, sucking off her socks. Ivy needed to get away from the snow the way you escape a dog or a bear: up a tree. She could see the little tree house, but she seemed to be in a nightmare, because it kept drawing away from her no matter how hard she ran. It couldn't be a nightmare, though. This was the most awake she'd felt in weeks. Needles were stabbing her feet, flames licking her hands. What was happening? She couldn't remember.

It was so hard to hold on to a thought these days, so hard to stay tethered to reality during this feverish, vomit-soaked dream. She stumbled, fell to her knees. The snow attacked her hands, and she cried out. She got up and lurched toward the tree house, clutching the waistband of her thin cotton pants. This was the one with a blanket, she was pretty sure of that. The one upstream of the Dumpster house, down the hill a bit. The one with the dirty magazines and the dirtier blanket.

She couldn't get up the ladder. She managed to clamp her fingers around the rough wooden crosspieces, but the ground kept leaping up to grab her. She raised one foot onto the ladder, her wet sock drooping over the end of her foot. She bounced a little, then heaved her weight up and over that foot, one arm reaching up to hook an elbow around the next rung. She rested a moment but knew she had to keep moving before everything turned to spaghetti and she fell backward into the snow.

Next foot up. She couldn't feel it touching the ladder, just a dull sort of pressure at the bottom of her leg. "Come on, Ivy," she muttered. "Up." Each time she got a foot onto a rung, it would take a few bounces to straighten her knee, and then she'd feel her weight sway backward and she'd have to gather every ounce of strength into her arms to pull herself back against the wood. Her breaths were coming faster and faster, her head feeling lighter and lighter.

Finally, with a squeezed kind of moan—*nnnggg*—she heaved her belly onto the floor of the tree house and swung a knee up behind her. After a moment, she pulled the rest of her body across the floor, sat up, tugged off her wet socks, and wrapped the stiff, dusty blanket around her legs and feet. She hugged her knees and rocked back and forth, white puffs of breath blooming from her mouth.

Stupid. Stupid. What did it matter if Agnes saw her like this, all sweaty and dull-eyed? Ivy could make her understand; she would fill her in on the plan. It was silly to hide from her. If only she'd had a chance to comb her hair, change her clothes. No more soap; the sliver had slipped down the drain. Agnes would make that face, but whatever. The important thing now was to rest, so she could get her head together when it was time to talk.

They'd talk in the morning, when light began to soak through the hem of sky above the trees. Now everything was going black. The threads of the sheets were sugared with broken glass, and something was coming in the night and cutting her hair, but if she didn't move, she'd be safe. Safe as houses, Gran always said, safe as Dumpsters, safe as swinging crystals in filthy cars. Crystals were growing all over her body. She could feel them flowering hungrily; she could hear the tinkle and clank through the darkness. And then, without warning, everything hardened into silence.

10

Mary Ellen stepped onto the deck, holding her phone up in the air. No signal. She spun around, walked the length of the deck, waved the phone back and forth like a flag. Nothing. She stared at the path of footprints leading into the woods, her head buzzing with alarm and indecision. Part of her wanted to run to the car; part of her thought the shoeless girl must be half-frozen by now. She felt confused. Who, exactly, needed saving? She jammed the phone into her coat pocket and went inside, where she fetched a long knife from the kitchen. Best to hedge her bets.

The footprints zigzagged a lot, yielding occasionally to what appeared to be hand- and knee-prints. They were easy to follow, having been punched clearly through the icy crust on top of the snow. Mary Ellen's large, heavy boots obliterated the prints as she matched the girl's stride, trying to imagine the story behind this barefoot flight.

The prints led to a ladder, which led to a deer blind jutted against a tree, about six feet up. Mary Ellen stopped a few yards away, watching.

"Hello?"

She coughed.

"Are you all right?"

She gripped the knife, waited a moment, drew a few steps closer.

"It's a little cold to be out here without shoes."

The trees were creaking; the forest sounded like an old wooden ship. Mary Ellen pulled herself up the first few rungs of the ladder so she could peek into the blind. The girl was asleep under a muddy blanket, her wet socks off to the side, her long hair covering her face.

"Excuse me?"

Mary Ellen dropped the knife in the snow, then pulled herself up farther and reached her hand in to touch the girl's leg. She didn't move. Mary Ellen climbed into the little structure, knelt next to the girl, and brushed her hair back.

"My God." She pulled off a glove and pressed two fingers against the girl's neck, but the angle was awkward, and her fingers were turning icy and insensible against the girl's bluish skin. She shook the girl's shoulder. "Can you hear me? Can you wake up?" She patted the girl's cheeks, shook her again. She found the girl's hand under the blanket and squeezed it, but it didn't squeeze back. It felt like cold rubber. Mary Ellen sat back on her heels, breathed out a long, white cloud, then raised a hand to her mouth and closed her eyes.

So it was like that, death. Uninvited, thin, and dirty. Luring you into its home, a tree house made for killing. She hadn't ever met it face-to-face, even though she would have, gladly, if someone had only told her. Mary Ellen shuddered violently and forced herself to open her eyes. The girl was tiny but looked like a teenager. Fifteen? Sixteen? Mary Ellen smoothed back the girl's hair, and some of it came away in her fingers, long and dull. The child was turning to dust right in front of her.

"Ma?"

Mary Ellen gasped and backed against the wall of the deer blind. Then she pulled off her coat and swiftly wrapped it around the girl, over the blanket. She remembered her hat, in one of the coat pockets. She found it and pulled it over the girl's head. The girl was shaking, her teeth knocking together. "Okay, okay," Mary Ellen said. "You're going to be okay."

She scooted over to the ladder, looked down. Too far to jump. "How did you get up here?" she asked the girl, but she seemed to have died again. Mary Ellen pulled off her sweater. She lifted the girl into a sitting position and tugged the sweater over her lolling head. She laid her back down and fished for an arm through the sleeve, pulling it through, then the other arm. She put her gloves on the girl's hands, then spread her coat open on the floor and lifted the girl onto it. Her body was lighter than a pile of laundry. As Mary Ellen was threading the girl's arms through the coat sleeves, her eyelids fluttered and she started shaking again. "Can you wake up?" Mary Ellen asked, zipping the coat.

She remembered the time she'd tried to wake Shelby up for a feeding, when she was barely a week old, and couldn't get her to open her eyes. "I think she's unconscious," she'd said to Matt, bouncing Shelby in her arms.

"She's asleep," Matt had said, his head under a pillow.

"Something's wrong." Mary Ellen blew gently on Shelby's face, and the baby's eyes opened briefly, startled, then sank closed again.

"Put her back in the crib. She's not hungry yet."

So Mary Ellen had reluctantly put Shelby back to bed, then stood there, her hands clamped around the crib rail, until she couldn't stand it anymore and blew in the baby's face again and again and again until Shelby finally exploded in furious sobs.

114

Now Mary Ellen was taking off her boots and her socks. She pulled her socks over the girl's thin, bony feet and rubbed them vigorously. "Wake up," she said briskly. "Let's go." Mary Ellen was shivering now. She pulled her boots over her bare feet, then lifted the girl into a sitting position, leaning her against the wall. The girl's eyes rocked open like a doll's. "What's your name?"

"You're not..." The girl seemed drunk.

"I'm Mary Ellen. Who are you?"

"Where—" The girl swiveled her head slowly to one side, blinking.

"We're in a tree." The girl's sunken eyes were blue; freckles were just starting to rise out of her cheeks' pallor. She had a sharp overbite that gave her a rabbity look. "We have to get down. Do you think you can hold on to me?" Mary Ellen went to the doorway, turned around, and lowered her feet onto a rung. She held on to the two rails that flanked the door. "Come over here." The girl just stared at her. "Come on."

Life was seeping back into the girl. She drew her knees to her chest, lowered her chin. Her eyes darted around the little tree house. "There's no other way down," Mary Ellen said. "You have to come here." The girl didn't move. Mary Ellen held out a hand to her. "I have food in my car."

The girl crawled to the doorway. "Put your legs around here," Mary Ellen said, patting one of her hips. "And put your arms around my neck." The girl did as she was told, hesitantly at first, but then she clamped onto Mary Ellen's torso with unexpected fierceness, tucking her head into the space between Mary Ellen's shoulder and jaw. She smelled like a bad nursing home—urine and hopelessness. Mary Ellen leaned as far back as she could, pulling the girl out of the house, then slowly descended the ladder, feeling for the

115

rungs with her feet until they finally met the snow. Staggering backward a few steps, she hooked her hands under the girl, whose grip was weakening, then turned and headed up the hill around the side of the house, toward the driveway.

"Let's get you to a hospital," she said. The girl moaned and shook her head. Mary Ellen paused to catch her breath, stretching her chin away from the girl's hair, which kept sticking to her cheek and getting in her mouth. She took some sideways steps up the slope, her feet feeling their way over the rocks and branches hidden under the snow. Her hands were sliding apart, unable to stay interlaced under the girl's weight. Her thighs were shaking. "I don't know if I can make it to the car," she said. "Let's go through the house."

Just outside the sliding glass door, Mary Ellen lowered the girl to her feet so she could use one hand to push the door open. The girl cried out as her feet touched the snow. "Sorry! Sorry," Mary Ellen said, helping her inside and settling her into an armchair in the den. She pulled the wet socks off the girl's white, bony feet and rubbed the cold skin between her hands, then went to the bedroom to find another pair of socks. She opened a drawer and reeled back at the smell of vomit that came from the sheets stuffed inside. She quickly shut the drawer and picked up a pair of dirty socks from the floor.

After piling some blankets on the girl and bringing her some water, Mary Ellen found a pair of rain boots and brought them to her. "You'll have to put these on so we can go to the car. Do you think you can get up the stairs?"

The girl shook her head, her blue eyes dull and sunken. She didn't look at Mary Ellen. "Food."

"Food. Okay, yes, of course. You haven't eaten in a while. Let me just… I'll be right back."

The girl nodded.

Mary Ellen carried the groceries in from the car and warmed some butternut squash soup on the stove. She brought it in a mug to the girl, who had fallen asleep, her head leaned back against the chair, her mouth slack. Mary Ellen nudged her, then held a spoonful of puree to the girl's lips, her own mouth opening by reflex, the way it always had when she'd raised a spoon to her daughters' lips. The girl's eyelids lifted sleepily. "Eat," Mary Ellen said.

The girl accepted some soup from the spoon, then reached for the mug. She gulped greedily from it, letting the soup ooze around the sides of the cup onto her cheeks. "Slow down," Mary Ellen said. "You'll vomit," but the girl didn't listen. She handed back the mug, wiping her face with the back of her hand. She was still wearing Mary Ellen's leather gloves.

"Sorry," she said, looking down at the soup-smeared glove.

"It's okay," Mary Ellen said, sinking to the floor by the girl's feet. She put her head into her hands, suddenly overcome with a mixture of horror and relief. What if the girl had died out there? Mary Ellen wasn't sure she was equipped to handle another death on her watch, even the death of a total stranger, a squatter, a runaway. She reached up and pulled the gloves off the girl's hands. "Feeling better?"

The girl looked dazed.

"What's your name?"

"Have you called the cops?"

Mary Ellen looked away. "No, not yet."

"I'm sorry…" The girl coughed, cleared her throat. "I'm sorry I broke into your house."

Mary Ellen looked back at her.

"Thank you." The girl patted the sleeve of the coat she was still wearing.

"What's your name?" Mary Ellen repeated.

The girl's stare floated away, then pulled back, like a balloon on a string. "Rose."

"Rose. I have more food, but I think you should wait a bit. Let that settle. You've been sick."

"I know."

Mary Ellen put her hand against the girl's forehead. "You have a fever. Wait here."

She went upstairs and found the bottle of Numbitol she always carried in her bag. She brought it to the girl, along with a glass of water. "This'll bring it down," she said, putting the pill in the girl's hand.

"Thanks."

"I'm Mary Ellen."

The girl swallowed the pill, drank some water. "Very nice to meet you."

Hearing this caused tears to rise in Mary Ellen's eyes. What was this girl doing here, all alone, in this condition? "We have to go now," she said. "To the hospital."

"No thank you."

"I found these boots. I'm going to put them on your feet."

The girl pulled her feet up under herself in the chair, shaking her head.

Mary Ellen squatted next to her. "Listen, you're sick and dehydrated, and I don't know what else is going on with you. You need to see a doctor."

"I just needed to eat something. I'm fine now. Please let me go to bed. I'm tired."

"Listen to me, I know you might be feeling better now, but this is not something you want to mess around with. I'm taking you to the doctor—"

"No."

"Rose—"

"I'm going to bed." The girl pushed herself up out of the chair and shuffled into the bedroom, closing the door.

"Okay then," Mary Ellen muttered, standing up and going upstairs. She inspected the view from all angles, walking from window to window, scanning the trees, which were thin, prickly, and still. The lack of internet was exasperating; she had a thousand questions. Was vomiting normal with seasonal flu? Where was the closest twenty-four-hour clinic? Was this the kind of thing Social Services dealt with? Should she drive to town and call Justine right away? What would Matt say? Should she go home?

She began straightening the living room, throwing away food wrappers and dirty tissues. She found a sketch pad with all its paper torn out; in the far corner of the room, a drift of paper airplanes. She collected the planes, examining the childish cartoon figures scribbled on their wings and sides, then flattened them into a recycling bin. She gathered all the towels from the kitchen and bathrooms and put them in the washer, along with the dirty sheets she'd found in the drawer. She swept the slick bamboo floors, picking up all the pine needles, clumps of dirt, and dead leaves that had been tracked throughout.

Teenagers! It was one thing to break into someone's house; it was another to completely trash it. Mary Ellen went to the kitchen and began washing the dishes that were strewn across the counter, scrubbing vigorously at the moldy smears of food. It was supposed to be simple, this trip—just Mary Ellen and the woods. Just Mary Ellen, her Nikon, and an uninterrupted expanse of time in which to focus on her photography. Was that so much to ask?

After finishing the dishes, she wiped the windows, erasing Rose's handprints. The house was smooth, sharp, cool to the touch. The hard sofas, the lacquered cabinets, the tiny light bulbs: Mary Ellen was beginning to understand the point of such a retreat. It was a cool hand against a feverish forehead, a sip of vodka after a rich meal. It was also a warm, well-lit shelter against the frozen forest, which was swiftly darkening outside the windows.

Mary Ellen hugged herself, wondering if it was actually safe to spend the night with this stranger in the house. She tiptoed downstairs and pushed open the door to Rose's room. Lost among the blankets and pillows, the girl's head was so small she could almost be five or six years old. She breathed wetly through her open mouth; her eyes moved stealthily under tissue-thin eyelids. Mary Ellen backed away, starting to close the door, then changed her mind. She left it open a crack and turned on the hall light, in case the girl woke up having to go to the bathroom, or wanting a drink of water, or feeling scared.

—⁂—

Mary Ellen parted her eyelashes, her pulse drumming hard at the sight of movement at the end of her bed, on the other side of the glass. Long legs, flicking tail, black nose. Mary Ellen exhaled and opened her eyes the rest of the way.

She'd never been so close to a deer, much less while she was still in bed. She was astonished by its size, by the solid, heavy fact of it right there, in the spot where, in any other house, there would be a dresser or an upholstered bench. She knew the glass separated her from the animal, but she couldn't help feeling unsettled, lying there in her pajamas so close to its hard, nervous feet and muscular, breathing body. After a few moments, she sat up and raised her arms. The deer lifted its head and fixed her with an affronted stare, then leaped away.

Mary Ellen dressed and went upstairs to find the girl rummaging in the refrigerator, a half-eaten banana in her hand.

"Can I help you find something?"

Rose backed guiltily out of the fridge, lowering the banana and half hiding it behind her hip. "You can have the banana," Mary Ellen said. "Why don't I make some eggs too? Then I'll take you into town."

The girl nodded slowly.

"You're feeling better?"

"Those pills," Rose said. "They made my bones stop aching."

"Good," Mary Ellen said. She took some eggs out of the fridge. "Numbitol. It's my secret weapon." The girl laid the banana peel on the counter, and Mary Ellen picked it up and threw it away. "How long has it been since you've had a meal?"

"I forget. I don't know how long I was sick."

"Well, you seem like you're going to be okay." Mary Ellen agitated some eggs in a bowl, shook in some salt. "The police will probably want to take you to the hospital, though. To make sure."

"The police?"

Mary Ellen poured the eggs into a hot pan; they tensed up almost immediately. She fumbled with the dial on the stove. "I don't know where else to take you. I mean, you broke in here. And what about your parents? Someone needs to call them. My phone doesn't work here."

"So you haven't...called anyone yet?"

"No, not yet."

Rose backed away from the stove, then turned and hurried out of the kitchen. Mary Ellen switched off the burner and watched the girl go downstairs. "Do you want these eggs?" she called, but got no answer. She sighed, pushing the eggs around with a wooden spoon. They wouldn't be any good cold.

A few moments later, the girl reappeared, dressed in layers topped with a jean jacket and a backpack, wearing the rain boots Mary Ellen had found the day before. Without looking at Mary Ellen, she crossed the room and went out the front door. Mary Ellen stood for a moment, a plate of eggs in her hand, wondering where Rose was going. She went to the window and saw the girl trudging up the driveway, hands shoved in her jacket pockets.

So she was leaving—just like that—with nothing but a banana in her system, and no winter coat. Mary Ellen shook her head. On the one hand, her problem had just solved itself. On the other hand...

She hurried downstairs and pulled on her coat and boots, then took her car keys and went outside. She could just see Rose, halfway up the hill, walking slowly. Mary Ellen got in the car and drove up to meet her, lowering her window as she pulled alongside.

"Where are you going?"

"Away."

"You'll freeze to death. You've been sick. Get in the car."

Rose stopped and looked at Mary Ellen. She was breathing hard; her face was pale. "Can you take me to the bus station?"

"No." Mary Ellen shook her head. "The hospital, maybe. Or the police station."

The girl turned and walked off the driveway into the woods, headed uphill through the trees, stepping high over the tangles of vines and branches that poked out of the snow. She pulled a hand out of her pocket to steady herself, then shoved it back in.

"Rose!" Mary Ellen got out of the car. It wasn't right, letting this sick girl wander into the snowy woods. Mary Ellen could drive into town to get help, but she wasn't sure how

122

far it was, and the girl might disappear in the meantime, lost among the dying hemlocks. "Come back!"

When she got no answer, Mary Ellen threw up her hands and stepped into the woods. It wasn't hard to catch up with the girl, who was pausing occasionally to lean against trees and catch her breath. "Come with me," Mary Ellen said, grasping Rose's thin forearm. Rose pulled away. "You have to get in the car."

"No."

Mary Ellen reached for her again, but the girl stepped backward. Her face was frightened, and seeing this sent a jolt of regret through Mary Ellen. "Okay," she said, holding up her hands. "Just come back to the house. Have some breakfast. Then we'll figure out what to do. All right? You must be feeling terrible. At least have some food."

Rose brushed some hairs from her face, squinting at Mary Ellen.

"Do you like bacon?" Mary Ellen asked. "I think I have some. I'll make bacon and some more eggs."

"You're not going to call anyone?"

"I told you... My phone doesn't work here."

The girl looked up the hill, then back at the house. "All right," she finally said. "Fine." She stepped forward, stumbled a little, and Mary Ellen reached for her arm. "*Don't*"—Rose straightened quickly—"touch me. Thanks."

After breakfast, Mary Ellen cleared the dishes and sat back down across from the girl with a cup of coffee. "So what are you doing here?"

"I'm not a drug addict or anything," Rose said, stretching

her arms across the table. "I'm not, like, dangerous. I just needed a place to stay for a while, and then I got sick. I'm sorry I made such a mess of your house."

"Where are you from?"

"New York."

"City?"

"You don't usually come here in the winter, do you? It seems more like a summer place." The girl propped her chin on her fist and watched Mary Ellen's face.

"Sure, I guess." Mary Ellen shrugged. "So you ran away from home?"

"Not really. I have someplace I need to be."

"Well, how old are you?"

The girl rubbed her cheeks with both hands. "Eighteen."

"No you're not."

"I am."

"You're too young for me to let you just wander off into the woods." Mary Ellen sipped her coffee. "But you can't stay here. I'm supposed to be working on my photography, not taking care of some…kid."

Rose's face clouded over, then she straightened up. "You're a photographer?"

"Well…yes."

"I could tell this was, like, an artist's house. All the books and stuff, and the paintings," she said.

"Right." Mary Ellen wrapped her cold fingers around the mug. She hadn't seen any paintings.

"I guess that pays pretty well, huh." Rose swept her eyes to the side in a gesture that encompassed the furniture, the light fixtures, the leather sofas.

"Photography?" Mary Ellen laughed. "Not really. No."

"So you do something else?"

Mary Ellen took her mug into the kitchen and rinsed it out. The girl's curiosity was like a flashlight aimed straight at her face. Mary Ellen didn't feel like going into it all—her boring job, her predictable life. She'd come here to get away from all that. "I do what most artists do," she said, returning to the table. "Teaching...consulting. Freelance art reviews." Her face turned warm, but there was also a pleasant flutter in her stomach, a flicker of excitement. "And I did pretty well in my divorce." She moved her hands under the table, twisted off her wedding rings.

"Oh." The girl nodded slowly. "No kids, I guess. I mean, it doesn't look like a place you'd bring kids to."

Mary Ellen shifted her weight on the hard wooden bench. Clean, uncluttered rooms...vast expanses of glass...a view uninterrupted by swing sets or soccer goals. "I prefer a more unfettered lifestyle," she said. "Like now. This trip was very spur-of-the-moment. A gallery in Philadelphia is thinking about offering me a solo show, but they want to see some new work. So I came here to work on my portfolio. I'm playing around with some ideas about agency and intentionality." Rose's face screwed up in confusion, and Mary Ellen waved her hand. "Never mind, sorry. Sometimes I forget that not everyone likes to read critical theory."

"Yeeeah." Rose yawned and stretched her arms.

"You must be tired."

"Kind of, yeah."

Mary Ellen studied the girl for a moment, trying to decide what to do next. She seemed harmless enough, and Mary Ellen didn't feel like trying to get her back into the car. "Why don't you take a nap," she said. "I want to go for a walk, take a few pictures. We can talk more later about what...to do."

After Rose went downstairs, Mary Ellen dropped her rings into a zippered pocket on the side of her wallet. This didn't feel like a betrayal any more than coming to this house felt like leaving her husband. She was just taking a break from her life, auditioning for a part. Was she credible as an artist, as the owner of this house? Could she make a place for herself in this world?

She took out her Nikon and sat at the table, wiping it carefully with a cleaning cloth, inspecting the lens for dust. She peered through the viewfinder at the treetops outside the window. The hemlock boughs bounced lazily in the breeze, releasing light puffs of snow. It was a relief, actually, knowing she could inhabit this world not as herself, but as a person who belonged here. She might even learn something—a different way of looking at the world, or a better understanding of what it all meant. Maybe, as Justine, she could even let go of the things that were weighing her down—her job, the situation with Matt and the girls, her father's accident—and approach her photography from a place of clarity and peace.

Feeling a surge of excitement, Mary Ellen pulled on her coat, gloves, and boots, shouldered her camera, and opened the door. After pausing a moment, she turned back to pull her wallet from her purse and slide it into her pocket.

Outside, she walked around the side of the house to the back deck, still pocked with footprints from the day before. She went to the edge and looked down the slope, which was perilously steep, black rocks and fallen boughs poking up through the snow. She could barely see the creek at the bottom, just a grayish flattening of the landscape where it was frozen at the edges, a narrow black stroke down the middle. The sound it made was like a cold wind blowing through dead leaves.

Mary Ellen moved back toward the middle of the deck, wondering why there was no railing. Someone could so easily trip and fall over the edge, then plummet to the bottom. She followed the path of footprints off the side of the deck and into the woods, where the top of the snow was littered with needles and broken-off branches. All around her, trees leaned against each other like drunks at a party; some, snapped in half, bent to the ground, their upper branches held out stiffly to break the fall. Mary Ellen raised her camera a few times, but couldn't think where to aim it, her mind still preoccupied with the strangeness of the cluttered woods, and of the girl, her unexpected companion.

She found it hard to walk and look at the same time because the ground was so uneven, the snow concealing holes, sharp sticks, and rocks. Her boots crashed noisily through the icy bracken; she stopped every few steps to reassure herself that she was alone. She came to the deer blind where she'd found Rose the day before. It was crude—just a box on legs, a flat roof raised above the box on two-by-fours, the ladder nothing more than a few crosspieces nailed across the legs on one side. Mary Ellen approached it from behind her camera, her finger resting on the shutter, unsure what to do. One corner of the blind was hammered roughly into a tree, but it was hardly camouflaged, its yellowish wood glowing against the background. She climbed inside and found the dirty blanket as they'd left it and Rose's socks, now stiff with ice.

Mary Ellen knelt on the blanket and peeked out. She tried to imagine what Justine would make of the scene, what importance she would assign to the black branches against the white snow, the gray shreds of sky visible through feathery fronds. She turned to study the crushed beer cans, the magazine fanned open in one corner, dead leaves sprinkled over its fleshy pages. There was something sinister and depressing about the scene; it seemed like ideal subject matter. But the minute she began thinking about the ideas represented within the gloomy juxtapositions—nature and man, hunter and hunted—the ideas immediately became stale and embarrassing. She didn't even want to try squeezing off a few shots, because doing so would be a failure—an invisible failure, yes, but one with the power to demoralize her, which would imperil her creative process.

She climbed out of the blind and walked on, keeping the ravine within sight so she could find her way back. She tentatively raised her camera a few times but never pressed the shutter, her finger paralyzed with uncertainty. She reassured herself that this was normal; it was only her first foray into the woods, and she was distracted by thoughts of the girl. There would be plenty of time to think about what kinds of pictures she was going to take.

She couldn't remember it being that way in college, despite all the distractions of campus life. She'd spent hours in the painting studio without ever running out of ideas, probably because she didn't know enough to understand how immature her attempts were. It had been so fun, so absorbing; she could remember losing track of time, missing meals, losing sleep, painting until her wrist ached, painting until she felt dizzy from the fumes and the colors and the exhilarating rush of creation. She'd painted almost without thinking, and that had showed, of course. The work was amateurish and boring. But that was the trade-off, wasn't it? She was older and wiser now, with more intellectual ambitions, and so the work would have to happen more slowly. Deliberately.

She replaced the lens cap and slung the camera over her shoulder. Her thoughts turned back to Rose. She wondered what she could be running from, and where she might be headed. It worried her, the way the girl had taken off into the snowy woods, not even saying goodbye, just fleeing like a frightened animal, like that jumpy deer outside the window that morning. The poor girl must be escaping something terrible. If Mary Ellen took her to the police, they'd probably send her right back where she came from. Maybe that wasn't the best idea. Maybe she should back off a bit, give the girl some space, let her tell her story. Rose could probably use another day of rest, and if Mary Ellen could figure out what her situation was, it would be easier to decide what to do.

She brushed some snow from her hood and turned back toward the house. She wasn't sure how long she'd been gone, but Rose would probably be waking up soon and wanting lunch. For such a small person, her appetite was enormous.

11

Something about this lady didn't add up. The way her hand hesitated before she opened a drawer. The way she peered into closets. The pearls in her ears. The sweaters and corduroys a full size larger than the clothes Ivy had found in the dresser.

Ivy put an ear to her bedroom door, listening until she heard the lady come downstairs and leave through the sliding glass door. She waited a few more minutes, then went upstairs and watched the lady through the window. She seemed to be wandering aimlessly. She'd take a few steps, look around at the trees, bring her camera to her eye and then walk on, zigzagging through the snow. Ivy couldn't imagine what her deal was, but it didn't matter much. She'd brought tons of food, and she'd given Ivy some pills that were like a miracle drug, calming her fever, easing the piercing ache in her joints, pushing her off into a warm pool of sleep without any of those pouncing, slicing thoughts that had plagued her for what—weeks?

She'd also brought a car—a sporty little thing that looked like a toy. And a purse, which Ivy located by the front door. There was no wallet inside, though, just a phone. Ivy turned it on and examined the wallpaper: a picture of a family in front of a heavily decorated Christmas tree, Mary Ellen right there between two blond girls, wearing a bathrobe, not looking one bit divorced, just tired and kind of unsure what to do with her mouth.

So she was a liar. Maybe the cops were after her—like they were after Ivy. (Or *Rose*, the stupid-sounding alias she'd come up with in the nick of time, remember that the cops were probably hanging WANTED signs all over the place with her name on them.) The lady didn't seem squirrely, though, just vague and kind of self-conscious. Maybe she was crazy; maybe she had Alzheimer's or whatever, and she'd escaped her nursing home and come here thinking it was her house. But how could she have found the place, once Ivy had thrown away the numbers that were nailed to the tree? She must have known where it was.

Ivy shook her head and dropped the phone back in the purse, then went to the kitchen and filled some grocery bags with food. She checked all the windows, making sure the lady hadn't circled around to the front door. She gathered the bags of food, took the car keys out of the lady's purse, and quietly left the house. She got in the front seat of the car and, after taking a deep breath, turned the key in the ignition.

Nothing happened.

She turned it again. Nothing.

She searched around the steering wheel for the lever that would put the car in Drive, but it wasn't there. Looking around some more, she noticed that there were too many pedals, and a knobby stick with numbers on it right in front of the parking brake.

She'd heard of this. Her cousin Thomas had one of these cars; he'd offered to teach her how to drive it, but she never took him up on it because his acne was so bad she didn't want to be stuck in a car with it, and besides, what was the point? Ma's Taurus was a regular kind of car.

"Fuck," Ivy muttered, breathing on her hands, which were white with cold. Maybe the answer was in the pedals. She tried starting the car with her foot doing different combinations: pressing the left and right pedals, center and right, left and center. On this last one, the car startled awake. "All right all right all right," Ivy said, laughing a little. The gear knob had numbers on it; "one" seemed like a good place to start. She pushed the knob in the direction of the number, and after some fiddling, it slid into place. "That's right," she said. "That's right." All she needed to do was follow her gut, and everything would work out.

It was not obvious how to get the car to actually move. Every time she let up on the left pedal, the car quit. She kept it mashed down and pressed on one of the other pedals, but this just made the engine race and howl. She stopped periodically and scanned the woods, hoping Mary Ellen wasn't nearby. It was clearly going to take a lot of pedal-mashing and engine-racing to get this figured out.

The heat was pumping out of the vents now, and Ivy was starting to sweat. She tried different numbers on the shifter, but that always caused the car to die. She fiddled with all the buttons and knobs she could find, switching on the windshield wipers and turn signals and the radio and everything else. She tried different pedal combinations, which only made the car jolt into silence. Finally, she leaned forward and rested her forehead on the steering wheel and cried.

She just wanted to leave. She was so sick of this place, where time seemed to be frozen and you couldn't move forward or backward or anywhere at all. She wanted to get away—from the woods, from the snow, from this weird lady she couldn't understand or trust. And now that she had a chance, a golden ticket, she couldn't cash it in because of Thomas and his acne. Why couldn't he have used some motherfucking Clearasil?

She cried for a while, pounding her forehead against the leather-clad steering wheel, feeling the black rot of hopelessness creep inside the car and wedge itself between her situation and her dreams. More hitchhiking, more hunger, more cold and frustration. Was'it impossible, what she was trying to do? Would Gran call her a dumbass for thinking she could make it all the way out west on her own, for imagining that someone like her could create a life out of nothing?

Ivy leaned her head back. Yes. Gran would say it was dumb, and so would everyone else, because that's how they were in Good Hope. They couldn't imagine anything better for themselves. Going back, giving up, accepting the life she had coming to her—*that* was the dumb thing to do. Ivy hit the steering wheel with her fist, doing her best to summon the energy of anger, which seemed more faded than usual, probably because of the sickness. She sighed and gathered the bags of food from the back seat. She brought everything inside, returned the groceries to the fridge and the cabinets, and dropped the keys back in the lady's purse. She checked the windows one more time—no sign of Mary Ellen—and went downstairs.

At this point, she figured, she had two options: walk up to the road and hitchhike to the bus station, or get the lady to give her a ride. A ride was better, obviously, if she could just get Mary Ellen to drop the idea of turning her over to the cops. She couldn't figure out an angle for doing that, though. Normally, Ivy could size up a person's worldview and play to it pretty quickly, but Mary Ellen was a different story. She was weird, cockeyed. Ivy couldn't tell which side to come at her from.

Ivy pushed open the lady's bedroom door, scanning for clues. She knelt beside her suitcase, which was large and filled with basic older mom clothes, stuff McFadden would wear. Khakis and thick sweaters. High-waisted cotton underwear and flannel pajamas. Underneath it all, Ivy found a package of pads that looked like they were for your period, except the box said *for moderate leakage*, which she was pretty sure meant *peeing*.

There was also a cardboard box of boring-looking books about art and photography, and a laptop. Ivy tried going on the laptop, but it was password-protected and nothing she tried—*1234*, *MaryEllen*, *crazylady*—worked. She put the computer down and picked up a leather-bound journal she'd found tucked among the books. She opened it to a random page.

> *Today in class: Clive Bell—"Significant Form"— aesthetics cleansed of content/narrative. A pure experience of art that is timeless, universal, and autonomous. Purity absolves the artist of self-exposure, self-absorption...what Justine calls "the infantile inward gaze." This week we're supposed to focus on shape, composition, balance. Maybe I'll do some still lifes. Too staged? It might be better to find existing compositions—less contrived. I think Justine would have a stroke if I came to class with a picture of some carefully arranged fruit. "Stop trying to make things pretty!!!"*

Ivy rolled her eyes and flipped to another page.

Shelby wants to get microdermabrasion. At her age! With her perfect skin! The girls are so focused on the wrong things. At this point I don't even know if they want to go to college. They seem so disengaged. I suppose it's my fault, our fault, for bringing them up in this exclusive little private-school bubble.

She snorted, shaking her head.

I guess I grew up in the same bubble. It took me this long to realize I need to break out of it. I wish the girls were more open-minded. I think Sydney could be some sort of artist, a writer maybe. She has that imagination. I just wish she would listen to me... Whenever I try to encourage her or give her advice, she swats me away like I'm some kind of annoying gnat. I guess I am annoying. I just don't want the girls to make the same mistakes I did. I want them to go to college and explore and learn and try things out until they really figure out what they love to do—and not end up stuck in some kind of meaningless corporate track.

She read a few more pages, absorbing the details of poor Mary Ellen's horrible life, her photography class, her spoiled kids, her ramblings about art. It was starting to make sense, the way her edges seemed all blurry. It was like she'd decided she didn't want to be Mary Ellen anymore.

Ivy slammed the journal shut and shoved it back into the box of books. The lady was crazy, all right; it was the very definition of crazy to have everything you could ever need in life—a nice car, a fancy Christmas tree, a "private-school bubble"—and feel like your life was a failure. Ivy felt the low fizz of irritation begin to spill over into anger as her thoughts turned once again to the cold walk ahead of her, the heartless road, the dodging and panhandling that lay between her and the life she longed for. Fuck that lady.

She went upstairs and paced in front of the windows. She should take a kitchen knife and force Mary Ellen to drive her someplace. Force her to drive to an ATM and empty her bank account. Make her hand over her phone. But first, she'd make her erase that picture of her and the private-school-bubble girls.

Ivy caught sight of the lady coming through the trees toward the house. Her head was down, her shoulders slumped. The way she picked through the undergrowth was dogged and clumsy, like an older person who's turned all stiff and afraid. Ivy knew she couldn't pull a knife on someone like that. Her heart might be black, but not in that way. It was more her style to use her brain…to take a slower, more careful path, a path that could take her farther than the bus station. If she played her cards right, Ivy thought, she might be able to get all the way to Montana, all the way through rookie training, all the way up the Going-to-the-Sun Road and into the sky.

⸎

"Cheers," Mary Ellen said, raising her glass in Ivy's direction and settling onto the bench across from her at the table. She'd started drinking before making dinner; now that the dishes were washed and put away, she was back at it. She unbuckled her camera bag and arranged some tools in front of her—a little brush, a soft cloth, Q-tips, some kind of air pump. She took out the camera and began carefully cleaning every inch of it.

Ivy was eating a piece of cinnamon toast she'd made for dessert. "How's the photography going?" she asked, licking her fingers.

"All right, I guess." Mary Ellen set down the camera and sighed. "I'm really trying to push myself. As an artist."

"Why?"

Mary Ellen picked up a Q-tip and dipped it in a little bottle of liquid. "So I can create something worthwhile. Something that will make people think."

"Are you getting paid for it?"

"No. It's not about that."

Ivy pressed her finger onto the plate, coating it with sugar and cinnamon, which she licked off.

"It's about doing something with your life that actually matters," Mary Ellen went on. "Something that might outlive you."

"Isn't that what kids are for?"

"Mmm…no. I mean, maybe for some people." Mary Ellen swabbed the Q-tip around the camera buttons, probably trying to work backward through the story she was acting out. "Personally, I've never bought into the so-called 'reproductive imperative.'" She hooked her fingers in the air. "It's just a way to keep women from gaining financial independence, or to keep them from creating art."

"Oh." Ivy wondered what the blond girls on Mary Ellen's phone would think of that statement. "I never thought of it that way."

"Yeah, well, the system doesn't want you to think too much."

"What system?"

Mary Ellen waved her hand around. "You know, the patriarchy. Corporations. So do you have any brothers or sisters?"

"No." Ivy leaned a cheek on her fist. "I'm an only child."

"Ah. The center of attention."

"Not exactly."

Mary Ellen gave her a long look, her face full of sympathy and a kind of hunger. "Is that why you're running away?"

"Who says I'm running?"

"Well, you're a little young to be taking a vacation by yourself."

"It's kind of a long story."

Mary Ellen began putting away her cleaning supplies. "I'm not going anywhere."

Ivy slowly wiped the rest of the sugar-cinnamon mixture from her plate. She'd spent part of the afternoon imagining different ways to go with this, using all the details she'd gleaned from the lady's journal, combined with her knowledge of how college-educated know-it-alls like McFadden tended to see the world. "Well," she began, "things aren't so great at home. There's stuff I want to do, but they won't let me." She paused. "Like, my parents don't want me to go to college."

"What!"

"They want me to stay home and work in the family business." Ivy pulled a name out of a hat. "The Gardner Family Funeral Home."

"Oh gosh. And you don't want to do that, I guess."

"No. But if you're a Gardner, you go to work as soon as you get out of high school. My dad did it, and now he has this permanent smell of embalming fluid. No matter how many showers he takes, it never comes off. I think he might actually *be* embalmed."

"Have you tried talking to them about it?" Mary Ellen got up to make another drink.

"Yeah, sure, of course. But they're like 'Nope, sorry, you're gonna spend the rest of your life like the rest of us, making dead people look less dead.' So here I am. On the road. Taking charge of my destiny." She said this in an ironic announcer-y voice.

"Wow. Brave." Mary Ellen dropped the cap of the gin bottle, and when she bent to pick it up, it skittered out of her fingers and rolled under the table. She sighed loudly and lowered herself to her knees, groping through the forest of bench and table legs.

"Yeah, well, I could never work for my family. Buncha crooks."

Mary Ellen resurfaced. "Funeral home crooks? Oh boy."

"Yeah. The worst kind. If you're crazed with grief, they'll talk you into the stupidest overpriced casket, plus the Eternal Life protective lining and Gold Standard Embalming." Ivy's friend Eleanna's family ran the Good Hope Funeral Home, and Eleanna had told her everything. She'd even sneaked Ivy and Asa into the mortuary one night. No sooner had she pulled open the door of the refrigeration unit than Asa had screamed like a raccoon and dragged Ivy out of the basement with more urgency and sense of direction than she'd ever thought him capable of.

"So you want to go to college?"

"Yes! College unlocks a lot of doors." This, Ivy was pretty sure, was a trademarked McFadden saying. "I'm going to live with my aunt in Pittsburgh. She promised to help me with the SATs and everything."

"But how on earth did you end up here?"

"Well." Ivy pressed her sticky finger to the table and

gently pulled it away, feeling the skin stretch as it clung briefly to the wood. "I was hitchhiking, and this young couple picked me up. They seemed super friendly and nice, you know, smiley but not in a creepy way, just a couple of happy people out for a drive. They shared their snacks with me, gave me some soda.

"Then, about an hour into the ride, they started asking me if I had accepted Jesus into my life and stuff. The girl said she had these, like, sister wives that she thought I would really like, and she wanted me to meet them. I got kind of scared, so I asked them to stop so I could pee in the woods, and then I just ran away. They chased after me, and the guy actually grabbed my arm, but I kicked him where it counts and he let go." Ivy chuckled a little at this detail. "I kept running until I found this house, and the key, and I decided to take a few days off before hitching another ride. I was feeling a little freaked out, to tell you the truth."

"I can imagine."

"But then I got sick. I guess one of the Jesus people had the flu or something. So I got stuck here for a little while, and then you came along. Thank goodness. You really...you really saved my life."

"Yes, thank goodness," Mary Ellen said with a little laugh. Then she got serious. "But, Rose, your parents must be so worried."

Shit, Ivy thought. She wasn't letting it go. "Well, see, my dad..." she said, then fell silent.

"Yes?"

Ivy shook her head, looking down at the table. She was happy she'd never even met her father; that, at least, made it easier to wade into this deeper, muddier swamp of lies. "I had to get away from him. I can't let him find me."

"You mean…"

Ivy turned her face away.

"Does he…"

Ivy nodded, then wiped a hand across her eyes and pretended to compose herself.

"Oh. No." Mary Ellen looked troubled. "How awful. I-I don't know what to say." She spent a moment straightening out her face, then asked, "Does your aunt know you're coming?"

"Yeah, yeah, she offered. She wants to help. But if you take me to the cops, they'll just send me home." Ivy took a deep, determined-sounding breath. "I can't go back there."

"Well." Mary Ellen moved her head around, looking from the table to the windows to the sofas and back again. She took a brighter tone. "I think it's great you want to go to college. College gives you so many options. How did you put it? It opens doors. I mean, it did for me anyway. I may not have walked through them all, necessarily, but at least I was exposed to things I could come back around to—" She stopped herself. "What do you want to major in?"

"Writing. I want to be a writer. Of, like, plays and stuff."

Mary Ellen sat up straight. "Really!"

Ivy shrugged. "I like to make up stories." Which was basically true.

"Well, you should just go for it. Don't let anyone tell you otherwise." Mary Ellen drank deeply. "College is all about finding yourself."

This, Ivy decided, was exactly what she would expect to hear from some rich lady who had completely lost touch with reality. "That's what I always tell my parents," Ivy said. "I have to be free to pursue my dreams. That's what college is, like, *for*."

"Exactly," the lady nodded. "But you can't hitchhike, for goodness' sake. Do you realize how dangerous that is? You're lucky those cult people didn't chop you up and have you for dinner." She leaned back, remembering, just in time, that the bench was backless. "But you're still in high school, right? Are you transferring?"

Ivy fetched the gin bottle from the counter and refilled Mary Ellen's glass. "Yeah. I'm a junior. You know, if I could borrow a little money, I could take a bus the rest of the way. No more hitchhiking."

"Mmm." The lady used her finger to twirl the melting ice in her glass, then licked it. "Playwriting. Where'd you get that idea?"

Ivy shrugged. "I've always loved the theater." She liked the idea of it, anyway. She figured it was like TV, only classier. "It's always been a passion of mine. And I don't know, someday I'd like to, you know, be like, like…"

"What?"

Ivy was really laying it on thick, but the lady was giving her such a wide-eyed, encouraging look that she kept going. "Like you. An artist. Doing what I love. Doing something that matters. Not just, like, punching in and punching out every day, you know what I mean?"

Mary Ellen looked surprised, then embarrassed and almost tearful. "I… Well, of course I know what you mean." She thought for a moment. "But if you do it this way, running away like this, you won't be able to count on your parents helping you out."

"I don't need them."

"Well, how are you… I guess I don't… Is your aunt going to support you?"

"No. I don't know. She's kind of poor, like me."

142

"Rose." The lady spread out her fingers, hands flat on the table, composing herself for the hard truth she was about to lay down. "College is very, *very* expensive."

It was all Ivy could do to keep "No shit, Sherlock" from flying out of her mouth, but she held it together. "I was thinking I could get, like, some help? Financially?"

"Financial aid? Yeah, sure, that's definitely an option. 'Specially if your grades are good."

Ivy was about to interject that she was thinking about a different kind of aid, something a little more personal, like one friend helping another, but Mary Ellen launched into a long monologue about different kinds of scholarships and how to apply for them. Ivy did her best to look interested, but impatience was making her jittery. How much more of this playacting would she have to do before the lady finally decided to help her out?

"Now, if you get residency in Pennsylvania, then you can go to a state school," Mary Ellen went on, "and that's a lot less expensive than private, but the quality, *pff*..." She flapped her hand and rolled her eyes. "I mean, it depends. California and North Carolina? Fantastic. But Pennsylvania... I mean, you could do worse, I guess." Ivy got up to serve the lady more gin, but she pushed her glass away. "Oh gosh, I think I've had enough," Mary Ellen said. She pivoted and swung her legs ungracefully over the bench. "I've gotta... I should probably go to bed."

"Oh, okay. Thanks for all the advice."

"You're welcome. I know it's a lot to think about. But..." Mary Ellen swayed slightly, seeming to lose her train of thought. "Well, anyway. Night."

Ivy stayed upstairs for a little while longer, trying to think what to do next. The lady seemed less eager to get rid of her, which was good. Ivy would have a little more time to figure things out. And while all of Mary Ellen's lecturing was kind of annoying, in a weird way it felt nice to have somebody actually interested in what Ivy wanted to do with her life. Even if it was all made up.

It was also pretty damn refreshing to have someone making all her meals and cleaning up the house and doing laundry and stuff. Back home, it was never like that. Back home, it was practically a competition to see who could go the longest without pulling hair out of the tub drain or taking out the trash. Colin always won that contest; he could live with the smell of rotting meat for days without even wrinkling his nose.

Ivy lay her head down on the table for a moment, caught in a swirl of memories. There had been a time when Ma and Gran kept up with things—but mostly Gran. She and Ma raised the kids together but grieved separately for their dead husbands, Ma a furtive weeper, Gran an angry door-slammer, each one hating the other for it. Ma worked long shifts as a picker packer, and Gran stayed home and kept things in order, getting food from St. Gabriel, cleaning up everyone's mess. When Agnes was old enough to watch Ivy and Colin, Gran did her best to hold down a series of jobs, but she kept getting fired for being mouthy.

And then all of the sudden, after Agnes and Colin started college, Gran's anger seemed to lose all its life force, leaving her crumpled in a corner without much to say. She stayed that way even after they moved back home. Ivy found herself missing the hurled insults and ashtrays, because at least those were signs Gran's blood was still circulating. Nowadays it was hard to tell.

Colin thought she'd had a stroke; Agnes said she was just

depressed. All Ivy knew was that she hated seeing the living, breathing body of a person who wasn't there anymore, like a ghost who'd never bothered to actually die. If Gran had died, at least they could've paid their respects and given her a proper burial, instead of letting her shrivel up under a shroud of *PennySavers*. They could've raised their glasses, drunk to her memory, sung her a song.

Of course, Gran wasn't the only one who'd cashed in her chips. Ma couldn't help it—she was sick and didn't have energy for much more than staying alive. But Colin, who'd gone to college all fired up to become the breadwinner who would save the family—to become the *man* they'd all apparently been waiting for—came home crushed by debt and a worthless résumé. No amount of basement weight lifting could help him get out from under that load.

And as for Agnes, she just made herself scarce, staying out most nights with her friends, sleeping at her boyfriend's house. Ivy begged her to be careful, but she knew Agnes would end up pregnant any day now. She'd just let it happen, whoops, and that would be that—the next eighteen years of her life scripted out with the kind of certainty nobody wanted but everybody was always happy to accept.

They were stuck—all of them—and it was the kind of thing that just fed on itself. Ivy could see that plain as day, but she couldn't make them see it, as hard as she tried, as loud as she yelled and pleaded and slammed around the house trying to wake everyone up. In the end, all she could do was swear she would never let it happen to her. Not then, not now. If she couldn't get away in a car, she'd damn well grow wings.

Ivy lifted her head and stared at her pale reflection in the glass. She imagined herself geared up like the smoke jumpers she'd seen online, some of them women: helmet, pack, harness. The jumpsuits were thickly padded, with high, stand-up collars, making jumpers look bigger than they were. Ivy lifted her arms, making a strongman pose, baring her teeth. She knew how tough the training was supposed to be; she'd read about how few rookies made it through. But that was okay—she was ready to push herself to the limit and show everybody what she was made of. No one had ever asked that of her before. It was about time somebody did.

12

The 3:00 a.m. headache was distinctive. It was always accompanied by a dry mouth, a rumble of nausea, and wave after wave of self-castigation: *This has to stop. You're destroying your body. It's not even fun anymore. You're acting like an alcoholic.*

Mary Ellen groaned and pulled a pillow into the crook of her body. The thoughts were coming faster now, pummeling her from the inside. *You're weak... You're self-indulgent... You can't have one glass of wine like a normal person. You really want to be more like Justine? Try a little self-control.*

She tried to remember the details of her conversation with Rose, hoping she hadn't said anything stupid. She remembered giving her a lot of advice about college. The girl probably didn't have anyone to help her navigate that world; all the same, the information wasn't much good if it came from someone slurring her words and reeking of gin.

Four counts in through the nose, four counts out through the mouth. Tomorrow she would make a fresh start. She needed to start taking pictures, *any* pictures. There was no point in pretending to be a serious artist if she wasn't going to try producing some actual work. It was hard, yes, but she had to stop making excuses and just create something, anything. Tomorrow was a new day—a day when she would stop feeling sorry for herself and start acting like the person she wanted to be.

She could see a glow under the bedroom door; Rose had left the hall light on. Mary Ellen got up to turn it off, then noticed that the girl had left her bedroom door ajar. Was she scared of the dark? She acted tough, but Mary Ellen sensed a certain vulnerability under the surface. She peeked into the room, the way she'd always done when her girls were young, before they hung a DO NOT ENTER sign on their door. Rose turned her head sleepily toward the light and half opened her eyes.

"Sorry... I was going to turn off the light," Mary Ellen whispered. "Unless you want me to leave it on?"

"Okay."

Mary Ellen crept back into the hall, flicked off the light, and returned to her room. A few moments later, she heard Rose's footsteps, and another click of the light switch. The glow of the hall light leaked, once again, under Mary Ellen's door.

<hr />

Mary Ellen began with a healthy breakfast, a couple of Numbitol, and lots of water. After eating, she lay down on one of the sofas for a while, letting the food settle, finishing one of Justine's books on postmodernism. Then she unrolled her mat and ran through a few slow, easy yoga sequences, breathing deeply through her nose, trying to ease the pressure under her skull. The downward dog caused all of the blood to rush to her head, which was painful, so she moved quickly into the warrior pose, which always made her feel like a soldier on the side of a Greek vase. Arms as straight as spears, neck long, legs powerfully planted, she felt a surge of courageous resolve. Things were going to be okay. Today was going to be different.

Rose was still asleep, so Mary Ellen left a note telling her what was available for breakfast. She cleaned up her own breakfast dishes and wiped down the counters, scrubbing the sink and drying it with paper towels. Finally, she put on her coat, hat, boots, and gloves, only then realizing she had to go to the bathroom, requiring her to take it all back off. She spent a long time washing her hands, gazing into the mirror as if in a trance, enjoying the feeling of warm water on her cold fingers. Finally, after applying hand lotion and giving it some time to absorb, she put her coat back on, shouldered her camera, and headed out into the overcast chill.

Mary Ellen stood on the back deck for a few moments, staring into the splintery, sickly forest. She couldn't imagine a less photogenic place. What did Justine love about it, besides its isolation and lack of amenities? Was Mary Ellen too unsophisticated to see it? Or was she not enough of a masochist?

She stepped off the deck and walked through the trees, scanning the broken branches that littered the ground and pondering her creative paralysis. Of course, the problem wasn't that there was nothing to photograph—anything could become interesting subject matter with the right perspective. The problem was that the number of possible pictures was infinite, and each picture required an infinite number of decisions about composition, framing, depth of field, focus… In making even a single decision, she would be imposing her Mary Ellen–ness on the shot, and that prospect was even more frightening than the vertigo of infinity.

It was turning out to be easier to impose Justine-ness on

her circumstances. A harmless game, really, but one that was helping her inhabit the resolutely spare house and its strange, half-rotten surroundings. She was actually kind of enjoying it—submitting to the possession, taking a much-needed vacation from herself and her dark, self-pitying thoughts. Even the way she dealt with Rose was different from how she spoke to her girls. She was more authoritative, more sure of herself. It wasn't hard; it just happened, like one of those flying dreams. Suddenly, you're just doing it, and you realize you always knew how, you just never bothered to try.

Something red caught her eye. She'd seen a few shell casings lying here and there in the snow, bright bits of red-and-yellow plastic, but as she drew nearer, she realized that this wasn't an object; it was a stain, dark red and glistening. A few feet away she found another one, then another, and then she recognized the twin teardrops of deer hooves pressed into the ground along the way.

She followed the stains for a while, trying to read their story in the chaotic way they increased and decreased, sometimes gathering into a larger splotch, sometimes spattering like fireworks, the footprints punched through the crust of the snow for what seemed like half a mile or more. She couldn't tell, but she knew it was a long way to walk for an animal losing so much blood.

She began to wonder if she really wanted to catch up to the deer—it would probably be an awful thing to see. But there was something so urgent and full of life about these scarlet spots, here among the black, dried-up branches and the white, impassive snow. The color of life was impossible to ignore.

When she found it, the deer was lying on the ground. Mary Ellen approached slowly, knowing what she looked like—a predator ready to take its advantage. "Shh," she said, crouching down. "It's okay. Don't be scared." The animal lifted its head and stared, its belly rising and falling rapidly. Mary Ellen could see the shotgun wound in its side, a messy gash with a stream of syrupy blood running down and accumulating on the snow. The deer thrashed and struggled to its feet, stumbled a few steps, and then fell onto its front knees, where it stayed for a few moments, probably trying to locate the strength it needed to get back up.

Mary Ellen stood up and looked around. "Hey!" she cried out. "Your deer is here! It's still alive!" Her voice sounded pinched and weak in the vast silence of the mountain. "You have to do something!" The deer's head was nodding. It tried once again to raise itself but slumped forward with a crash. Mary Ellen cried out, turning away from the sight, pressing her glove to her mouth. She pulled the lens cap from her camera and put her eye to the viewfinder and turned slowly, the camera like a shield, stepping closer to the deer. She twisted the lens, the animal's black eye zooming into focus. It was so dark and bottomless, she felt like she could fall into it and never find her way out. She put her finger on the shutter and held her breath, but before she could press the button, the eye rolled back, flashing white, and the deer arched her head back and bawled, *"Bwehhh-oh."*

Sharp, nasal, pleading, the two syllables vibrated deep in Mary Ellen's chest. *"Bwehhh-oh,"* the deer screamed again. *Help me!*

Mary Ellen gasped and stepped backward. Clutching her camera to her chest, she turned and started running, back the way she'd come, her feet crashing through the undergrowth in clumsy, terrifying slow motion. She stumbled, almost dropping her camera, then righted herself and looked around, hoping to catch a glimpse of a fluorescent-orange vest, a camouflage cap, something. "Hello?" she cried. "Your deer!" The only response was the creaking of the trees.

She started running again, her hat sliding down over one eye, her camera's lens cap bouncing crazily on the end of its tether. She followed the blood trail, hoping to find its origin and, nearby, its creator. But when she drew close to the ravine, she saw the trail veer off the right, in the opposite direction from Justine's house. Mary Ellen stopped, slung the camera around her neck, and bent over, hands on her knees, great gasps of air billowing out of her. She straightened and looked around, listening for footsteps, trying to think what to do. Maybe the hunter would find the deer on his own and put her out of her misery. But what if he didn't?

Some passing crows barked hoarsely in the sky, and the sound filled Mary Ellen with loneliness. She turned to the left and hurried back toward the house. When she got inside, she found Rose upstairs in the kitchen. Mary Ellen stripped off her hat and gloves, still out of breath, and threw her camera down on the counter.

"What's—" Rose pulled her head back, narrowing her eyes.

"A deer," Mary Ellen panted. "She's been shot. She's still alive, she's in terrible pain, we have to do something."

"Like what? I don't—"

"I don't know. I think we have to put her out of her misery."

Rose stared at Mary Ellen for a moment, then screwed the lid back on the peanut butter jar she'd been eating from. "No thanks."

"We have to, Rose. We can't just leave her like that. Can you imagine? It could take her hours to die. She needs our help."

"The hunter will find it."

"But what if he doesn't? She's been walking around like that for a long time." Mary Ellen wiped her mouth with the back of her hand. She was shaking. "She asked me to help her."

"The deer."

"Seriously, Rose, she cried out; she was begging. I wish you could've heard it. It was—" Mary Ellen shook her head, the memory of the sound as deep and painful as a bullet hole. "It was awful."

"And you want to kill it how?"

Mary Ellen looked around.

"There's no gun in the house," Rose said.

"I know that."

"Well, whatever you have in mind, I can't." Rose swiped the air with her hand.

Mary Ellen yanked open a drawer and pulled out a chef's knife. Then she thought better of it and chose a boning knife instead. She turned to Rose, who took a step back, her eyes wide. "I'll just have to cut her throat," Mary Ellen said, tears rising in her eyes. "It'll be quick. Quicker than what she's going through now." Her breath caught up in her throat. "Will you at least come with me? I don't want to do it alone."

The girl watched as Mary Ellen pulled on her gloves; then, she sighed heavily and retrieved the rain boots from beside the front door, and pulled on her jean jacket. She followed Mary Ellen outside and into the woods.

Mary Ellen traced her own footprints back to the blood trail, feeling bolstered by Rose's presence. "She's a little ways on from here," she said over her shoulder. "She walked pretty far, considering how bad she was hurt. She's not a big deer, but strong. Animals are amazing. They have that,

I don't know, life force. Survival instinct. They don't sit around feeling sorry for themselves; they just get on with it."

"Yeah."

"There." Mary Ellen stopped and pointed at the brown heap a few yards away. "See her?" She took a deep breath. She couldn't back out now; Rose was watching.

Mary Ellen drew closer to the deer, calling softly, "I'm here. Everything's going to be all right." The deer didn't move. "I came back to help you." Mary Ellen crouched next to the deer and gently placed a hand on her flank.

"Oh," she said.

"What?" Rose asked.

Mary Ellen set the knife down on the snow and put a hand over her mouth. She leaned forward and looked more closely at the deer's face. "She's gone," she said. "We were too late."

"Oh, thank Jesus."

Mary Ellen shook her head, suddenly overwhelmed. She couldn't speak.

"That's good, right?" the girl asked. "You don't have to kill it."

Mary Ellen tried to swallow whatever was crowding her throat, but she couldn't. She closed her eyes, trying to remove herself from the moment, but the images couldn't be stopped. They came barreling straight out of her imagination—not her memory, because she'd never looked at the police report, she'd never seen the photos. She had to assemble the image herself: her father's naked body lying in the bathtub. The bluish tint of his skin. "He was all alone," she said through the swell of tears.

"It's just a deer." The girl patted Mary Ellen's shoulder. Mary Ellen opened her eyes and stood up quickly, wiping the wetness from her cheeks.

"I know." She sniffed, the cold air clearing her head. "Sorry, I don't know..." She swallowed. "I guess this is nature, right? Predator, prey. Although in this case..." She shook her head. "I don't know what's wrong with people. Wounding an animal like that and letting her wander off."

"Well, if the hunter doesn't come get it, something else will," Rose said, looking around. "Like, a bear or something."

"Oh, I don't think there are bears around here," Mary Ellen said. "Are you scared?"

"No."

Mary Ellen watched Rose's pale face take on a look she was coming to recognize: bravado laid like a thin sheet over uncertainty.

"It's getting dark," Mary Ellen said. "I know you don't like that."

"What do you mean?"

"Well, nobody likes being in the woods after dark. It's...creepy."

"Yeah." Rose looked embarrassed. "I'm not a big fan of the dark. I know it's dumb, but it's just how I am."

She was so young. Mary Ellen felt herself being drawn in by her youthfulness, by the beauty and mystery of it, by the hazy memories it provoked and the ugliness it outshone. She'd made so many mistakes. Was she being offered something now? A chance to do better?

"Come on," she said, starting to reach for a strand of hair hanging in Rose's face, then stopping herself. "I know a place with lots of lights. And food. Do you like chicken?"

"Yeah."

"Then you're in luck. Let's go."

13

Mary Ellen started the dinner routine as soon as they got back, pouring herself a glass of booze and spreading a bunch of groceries out on the counter, getting out all of her bowls and pans, arranging them just so. The whole time she had a kind of pinched look on her face, a look that reminded Ivy of people back home. The look that meant someone was hurting and not talking about it.

"Need some help?" Ivy asked.

"Do you like to cook?"

"I don't really know how. I should probably learn sometime, huh."

The lady seemed to like that—she liked anything that gave her a chance to talk about stuff she knew. She showed Ivy how to cook the chicken in a pan, using the brown bits stuck on the bottom to make a sauce. She taught her how to cook mushrooms with garlic and butter, which smelled like Christmas. And she explained how to make salad dressing, which Ivy had never heard of before. She thought everyone just got it out of a bottle.

Ivy was playing up her interest, but the cooking lesson actually turned out to be kind of useful. She could see herself making a meal like that when she was finally living on her own, maybe even inviting some friends over to her place, having a little party. She'd learn to make hamburgers and chili too. Put some music on, maybe show a movie on her TV, everyone hanging out on her sectional. She was planning to have a pretty sweet setup in her apartment, once she started smoke-jumping. Comfortable, not like this place.

"Sure, I know how to make chili," Mary Ellen said when Ivy asked. "I used to make it all the time when I first moved to Philadelphia."

"Can you teach me?" Ivy asked. "So I can make it, like, at college?"

"Of course," Mary Ellen said, bringing their plates over to the table. "It's good student food. Not as cheap as ramen, but close."

"Yeah, I guess I'll be eating a lot of day-old bread and peanut butter." Ivy tried saying this like it was a romantic dream of hers. "It'll be worth it, though."

"Definitely."

"It was for you, right? Paying all that money so you could get a college degree?"

"Well, sure—"

"I mean, that's how you got to be a painter and all. It seems like it worked out really well for you."

"It did. Yes." Mary Ellen chewed her chicken for a moment, then crinkled her forehead and looked out the window. "Did we talk about me being a painter?"

"I just hope I can figure out the whole money thing. I've been thinking about what you said, about how expensive college is. It's a little scary."

"It is, but you'll figure it out."

"Did you have any help? Like, did anyone take you under their wing? Make sure you had everything you needed?"

The lady picked at her salad. "No. Not really. I mean, my parents paid for college. But they weren't very supportive of me being an artist. I could've used a mentor or a role model."

"Huh." It seemed to Ivy that paying for college was pretty damn supportive, but what did she know. "That's hard, when your parents don't want to let you to do your own thing."

The lady drew herself up and started cutting her chicken into a million tiny pieces, silently nodding her head.

"My parents used to tell me all the time what a waste it was to go to college, how dumb I was for thinking I could ever make it as a writer. I'll tell you what, though." Ivy stabbed some mushrooms with her fork. "When I make it—when I'm a successful writer—what I'm gonna do is help some other kid. Give a chance to someone else who was in my shoes. As a mentor or whatever, but with money too. So they don't have to worry." She ate the mushrooms, a smile breaking out around her fork.

"Ah." Mary Ellen put her chin in her hand, smiling back at her. "How generous of you."

"We artists have to stick together, right?" Ivy licked her fork.

"Mmm." Mary Ellen began gathering their plates and silverware. "By the way, have you ever seen any hunters out there? In the woods?"

"No. I've only seen their stuff. In their, like, hideouts."

"But you haven't run into one?"

"They're not supposed to hunt around here, around the house," Ivy said. "There are signs."

"I guess. But that deer today. It made me think," Mary Ellen said, turning her head toward the expanse of windows.

"We're so exposed here. At night? When the lights are on? It's like we're on TV."

"You think they're watching us?" Ivy asked.

"I don't know. How would we ever know? It's so dark out there." Mary Ellen pressed her knuckles against her lips, eyes wide.

Ivy looked over to the black windows, then back at Mary Ellen. "Oh, come on," she said. "You think we're so interesting? Two white girls cooking chicken?"

"I don't know. I don't like them knowing we're here alone."

"Oh God." Ivy laughed. She got up and went to the window, waving her arms. "Hey, rednecks, free shows nightly!"

"Rose—"

Ivy waggled her butt back and forth, doing a little dance, watching herself in the reflection.

"Rose, come away from there."

Ivy started doing a little striptease, pulling her hoodie down slowly off her shoulders. The expression on the lady's face, which Ivy could see in the glass, was hilarious. She dropped the hoodie to the floor and began lifting the hem of her T-shirt. Was there really someone out there watching? Ivy felt the skin on her arms prickle at the thought. She cocked one hip to the side as she slowly raised the shirt past her waist. She wasn't wearing a bra.

"Rose!"

Ivy dropped her shirt, bent, and swept the hoodie off the floor. "Sorry," she said, sitting back at the table. "I'm just kidding around. The whole time I've been here, I've never seen anyone out there. No footprints either."

"Still." Mary Ellen's nostrils were flaring. "I don't know why you would—"

"Sorry, sorry." Ivy reminded herself to stay on task. The

lady was looking skittish, like there were questions forming in her mind that she hadn't bothered asking before. "Sometimes I act silly. I don't know why," Ivy said. "It's like I'm making up a character or something. It's immature, I know."

"Huh." Mary Ellen took the dishes into the kitchen and came back to the table with the gin bottle. "Maybe hold off on playing that particular character while we're in here alone, you know? Don't borrow trouble."

"Okay." Ivy twisted her fingers around themselves. "My ma says that. 'Don't borrow trouble.'"

"Oh yeah?"

"Yeah." Ivy calmed her fingers down, cupping her hands together on the table. "She's sick," she said. "She's got this, like, lung disease." Ivy wasn't sure how this bit of truth managed to slip through, but there it was, and there was Ma, poking at her heart.

"Is she on oxygen?"

"She should be, but she says she doesn't want to drag that tank around, looking like a freak. The doctor says she's going to end up flat on her back for the rest of her life."

Mary Ellen reached over and patted Ivy's hand. "It must be hard, seeing your mom like that," she said. "I'm sorry."

Ivy withdrew her hand and looked down. A tear plopped on the surface of the table, and she quickly wiped it away, rubbing her hand on her jeans. The sadness-anger-guilt tornado was ramping up inside her, and she needed to shut it down before she lost her shit and blew it all.

"Oh, honey, I'm sorry," Mary Ellen said again. "Do you miss her?"

Ivy shook her head.

"It's normal to feel a little homesick—"

"I'm not a baby," Ivy said sharply.

Mary Ellen was silent.

"I'm not the kind of person who looks back and, like, feels bad about everything, okay? If I did that, I'd never get anywhere. I'd just sit around crying all the time."

"But, Rose, it's okay—"

"No, it's not." Ivy squeezed her eyes shut, sending the tears back to where they came from. *You're Rose now*, she reminded herself. *A good girl running from an abusive father, a girl with a soft, pink heart who just needs a little cash to get where she's going.* She took a deep breath and looked Mary Ellen in the face. "Are *you* homesick?" she asked.

The lady looked surprised. "Me? No. Why?"

"I don't know." Ivy picked at the skin around her thumbnail. "You were really upset about that deer. I was just wondering if there was something…else."

"Oh, that!" Mary Ellen waved her hand. "I guess I was thinking about my father. I don't know why. I mean, I guess because he passed away last year. And that deer, when she died, it kind of took me by surprise."

"How did your dad die?"

She waved her hand again. "In his sleep."

"That's a good way to go," Ivy said. "All peaceful. You don't know it's coming. You just go to sleep, and…that's it."

Mary Ellen nodded slowly, misery working its way across her face. She took a long drink and said, "Nobody should have to die the way that deer did. Hurting and scared. Wanting help." Her eyes started turning pink and watery, but she shook it off. "Anyway. I'm sorry about your mom." She gave Ivy a half smile. "I'm sure her doctor is taking good care of her."

"Yeah." Ivy sucked on the side of her thumb, which had started bleeding. It tasted salty and metallic. "After I get my degree and a job, I'll probably go back and help out." Rose wasn't salty on the inside; she was soft and sweet, like a cream donut.

"Are you thinking you'll work for a theater company? Or do you want to teach?"

"I don't know. I guess. All I really care about is the writing, you know? So I can put myself out there." Ivy sat up straighter. "Isn't that what it's all about when you're an artist? You say, this is who I am, this is what I'm all about, and if you don't like it, tough sh—too bad. Right?"

"Well, kind of, but it should really be about more than that. It should be about ideas. The concept of art as a means of self-expression is kind of..." Mary Ellen made a face and shook her head.

"Oh."

"Like, for example, I've been reading a lot about what Michael Fried called 'good objecthood' and trying to find ways to bring that into my work."

"Objecthood?" Ivy asked, leaning her chin on her hand and widening her eyes.

"It's a kind of specificity, what Fried called 'thingness,'" Mary Ellen said.

"Thingness?"

"I know it sounds strange. But it's about the ontological status of the object being portrayed. See, it all started with the minimalists." Mary Ellen brightened. She started going into a whole explanation about objects and things, and things other people thought about things, and how still other people disagreed with those people about things. It was crazy and stupid-sounding, but as Mary Ellen talked, Ivy let herself be lulled into a trance by the circular swirl of words, until she felt her sadness dip underwater once, then twice, until it finally dropped out of sight.

must be boring you. I'm sorry."

"No! I'm just sleepy." Rose's face had gone slack. Mary Ellen knew she was throwing too much at her at once; the girl hardly had the background to absorb so much art theory in one evening. It just felt good to talk about it. Putting the unwieldy ideas into words helped Mary Ellen feel more in control of the information.

"Do you want to go to bed?"

"Maybe." Rose yawned. "Thanks for teaching me all that stuff. And how to make chicken too."

"Sleep well, okay?"

"Okay."

Mary Ellen poured herself another drink and took out her camera-cleaning supplies. Her adventures in the woods had probably caused all kinds of dirt and snow to work their way into the camera's delicate mechanisms. She powered it on and checked the display. She was surprised to find fifty-four shots on the memory card; she couldn't remember having taken a single one. She scrolled through them and couldn't make out what they were. She went downstairs to get her laptop from the bedroom, then hooked up her camera to it and uploaded the pictures.

A smear of gray sky interrupted in one corner by a bent, scrawny branch; a brown blur against white snow; a froth of pine needles filling the frame. Apparently, she'd mashed the shutter button while running away from the deer, and her camera had been in continuous shooting mode. Mary Ellen scrolled quickly through the shots and could see her frame-by-frame progress through the undergrowth.

She enlarged one of the pictures. There was something energetic about the way a branch slashed through the frame, a black streak against a mottled gray background. The composition, if you could call it that, was unbalanced and haphazard, making the photo feel artistic but not contrived. Actually, it was the opposite of contrived, Mary Ellen real-ized, the blood quickening in her chest and her head. There was no Mary Ellen–ness imposed on the picture whatsoever, no evidence of struggle, no pitiful attempt to be liked. She'd finally managed, as Justine had predicted, to "strip away all the bullshit."

Mary Ellen enlarged a few more of the pictures and found them equally compelling. She deleted the ones that showed a glimpse of her leg or her coat, leaving her with twenty-eight unadulterated photos. She tried cropping a few of them and tweaking the exposure, then shook her head and undid all of the changes. Purity was the idea here. She needed to just let the photos be what they wanted to be.

She drained her glass, savoring the euphoric tingling in her extremities. The pictures were so wild, so uncontrolled. They weren't trying too hard; they weren't trying *at all*. She couldn't wait to send them to Justine.

She'd go to town in the morning. Justine had told her

the local library had Wi-Fi, so she would go there to send the files. Then maybe she'd check her email, give Matt a call. If the library had a printer, she could bring Rose some information on scholarships.

Of course, she'd picked up on Rose's hint about helping a younger person trying to make it in the world. Mary Ellen actually thought it was cute, the way Rose had promised to pay it forward. "We artists have to stick together," she'd said, and Mary Ellen supposed she had a point. If only she'd had a mentor back when she was in school—someone like Justine, who could have recognized her potential and urged her to stick with her art major. Someone who might have persuaded her to turn away her parents' money and all its messily attached strings. A word or two of encouragement—that's all she'd really needed.

Her mind was whirling now; she'd had too much to drink. She decided to go to bed so she could leave early in the morning, before Rose woke up and asked to come along. She wasn't ready to put the girl on a bus to Pittsburgh. She still had so much to tell her.

⸻

That night, Mary Ellen dreamed about a man who wasn't Matt, someone with black hair and a low voice and a face always in shadow. She was in bed with him, but it wasn't a betrayal because in her dream, there was no Matt, so there was no sense of alarm or shame the way there was sometimes in her other dreams. She and the man were both undressed, but they weren't having sex. They were just melted together in a full-body embrace, their protrusions and recesses locked like the teeth of a zipper. Something intense was pulsing between them, passing back and forth like an alternating current—anxiety/acceptance, longing/gratification, questions/answers.

As dawn broke and she emerged from sleep, Mary Ellen kept her eyes closed for as long as she could, savoring the dream's vapor trail. She felt a little guilty that it wasn't Matt in her dream; it was never Matt. These sorts of dreams were almost never about a specific person. She wasn't fantasizing about men with broader shoulders or wider jaws or more imaginative wardrobes than her husband. It was just her subconscious conjuring an abstract "other," a warm body with which she could pulse and thrum and experience a kind of urgent, transporting closeness that simply didn't exist in real life.

She opened her eyes and gasped. The deer was back, right outside her window, as if risen from the dead. She was nosing at something on the ground, lifting her head now and then to glance around, ears swiveling. She looked straight at Mary Ellen, almost boldly, her nose sugared with snow. Mary Ellen stared back. Had she dreamed the deer's death in the woods? No, she could clearly remember the fading warmth of the flank under her hand, the seep of snow through her pants. This had to be another one. She raised herself up on one elbow, and the animal startled away. Mary Ellen smiled, reassured to see a deer looking so alive, so peaceful, so uninterested in her mistakes.

It was early; the snow was just beginning to catch the reluctant morning light and drag it through the trees. She fell back against the pillows. Matt would like that—a deer at the foot of the bed! She'd have to tell him about it when she called him from town. She wondered what he was doing, if he was sleeping in, enjoying the quiet of the empty house. Probably not. The ability to sleep late was one of those things they were both losing in middle age, along with eyesight and an interest in new music. If she had to guess, he was probably at the diner, sitting at the counter eating pancakes with whipped cream.

She remembered how adorable she'd found it, the first time he ordered his favorite breakfast in her company. There had been something so sweet and boyish about Matt, with his messy hair and messy apartment, a kind of jovial helplessness that stirred tender feelings in her. He'd always resisted her mothering, though. He wouldn't let her clean his bathroom, no matter how forcefully she claimed not to mind, and he refused to let her take him shopping for clothes. To his credit, he did grow up a lot during those early years. He learned to cook and clean; he started going to an actual hairdresser. Mary Ellen understood, and loved, that he did these things to make her happy, and because he wanted a partner instead of a parent.

He kept eating pancakes with whipped cream, though, and ice cream with sprinkles. The charm of this had long worn off—she supposed her own adorableness had faded just as much, was there any point in pretending otherwise?—but now they were bound by an intense familiarity that exerted its own gravity. No one knew her as well as Matt did. No one else could predict, even before she knew herself, what she was going to order at a restaurant. No one else could read her eyebrows, her neck tendons, her grip on a tooth-brush like they were complete sentences written in his own handwriting. No one else could find that knot of nerves just behind her shoulder blade and smooth it out with a few well-placed rubs of the thumb.

Sometimes it had a whiff of the supernatural, the way Matt knew things—*felt* things. Like when her father died. She'd gotten the call at the office, and just few minutes later, while she was still staring dumbfounded at her phone, Matt had appeared out of the blue with a bag from the Marathon Grill. "It feels like a soup kind of day," he'd said before seeing her face and the terrible news written there. He'd taken charge immediately, allowing Mary Ellen to float apart into a million useless pieces while he met with the coroner, and the police, and the funeral home, and all the rest. And when it was over, he'd done exactly what she wanted, without being asked. He'd never spoken about her father or his tragic, lonesome death again.

And now…this inability to understand the changes she was going through. His confusion hurt, because it seemed to say he'd lost interest. But wasn't that to be expected after so many years of familiarity? Hadn't they just lost the habit of exploring each other's dark, mysterious corners?

She dressed quickly, gathered her things, and went out to the car, moving quietly so as not to wake Rose. The gray sky, which she could just glimpse through the treetops, seemed to be hanging lower than usual, pressing down on the world. She got in the car and turned the key, and it lunged forward violently before stalling. She stared dumbly at all the red lights on the dashboard. It was strange; she never parked it in gear. But then, she hadn't really been herself since coming down that snowy driveway. Mary Ellen put the car in neutral, shaking her head, then restarted it and climbed up the hill to the road.

Justine had told her Agloe was just a few miles down the road; cell service started about halfway there. Sure enough, Mary Ellen's phone started purring with texts as she descended the mountain. She rolled into town and pulled into the Price Chopper parking lot, where she glanced through her messages, then dialed Matt's number.

"Matt, it's me. Were you asleep?"

"No, yeah, but it's okay."

"I figured you'd be up by now. I'm sorry."

"It's fine," he said. She could hear him pushing himself into a seated position against the pillows. "Everything okay?"

She imagined him peeling off his anti-snoring nose strip and rubbing the skin underneath with his thumb and forefinger. "Everything's great," she said. "Sorry I haven't called until now."

"That's all right," he muttered.

"The house is really nice. It's very Justine, you know? Really modern and minimal, in a very expensive way. You'd probably hate it." She paused, fiddling with the gearshift. This was the point, of course, when a normal wife would tell her husband about the runaway she'd found hiding in the house. But it was all too hard to explain, and she knew Matt would insist on calling the police. She didn't feel like going into the playwriting, the funeral home, the aunt in Pittsburgh. Nor did she want him calling Justine. "There's a deer that always comes in the morning, right outside my bedroom window. When I wake up it's always there, just a few feet from the bed. It's so strange."

"Huh."

"Anyway," she said, "it's nice and quiet. No distractions. I'm taking a lot of pictures. In fact, I think I made a real breakthrough yesterday. I shot some great stuff."

Matt made a sinus-clearing noise.

"Have you talked to the girls?" she asked.

"I sure have. About that—"

"Are they having a good trip?"

"It's over, Mary."

"What?" Her head buzzed with alarm.

169

"They got sent home."

"Wait, what? I don't—"

Matt sighed heavily. "They got caught buying beer. They had fake IDs."

"Sydney and Shelby? Fake IDs?" Mary Ellen put a hand over her mouth, noticing, in spite of her shock, that her glove still smelled like butternut squash soup. "That can't be. No. It must've been someone else."

"Look, Mary, it happened, and I can tell you that because I'm here, dealing with it."

"Well, I'm sorry. I had no way of knowing—"

"They took all the blame. Nobody else was sent home, even though Syd and Shel were buying for the whole team. Everyone chipped in and sent them to the store, and they're the ones who got sent home."

"Well, Matt, they shouldn't have done it. I mean, come on—"

"Mary, it's *what you do*. They're teenagers on a ski trip. Christ."

"Don't make excuses for them, Matt! They knew they were breaking the law. But you make it confusing for them, because you let them get away with this stuff, like it's okay, and it's not. And now look."

"You're blaming me. You're not even *here*."

"You're just so easy on them, Matt. You let them get away with so much. And then when I try to stop it, they say, 'Yeah, but Dad lets us.' And now, oh my God."

"You're acting like I went out and got them fake IDs."

"Well, did you?"

"Jesus Christ, Mary."

"You're the one who wanted to buy beer for the lacrosse team."

"Yeah, so they'd drink in our house, while we were home. Instead, they went to Dani Morrison's house, and I can guarantee her parents weren't there."

"What? When was this?" Mary Ellen pinched the bridge of her nose.

"Never mind. Are you coming home?"

Mary Ellen opened her mouth, then closed it. She couldn't leave now, when things were beginning to go so well. She'd finally taken some pictures; she was just getting started. And Rose—what about her? "I just don't see what good that would do."

"What do you mean?"

Mary Ellen looked at the ceiling of the car. Well, of course they were her daughters. But the damage was done; they'd already been sent home. The whole situation was entirely Matt's doing, and he could perfectly well deal with the aftermath. "I just mean there's nothing I can do at this point."

"You could come here and talk to them about what happened. You know... Be their mother."

"I think you took over that job years ago," Mary Ellen snapped. "I'm just the breadwinner, remember?"

"Oh, come off it. You love your job. I made that *possible* for you."

"Except I don't, Matt. I don't love it. I just happen to be good at it." Mary Ellen felt something surge in her chest. "What you need to understand is that I love what I'm doing now—creating something interesting and new. You should try it."

Matt was silent.

"Look," Mary Ellen said. "I'll call the girls in a couple of hours. After I run some errands. Okay? Tell them I'll call and... and...we'll talk about what happened. But I'm not coming home. I'm staying a little longer. I have more to do here."

"What? But you said one week."

"Justine said I could stay longer if it was going well, and it's going well."

"What are you going to tell Gallard?"

"Would you stop worrying about my job? I've got plenty of vacation time, okay? The paychecks will continue to flow. God."

"You know that's not what I mean."

"I know, I know. You just don't like it when plans change. But that's how life is, Matt. Things change. I'm sorry."

Inside the Price Chopper, Mary Ellen browsed the aisles impatiently. It was the worst of the worst—nothing remotely organic, just shelf after shelf of colored, processed, individually packaged GMO-tainted crap. Rose needed nutrients; she needed protein. She probably needed fiber. Mary Ellen hesitated in front of the meat case. The shrink-wrapped chicken breasts were grotesquely swollen, like the girls in the awful men's magazines Matt kept in the bathroom. She chose some ground beef instead, remembering that Rose wanted to learn to make chili.

Why did Sydney and Shelby always have to be so short-sighted? They only thought about what was right in front of their eyes: A game. A screen. A party. Of course it wasn't all Matt's fault, it was hers too; she hadn't tried hard enough to get through to them. And now they were fully formed and leaving home. Completely out of her reach.

Were they going to be okay? Mary Ellen picked up a can of beans and stared at the list of ingredients. She remembered the kids who partied too hard in college. Everybody laughed about the ones who passed out in the quad or threw up all over Frat Court. But nobody talked about the pledge who ended up in the emergency room with alcohol poisoning.

No one ever mentioned the girls who stumbled back to their dorms with troubled looks on their faces…who withdrew into themselves, sleeping too much and missing classes. Where were those girls now?

Mary Ellen threw the can into her cart and moved toward the checkout counter. It came down to trust, she supposed. She would just have to have faith that her daughters could take care of themselves…that their expensive education and proper upbringing had prepared them for whatever challenges lay ahead. And, of course, that she and Matt had been good role models. They'd done all right at that, hadn't they? They were law-abiding, civilized people. She liked her evening cocktails, but it wasn't like she was blacking out in the middle of the day or creating scenes at parties. She knew when to stop.

She loaded the groceries into the trunk of the car, then took her laptop bag and walked to the edge of the lot to look down the street. A group of old brick buildings was clustered on the next block, like an antique bobbin around which the village was wound. She crossed the street, hands tucked under her armpits. A light snow was falling. She walked briskly toward the brick facades, hoping the library hadn't been relocated to some flat, sprawling building on a parcel of land that would be hard to find.

But no, it was right there, tucked between Village Hall and a stationery store. Mary Ellen looked in the store window, attracted to a display of leather-bound journals next to the more ordinary spiral-bound notebooks and three-ring binders. The journals looked handmade; she wondered if there was a bookbinder living in the woods nearby, turning deer hides into these pretty, floppy-looking books stamped with floral designs and closed with a loop and a wooden button. She pushed through the brass-trimmed door and asked to see them.

"I don't know where they're made." The teenage shopgirl shrugged as she handed a stack of the books to Mary Ellen. She ran her fingers over the designs, trying to decide which one would be the best addition to her collection. One of them, the simplest, was stamped with a single rose. She smiled at the coincidence and thought about her conversation with the girl the night before. Rose was clearly asking for her help—how could she ignore that? This was her chance, Mary Ellen thought, to make a difference for someone. To throw a little light back into the world for a change, instead of wallowing in the shadows.

"I'll take this one," she said, putting it on the counter. She also chose a weighty black pen in a gift box. The girl rang them up, then shoved them briskly into a plastic shopping bag.

It was snowing harder when Mary Ellen got back outside. She entered the library and inquired about Wi-Fi at the front desk, then settled into a worn armchair in a far corner of the high-ceilinged room. She opened up her photo software and began uploading her "accidental" photos to a file server where Justine could view them.

She spent time on her email to Justine, wording it just right, trying not to sound too proud or excited, maintaining a tone of serious contemplation. "I see this as an exploration of postmodernism's obsession with eradicating agency," she wrote. "The images are as blurry, ephemeral, and meaningless as any individual's sense of self." That sounded good. She pushed Send, savoring the sense of accomplishment, and moved on to her work emails.

Her department seemed to be in a state of chaos. The ad agency was pushing back on the need for focus groups; regulatory was giving them grief about the new tagline; budgets and timelines were being tossed overboard like bags of kittens. Mary Ellen rubbed her temples, wondering where to begin. She plumbed several email chains, trying to determine when, exactly, things had gone wrong, who needed a stern talking-to, and where she could even hope to make a difference. The more she read, though, the more her spirits sank. Everybody was so dug in, so invested in defending their tiny little corners in their tiny little world. They were acting as though lives were at stake. Where was the sense of perspective? She hit Reply All on one of the emails and wrote, *It's only advertising. Get a life.* Then, half laughing to herself, she deleted the message and snapped her laptop shut.

She got up and browsed the library stacks until she found some collections of plays. She skimmed through a few, looking for accessible texts, something Rose could read during the next few days while Mary Ellen explored her new approach to photography. She was absorbed in a collection of Stoppard plays when the librarian appeared beside her.

"We're closing early," she said. "For the storm."

"Oh!" Mary Ellen said, blinking at the window, which was busy with clumped snowflakes tumbling fast and heavy. When had it gotten so bad? She gathered her books and checked them out with the library card Justine had given her.

"Careful out there," the librarian said as she locked the front door. "It's a big one."

The Price Chopper parking lot was empty now; the few cars still on the main road drove slowly, their tires spitting slush, wipers frantically waving. Mary Ellen got into her car and started the engine, holding her hands in front of the heat vents. She couldn't believe she'd blown off work like that. Was she crazy? It was only going to be harder to fix things when she got back. Still, there was a hum of excitement in her bones, mixed with self-satisfaction. Her photos…

They'd been launched into the world! She couldn't wait to hear what Justine thought of them. She'd have to come back to town in a few days to check her email again.

Mary Ellen took the journal and pen out of the bag from the stationery store. She opened the book to the first page and sat thinking for a few minutes, watching the snowflakes rapidly darken her windshield. She started writing, slowly and carefully, not wanting to mar the beautiful book with any mistakes.

Dear Rose,

When I saw this journal, I thought of you, not just because of the rose on the cover, but because of all the potential contained in these empty pages. Your life is a story waiting to be written, and I can tell, having spent this time with you, that you are going to create something wonderful. Just remember to pay attention to the things that make you happy, and never let anyone tell you they're not worth doing.

She stopped writing, looked something up on her phone, then continued.

"Only through art can we emerge from ourselves and know what another person sees." —Marcel Proust
I wish you much success with your writing, your education, and your future career.

Your friend,
Mary Ellen

She waited until the ink was dry, then placed the journal

and pen in her purse. By that time, the windshield was packed with snow too heavy for the wipers to clear, so she got out of the car and used the scraper. Finally, she rolled slowly out of the parking lot, squinting into the whirling torrent. A guardrail appeared on the right side of the road, so she focused on keeping it in sight, following it up the mountain. Normally Mary Ellen would have been terrified to drive in these conditions, but she felt a thrill as she plunged through the storm. She was doing this. She was totally doing this. It was a new feeling, this invincibility, and the novelty itself was exhilarating. Most of all, though, she enjoyed the feeling that she was in charge: of her art, her protégé, her *car*.

The GPS told her the turnoff was coming up, so she slowed to a crawl. At the gap in the woods, she bumped over the edge of the road onto the driveway. The snow was falling a little less heavily under the trees, so she was just able to make out the switchbacks ahead of her, and then, down the slope, a glimpse of rust-colored walls. Mary Ellen downshifted and urged the car around the bend, its engine protesting against the low gear. She could feel the snow brushing against the underside of the little car, so even when the drive steepened on the next switchback, the car descended sluggishly. "Come on," Mary Ellen growled, impatiently shifting back up to third, letting the snow do the braking for her. At the bottom of the drive, where the trees cleared away, was a small rise, and Mary Ellen, eager to go inside and give Rose her gift, accelerated confidently to climb over it. But instead of going up and over the little hill, the front of the car plunged straight into it, lifted upward slightly, and stuck there with a crunching jolt.

"Shit," Mary Ellen said, touching her forehead to the steering wheel.

She'd forgotten to call the girls.

15

Nice going, lady, Ivy thought, watching Mary Ellen spin her tires deeper and deeper into the snowdrift. Even if she managed to get the car out—which wasn't looking too likely—Ivy could tell they wouldn't be going anywhere for a while. It was snowing the way it did sometimes in Good Hope—lake-effect snow, they called it. It was the kind of snow that meant you were going to be stuck inside for three or four days, so you'd better be prepared to spend some serious quality time with your antsy, not-making-any-money relatives. The last time it happened, Colin spent so much time doing curls in the basement that his bicep popped and balled up in his arm. It took the ambulance forever to show up, so he ended up walking to the emergency room.

Why did she have to sneak off like that, without giving Ivy a chance to go into town with her? Ivy would've appreciated a change of scenery, and maybe a chance to have a say in the grocery selection. She also could've dropped a few more hints about college tuition, and maybe helped the lady find a branch of her bank.

"I got some more food," Mary Ellen announced, bursting in the front door with a bundle of grocery bags and a gust of freezing air. "Which is good, considering I got the car stuck." She heaved the bags onto the kitchen table and shrugged off her coat. "I left early...didn't want to wake you. I hope you weren't worried."

"I would've liked to go."

"Oh." Mary Ellen pulled out a can of beans and set it on the counter. "I'm sorry. I thought you'd rather sleep. I had to do some work stuff, make some phone calls." Her face clouded, and she continued putting away groceries. "Oh, and! Don't worry... I remembered what you said last night."

"You did?"

Mary Ellen pulled a package of ground beef out of a bag. "Chili! I'm going to show you how to make it."

"Oh." Ivy went over to the sofa and sat down.

"No better time than a snowstorm, right? Snow always makes me want to cook something in a big pot. Chili...beef burgundy...coq au vin." The lady started humming. Ivy didn't know what she had to be so cheerful about.

"Is anyone going to come plow the driveway?" Ivy asked.

"Um." The lady had her head in a cabinet. She stayed that way for a moment, tapping the door with her fingers. "I think I have that set up, yes. They're supposed to come after a big snow. But they're a little flaky, so we'll see." She slammed the cabinet shut and started folding paper bags.

"'Cause if they don't, you know, we're going to be here till March."

"Don't worry. My car can get up that hill. We just have to dig it out of that drift is all."

We? Mario Andretti here buried her car up to its tailpipe, and now Ivy was supposed to dig it out? With her hands? "There's no shovel, you know."

"Oh, I'm pretty sure I have one around here—"

"No, you don't. You don't come here in the winter. Remember?"

Mary Ellen stared at Ivy for a second, working her jaw back and forth, then pressed her mouth into a smile. "We'll figure something out. Are you worried? We have plenty of food."

"No." Ivy sighed. "I just don't like feeling trapped."

"Well, I think it's kind of cozy. When you're nice and warm inside, watching the snow fall, good smells coming out of the kitchen. You don't have to go anywhere or do anything because, well, you *can't*."

Don't roll your eyes, Ivy commanded herself. *Do not. Roll. Your eyes.*

Mary Ellen picked up her purse and a pile of books and came to sit on the sofa opposite Ivy. "So," she said.

"So."

"I was thinking about what you said last night."

"About the chili?"

"No." Mary Ellen smiled, crinkling her eyes. "About how everyone needs help along the way as they go after what they want. Especially if they're taking the, you know, less-traveled path. It's hard to do it all on your own. I realize that." She clapped her hands on the tops of her thighs. "So if it's all right with you, I'd like to be there for you. As a mentor. Not just now, but later. While you're in college, and maybe afterward too? I'd like to stay in touch and, you know, offer my help along the way."

"Oh," Ivy said, feeling a dumb, surprised smile tug at her mouth. "Wow. Thank you. That would be amazing."

Mary Ellen opened her purse. "Wonderful." She put her hand inside her purse and drew a deep breath like she was nervous or excited or something. "So I have something for you."

Ivy sat up. Okay. Maybe she'd have to endure another couple of days imprisoned with a crazy lady, but it would be easier knowing she had enough money to get to Montana when she finally got out. *Way* easier.

Mary Ellen pulled something out and laid it on the coffee table in front of Ivy. Ivy leaned forward. It was a leather book and a black box. She waited for the lady to pull out an envelope too, but that didn't happen, so she picked up the black box and opened it. A pen. She picked up the book and flipped through the pages, but there was nothing tucked inside.

"Aren't you going to read it?"

Ivy went back to the first page and skimmed the inscription, then closed the book and set it down on the table. "Was there...anything else?"

"What do you mean? It's a gift. I saw it and thought of you. I wanted you to have it. I also got you these books from the library. They're plays. See? Arthur Miller, Tennessee Williams..."

It was coming on now. Ivy could feel it—that familiar squeeze, like there was a locked seat belt crushing her chest, tightening its grip every time she tried to move. No way out, no way forward, just glass and snow and the suffocating weight of this lady's need, her hot, hopeful breath and hungry, empty eyes looking at her like she wanted to swallow her whole. A mentor. Fuck. A mentor and an empty book. How far would that get her? About as far as the front door. About as far as the car that was stuck in a snowdrift and probably would be till March. She tried to take a deep breath, but her chest was too tight.

"Who—"

"Yes?"

Ivy gripped her knees. "Who are you?"

Mary Ellen blinked at her, still smiling. "What?"

"Whose house is this?"

"It's mine, of course. I don't know what you—"

"No, no, no, stop that. I don't want to do this anymore. I know this isn't your house; I know you don't belong here. Just tell me. Who are you?"

Mary Ellen sat back, shaking her head in small, trembling movements. "This is how you *thank* me?"

"Tell me the truth."

"I've been telling you the truth."

"So you're saying this really is your place. These are your books; these are your clothes." Ivy yanked the hem of the shirt she was wearing. "Those are your paintings in the basement."

Mary Ellen rolled her lips between her teeth.

"See? See? You don't even know about them. Because you didn't paint them. They're not yours."

"Of course they're mine," Mary Ellen hissed, standing up and brushing invisible crumbs from her lap. "Of course they're mine. I just…" She walked to the stairs, went down one step, and stopped. "Forgot."

16

Mary Ellen hurried the rest of the way downstairs. It took her a couple of tries to find the basement door; there were two closets in that hallway, which was confusing. When she found the right door, she descended into the musty smell and flickering fluorescent light, pausing to lean against the railing at the bottom of the stairs.

Teenagers! What had made Rose turn so *hostile*? After Mary Ellen had been so thoughtful, so generous with her time and encouragement. She couldn't believe the way the girl had tossed the journal aside, barely reading the inscription, not even pretending to be grateful. And then to accuse Mary Ellen of lying. What had set her off? She was just like Sydney and Shelby—on hair triggers, all of them! Had Mary Ellen been that way at that age? She honestly couldn't remember.

She walked to the corner and lifted a sheet from the stack of medium-size canvases that were leaned against the wall. She picked up a painting: a grotesque still life, tampons spilling out of an antique vase, some maxi pads arranged in a fruit bowl. She studied the flat, poorly proportioned objects, the uncertain lighting, the overworked velvet drape.

She picked up another canvas, feeling her heart sink: a child pulling a gun out of a cereal box—his arm oddly bent, one eye higher than the other, the table slightly foreshortened. Another one: a Barbie doll clamped in a vise. Mary Ellen paddled through the stacks, impatiently scanning, searching for something she couldn't name. Canvas after canvas revealed little more than a churlish contempt for traditional painting and some flippant swipes at contemporary culture—but no sign of Justine besides her meek initials, JMV, painted in one corner.

Mary Ellen backed away from the paintings and sat on the basement steps. It was hard not to feel cheated. Not by the realization that Justine was a terrible painter—that was useful, even touching, assuming Justine cared about something as uncool as technique. But Mary Ellen had been hoping to find something more substantial under that drape. Something to fill out the armature of Justine's persona, to put a little flesh on the bone.

Mary Ellen could hear Justine scolding her for her childish notions about art. "I'm not interested in your insides," she'd always said in class. "Self-expression is an elitist practice. I won't allow you to penetrate me with your point of view." And Mary Ellen got it—she really did. She'd read all the literature dismantling modernism and its self-centered, white male privilege; she understood the arguments against identity, individualism, authenticity. Reading about these ideas excited her—They were so counterintuitive! So full of bravado!—and when faced with a work of art, she normally reveled in the game of criticality. But now, here, in this flickering basement, she felt only disappointment. She wanted more. Not just from Justine as a person, but from art.

Mary Ellen rubbed her eyes with the heels of her hands.

What was she doing? The whole idea that she could go off to the woods and become an artist was ridiculous. It was the kind of thing people did on reality shows—frumpy housewife turned supermodel! Homeless drug addict turned master chef! The myth of reinvention was etched so deeply into the culture that it resembled the very grain of life. But now Mary Ellen was beginning to see it for what it was: the foolish dreams of the teenage mind, acted out with costumes and scripts and two-dimensional scenery.

She stared glumly at Justine's swiping brushstrokes. The paintings were too easy—that was what really bothered her. Jokey, tossed-off remarks, like an anonymous comment on the internet. Not that she was in any position to judge; the photos she'd just sent to Justine hadn't even required conscious thought. Accidental photographs! She'd actually thought they were an artistic breakthrough. She'd actually thought they were good.

What was it her father always said? "Good things come to those who work their asses off." She smiled, imagining him rolling his eyes at Justine's pictures, at the very idea of turning one's back on talent, skill, beauty, truth. He'd probably take the opportunity to bring up the tumultuous career of his beloved John James Audubon, a favorite happy hour topic. *He was the real thing, that one. Never let anything get in his way. Did you know rats ate all of his drawings, forcing him to start over? Rats!*

Justine, on the other hand, seemed to feel that an artist could be cobbled together by anyone with the right nuts and bolts—the right buzz, connections, contempt for sincerity, demographic disadvantage, friends at *BOMB*. She was wrong, of course—the proof of that was piled against the basement wall. And yet, for some reason, she seemed determined to apply her formula to Mary Ellen.

Mary Ellen still couldn't fathom what that reason could be. Her memory of that night on the roof deck was fuzzy, but she knew she'd put the question to Justine at one point. Justine had said she wasn't in it for any sort of commission; she just wanted to help. And she'd said something about people thinking she was washed up, since she'd been fired from that fancy art school. "Justine never does anything just to be nice." Hadn't someone told Mary Ellen that at the party? She was beginning to come up against the hard edge of that truth.

And okay, maybe that was how it worked. If the art world was like any other business, then of course it was about who you knew and how you positioned yourself and what the market was looking for. She couldn't fault Justine for working the system. But sitting here, looking through her fingers at the garish colors splashed across Justine's canvases, Mary Ellen began to suspect she'd wandered into a fun house-mirror version of the very career she was trying to escape.

She groaned and rubbed her temples. She couldn't believe she'd come all the way out here on a fool's errand. Leaving her job, imperiling her marriage, abandoning her children. Her children! Poor Sydney and Shelby, waiting for a call that never came. She'd been so focused on her own self-serving mentorship—another pointless exercise—that she'd forgotten about her own flesh and blood.

She felt a crushing wave of guilt, spiked with anxiety about what Matt was thinking and saying about her now. She was a terrible mother; he had every right to think that. What he probably didn't realize was that she wanted very, very much to do better. She'd made it sound like she didn't care one way or the other, but she did care, she cared so much, and she wanted him—and the girls—to know that.

Mary Ellen stood up quickly and went upstairs. The living room windows were frantic with fast-falling snow. She crossed the room and looked out at the driveway, but she couldn't make anything out through the rushing whiteness. "I need to make a phone call," she said to Rose, who was curled up on the sofa. "I've got to dig the car out and go back to town."

Rose didn't move, except to draw her eyebrows together. "In this?"

"I have good tires. I just need to get out of that drift. Anyway, if we wait any longer, we're going to be stuck here forever."

Rose didn't say anything. Mary Ellen began pulling on her coat, boots, hat, gloves. "Don't you want to get out of here? I can take you to the bus station."

Rose sat up slowly. "I told you. There's nothing to shovel with."

Mary Ellen went to the kitchen and began slamming through cabinets. She pulled out saucepan and a ladle and returned to the living room, holding them in the air. "Voilà!"

Rose rolled her eyes and lay back down.

"Okay, thanks a lot," Mary Ellen said. She pulled her car keys out of her purse and shoved them in her coat pocket, then took a deep breath and plunged into the swirling cold.

It really was snowing quite hard. The wind, which had become ferocious, made it almost impossible to walk in a straight line. Mary Ellen held up the saucepan to shield her face from the stinging flakes. The snow on the ground was deep enough to crumble into the tops of her boots, and she could see that the drift where her car was stuck had been sculpted into a smooth, car-enveloping dune.

She began scraping snow away from the hood and

windshield. The ladle did little more than make short, narrow channels, so Mary Ellen tossed it aside and focused on taking larger scoops with the saucepan. The cuffs of her coat soon filled with icy wetness, and wind-hurled snow-flakes burned her cheeks. She alternated swiping at the car with the pan and with her left forearm, but as she worked, the snow packed down and became hard, so she cleared less and less with each swipe. She clawed at it with her fingers, but it just jammed up against itself, becoming dense and heavy under her hands.

Her arms were starting to ache. She leaned against the car for a moment, pulling her fur hood around her face. Through the curtains of snow, she could see a figure staggering toward her. It was Rose, hood drawn into a tight O on her face, jean jacket buttoned up over the sweatshirt. There were socks on her hands, and she was carrying two canoe paddles.

"Brilliant!" Mary Ellen cried, but the wind carried her voice away, so she showed her enthusiasm with exaggerated clapping motions. Rose handed her a paddle, and she slid it into the hard-packed snow on the windshield, leaning on the handle until the blade popped up, spraying her and Rose with snow. Rose put her head down and went around to the other side of the car, where she began scraping at the snow around the front tire.

They worked like that for a long time, until finally there was enough snow cleared from the doors and the tailpipe for Mary Ellen to get inside the car and start it up. She pushed open the passenger door and yelled out to Rose, "Get in!"

When Rose shut the door behind her, the silence fell over them like a heavy quilt. Mary Ellen leaned her head back and closed her eyes for a moment, breathing hard, feeling the burn of blood rising to the tips of her ears, her fingers, the edges of her nostrils. She pulled off her gloves and held her fingers in front of the heat vent. She looked over at Rose, who was using her teeth to tug at the wet sock on one hand. The sock was caked with snow, and the girl didn't seem to have the strength to pull it off. "Oh no," Mary Ellen said, reaching over and peeling the soggy bags from Rose's hands, which were bright red and shaking. "You need to go inside and put on some dry clothes. You're not dressed for this."

"Yeah."

"Thank you for helping. You shouldn't have stayed out here this long. My God, you're really frozen."

Rose loosened the sweatshirt hood and cleared it away from her face, which looked paler than usual. She shifted suddenly to the side, looking under her rear with alarm. "What the—"

Mary Ellen laughed. "Heated seats."

"Oh." Rose looked embarrassed. "I thought I peed myself."

"It takes a little getting used to."

"Do you think you can get the car out?"

"I'm going to try." Mary Ellen got the front and rear windshield wipers going, then put the car in reverse. The tires spun, and the car didn't move. She put it into first. "Sometimes you have to work it back and forth," she said. But the car seemed to have no interest in going either direction. She shifted a few more times, varying the pressure on the gas.

"Turn the wheel," Rose said.

"I don't think it'll help."

"Well, this isn't working."

"See?"

"Try it in reverse again."

"Rose, the wheels are spinning. There's nothing I can do about it!"

189

"Don't gun it so hard! Try it slower!"

Mary Ellen tried a few more times, then slammed the car into Park. "It's not working, okay?" She put a hand on her cheek and tried to calm her breathing. "I think the middle of the car is up on a pile of snow. The tires are barely touching."

"Maybe we can jam something under them. Like branches or something."

Mary Ellen stared at the windshield, which was newly blanketed with snow. "I'm starting to think I can't drive in this."

"But you said!"

"It's late… Look how dark it's getting. And it's coming down harder than ever."

Rose huffed and flopped back in her seat.

"Trust me, I want to get out of here as bad as you do. I need to call my…my…"

"Husband? Daughters?" Rose was staring straight ahead.

Mary Ellen looked at her for a moment, calculating. "Did you go through my things?"

Rose laughed and got out of the car, slamming the door behind her. A swirl of snow blew in and settled into clear droplets on the dashboard. Mary Ellen switched off the engine and pulled her gloves back on, steeling herself for the blustery walk back to the house.

She didn't necessarily owe Rose an explanation. So she'd changed a few details of her life. Who didn't do that when they met someone new, someone they probably wouldn't ever see again? Rose probably wasn't being 100 percent honest about everything either. The way she'd been acting since Mary Ellen got back from town—so different from the sweet, vulnerable girl she'd first found in the deer blind— was disconcerting. She was probably as full of secrets and lies as any other teenager.

Mary Ellen tugged her hood around her face and left the car's warm stillness. The light was fading fast, but she could see enough to tell that the car was once again caught in a wave of drifting snow. She picked up one of the canoe paddles and used it to steady herself as she staggered toward the yellow glow of the living room windows.

Once inside the house, she took a hot shower and put on dry clothes, feeling her agitation soften with the stroke of a hairbrush, the comfortable slip of wool socks on the bamboo floor, the lighting of the stove. Exertion followed by relaxation; cold followed by warmth; disappointment followed by a good drink and a bowl of hearty food. The older Mary Ellen got, the more she appreciated this simple sort of ebb and flow; the more she depended on it, really, for any sort of equilibrium.

Rose was nowhere to be found, but when chopped onions hit the hot oil, she appeared on the stairs.

"I'm making chili if you want to watch," Mary Ellen said.

Rose hesitated, then came into the kitchen and leaned her hip against the counter, arms crossed.

"Some people add garlic, but I like it without." Mary Ellen pushed the onion around the pan, watching it relax. She shook some salt and pepper into the pan. "Chili's one of those recipes you can change to your own taste and it'll still be good, you know? Beans, no beans. Some people add cinnamon."

Rose made a face.

"I know! I don't do that. Can you open this for me?" She handed Rose a can of tomato paste. "My secret ingredient is beer. I didn't buy any, though, because they only had Budweiser and Coors. That stuff's terrible. You might as well just use water."

"I don't like the taste of beer anyway," Rose said, pulling the can opener out of a drawer.

"Well, good. You're too young for it." Mary Ellen paused her stirring and put the back of her hand against her mouth.

"What?"

"Nothing."

"What?"

Mary Ellen scooped tomato paste into the pan and added some chili powder. The fruity, fiery smell filled the kitchen. "I guess you saw the picture of my girls in my wallet?"

Rose shrugged.

"Did you take anything while you were in there? Money?"

"No! God."

"Okay, it's just, I don't know what to think anymore." Mary Ellen got the ground meat out of the fridge. "You should try to get organic beef if you can. This was all they had."

"How old are they?"

"My girls? Seventeen." She popped a finger through the plastic covering the meat and stripped it away. "They were on a ski trip last week, in Colorado. But they got caught buying beer, so they were sent home."

"Oh man."

"I was supposed to call them this morning. But I got caught up in buying you that journal, and I don't know. I forgot."

Rose's face clouded over. "Well, nobody asked you to do that."

Mary Ellen tipped the meat into the pan. "I'm not blaming you." She shook her head. "They probably don't even want to hear from me. They're so much closer to their father. If I yell at them, I'm just going to push them even farther away."

"You should definitely yell at them."

Mary Ellen looked at Rose's face, but she didn't seem to be joking.

"I mean, how else will they know you care?"

Mary Ellen mashed the beef with a spoon, coaxing it into smaller pieces. She'd never really let loose on the girls—it wasn't her style. When they misbehaved, she worked hard to remain calm, explaining their transgression in a levelheaded way, encouraging them to use better judgment next time. And when they spoke to her disrespectfully, she simply rose above the situation, refusing to engage.

"My gran used to yell at me all the time," Rose went on.

"And that was a good thing?"

"Well, I didn't realize it was good until she changed. When she got all withdrawn and stopped giving a…a darn. That felt worse than getting yelled at."

Mary Ellen wondered if her way of dealing with the girls—which she'd always assumed was the enlightened, civilized parenting style of successful people—might have been too soft. Maybe they would've benefitted from the occasional flash of anger. She poured in the canned tomatoes and beans and set the pot to simmer. "We'll let that cook for a little while. Doesn't that smell good? All that shoveling made me hungry." She made herself a drink and sat at the table, staring out at the storm.

Rose sat across from her. "Do you even know whose house this is?"

Mary Ellen kept staring at the gusting, blowing snow. "Yes," she finally said. "My friend Justine. She invited me to come here and work on my photography."

"So you're really a photographer?"

"No." Mary Ellen took a drink. "I'm vice president of marketing at Gallard Pharmaceuticals." She watched Rose's face for signs of disappointment, but the girl remained impassive. "Justine's been helping me get back in touch with my

193

artistic side. I took a class she was teaching, and then this gallery owner... Oh, whatever. The whole thing is stupid."

"So you were pretending to be her? Justine?"

Mary Ellen frowned into her glass.

"Why, exactly?"

"I don't know. It was just easier that way."

"Easier to make stuff up twenty-four hours a day?"

"Okay," Mary Ellen said. "So you know how they say 'Dress for the job you want?'"

"They do?"

"'Fake it till you make it,' 'act as if.' It's all about making people think about you a certain way. Until it comes true."

"You believe in that?"

"Well..." Mary Ellen had no idea what she believed anymore. "I guess it helps you visualize success."

Rose squinted at her. "So let's say I want to become a fireman," she said. "Fireperson. All I have to do is get a Dalmatian and a pair of suspenders and walk around telling everybody I'm awesome at fighting fires, and—*bam!*—I'll turn into a real one?"

"No, obviously—"

"You want to know what I think?" Rose waggled her eyebrows at her. "I think you've just been showing off. This was all some kind of ego trip."

"Oh, please," Mary Ellen scoffed. "Like I need to impress you? Some random girl hiding out in my friend's house?" She swung her legs over the bench. "Anyway, it doesn't matter why I did it." She went into the kitchen and stabbed at the chili a few times with a spoon. It looked done enough. She started pulling out bowls and silverware and napkins.

"So how come you didn't turn me in?" Rose called from the dining room. "Go into town, call the cops?"

Mary Ellen brought the bowls of chili to the table and

set them down. "Can we just eat? I'm starving." She tasted the chili. It was missing something probably the beer. She shook some salt over it.

Rose kept staring at her. "I think it's because you wanted an audience. You kept me around so you'd have someone to show off to. Someone to lecture and preach at."

"Rose." Mary Ellen dabbed her mouth with a napkin. "I wanted to help you. I didn't think turning you over to the authorities was the best way to do that. I thought it would be better to give you some guidance, some encouragement, and yes, okay, maybe I thought I could be kind of a role model. Something I could've used when I was your age."

Rose finally picked up her fork and started to eat. "You keep saying that," she muttered around a mouthful of chili.

"What?"

"That you could've used a mentor or whatever. Like your life is a big failure because the right person didn't come along and tell you what to do. Seems to me you did all right, Miss Vice President of Blah-Di-Blah."

"It's a pointless job." Mary Ellen rested her cheek in her hand. "It just pays well is all."

"Oh man. I'm so sorry." Rose lowered her head and shoveled chili into her mouth, scraping the bottom of her bowl.

"You'll understand some day—"

"No I won't." Rose threw down her spoon. "Excuse me, but fuck that noise."

"Rose! Please."

"You had someone to pay for college, okay? You could do whatever you wanted after that. Be a photographer, be a painter, whatever. You didn't have to pay back eighty grand. You could do anything. *Jesus*."

Mary Ellen felt her nostrils flare. She took a deep breath,

willing herself to stay calm. "I'm sorry, but you're wrong, Rose. My father made me change direction. I was majoring in studio art, and I loved it, but it wasn't good enough. He made me go into marketing."

"So he threatened to cut you off? Or he said he'd beat the shit out of you?"

"Of course not." How could she make this girl understand? It was real, the pressure her parents put on her. The pressure to make them happy and proud. The pressure to eat what they ate, to wear what they wore, to fund her 401(k) and buy a house in the right neighborhood and get her children the best education money could buy.

"Then why didn't you just tell him no?"

"I couldn't. I didn't have a choice."

Rose barked out a laugh. "You had nothing but choices. Please."

Mary Ellen shook her head violently, the way her daughters used to do at the sight of mashed peas.

"Your kids are going too, right? Harvard, Yale. All expenses paid."

"Good lord no. They could never get into those schools."

"Okay, but they're going somewhere, right?"

Mary Ellen blinked at the girl, not fully understanding. "For college? Of course. I mean, how else would they get anywhere in the world?"

"You can get somewhere in the world without college."

Mary Ellen snorted. "Well, sure, it's possible, but come on. *You* know what a dead-end life that usually means. You'll never get very far. I mean, look at your whole situation, the life you're running from—"

"*Jesus fuck*ing Christ." Rose stood up, swiping her bowl off the table.

"Excuse me?"

"It's a trap, okay?" She went to the kitchen and threw her bowl into the sink with a clatter. "For people like me anyway. They say 'Oh, college is your ticket out of here; it's your big chance.' They get the guidance counselors working for them. My counselor? McFadden? She goes on these boondoggle trips every year, on the school's dime. It's fucking ridiculous. Then all the kids get in, of course, and everyone throws a party, and then—*then*—they decide to mention you need eighty, ninety, a hundred grand. Us! People like us!"

"Okay, but—"

"'But you can get financial aid! You can get a scholarship!'" Rose waggled her hands in the air. "Yeah...for two thousand dollars. And by that time, you've had the party and you've bought your extra-long twin sheets and you've seen your ma cry *tears* of motherfucking *joy*. So you borrow the rest, and bam, game over. You lose." Rose shook her head.

"No, but I guess I'm confused?" Mary Ellen pushed her hair away from her face. "I thought your family didn't want you to go to college."

"That's Rose's family." Rose sat back down at the table and gave Mary Ellen a hard look.

"What?" Mary Ellen shook her head. She was having a lot of trouble following this conversation, and she hadn't even had that much to drink.

"I'm not Rose," Rose said, balling her hands into fists and lowering them gently to the table, unfurling her fingers into two open fans.

"Excuse me?"

"I'm not Rose. I'm Ivy."

17

If she'd known how good that was going to feel, she'd have done it days ago.

The lady was opening and closing her mouth like a confused fish. "You mean, Rose isn't your name?"

"I mean, Rose isn't who I am."

Mary Ellen jerked her head back, squinting. "Then who are you?"

"I'm Ivy."

"But the whole college thing—"

"Was bullshit. I'm not running away to go to college; there's no aunt in Pittsburgh; my dad's been dead since before I was born. I've never written a play. I've never even *seen* a goddamned play. Unless you count school plays, which are fucking stupid." Ivy paused, enjoying the gush of truth, hoping she wasn't going too far. "I'm headed out west. I have other plans."

The lady had turned kind of white, and it occurred to Ivy that she didn't know CPR. They'd taught it in health class, but she'd cut school that day. "Don't worry," she added. "I'm not, like, a psycho or anything."

"Well, I should *hope*..." Mary Ellen shook her head and

got up to refill her drink. When she came back, she edged warily around Ivy's side of the table, keeping an eye on her like she was a hairy spider or something. She set her drink down, then casually reached for her camera bag, which was at the end of the table. She shouldered it and picked up her laptop.

"And I'm not gonna steal your stuff," Ivy said.

"I'm just making sure I don't forget anything. I want to get packed tonight so we can leave first thing in the morning." Mary Ellen went to the door and picked up her purse, rooting through it to make sure everything was there. She took everything over to the living room, where the journal and pen were still sitting on the coffee table. She put down her belongings, picked up the journal, and stood for a moment, reading what she'd written inside. She shook her head sadly. "I just—" She closed the book.

"What?"

Mary Ellen came back to the dining room table. "Are you sure you don't want to be a writer? I mean, I could just see it. You seem so creative." She gave a half-hearted little laugh.

Ivy rolled her eyes. "No, I'm telling you, I'm not that person." She went to the hooks by the door and took her wallet out of her jacket pocket. She pulled out the Montana newspaper clipping and looked at it. The picture had always explained everything—to her, anyway. Now she realized the lady wasn't going to understand a damn thing about it.

"What's that?"

"Nothing."

"Let me see it."

Ivy huffed impatiently and slapped the clipping onto the table. "It's a baby deer hanging from a telephone wire. It's in Montana. Okay?"

Mary Ellen sat down and studied the clipping, reading the brief story under the picture. "How sad. Why do you have this?"

"That's where I'm going."

"Missoula, Montana?"

"Yeah."

"To see the baby deer? I think it's probably gone by now. Look, the guy in the picture is—"

"I know it's gone. Jesus, no. I just want to see stuff *like* that. Eagles. Mountains. *Real* mountains, not like this bullshit. The Going-to-the-Sun Road."

Mary Ellen looked really confused now. "But how are you... I mean, what's your plan? You're just going to travel around sightseeing?"

"I have a plan, don't worry. I'm gonna be a smoke jumper." As soon as Ivy said this, she knew it was a mistake. The lady's face screwed up like a stiff old sponge.

"You mean one of those skydiving firefighters?"

"Yes."

"You're going to... Oh wow." Mary Ellen laughed a little, rubbing her eyes like she had a headache. "You're going to, I don't know, walk to Montana, in the middle of the winter, and magically get hired to do one of the most physically demanding jobs on the planet. That's great. That's perfect."

"What?"

"Everything. This trip, my photography, Justine, you. I don't know." She plunked her chin into her hands and said softly, as if to herself, "It's all just turned to shit."

"Excuse me?" Ivy crossed her arms and grabbed handfuls of her shirt.

"Nothing. Never mind."

"You think my plan is shit? Well, screw you. I don't care what you think."

Mary Ellen shook her head slowly. Suddenly, her face began to swell with tears. "It's just... I liked Rose," she said, stretching her hand out. "Okay? I really, really... She was like a—"

"Oh, fuck off!" Ivy yelled. "This is me, okay? This is what you get. Accept me as I am, or leave me the hell alone."

"No!" Mary Ellen sluiced a tear from her cheek with the flat of her hand, like a little kid. "I don't have to accept it! You don't either... You can do something with your life! Get educated, expand your horizons!"

"That's what I'm *doing*! God *damn*." Ivy snatched up the newspaper clipping and shoved it back into her wallet. She sat heavily on the bench opposite Mary Ellen, her back to the table. She could hear the lady slurping from her glass, and the sound plucked violently at her nerves. If they couldn't get the car out in the morning, she was walking up to the road and hitchhiking. End of story.

"Do you even know anybody out there? In Montana?" Mary Ellen's voice sounded all quavery.

"No."

"Where were you planning to stay?"

"I'll figure it out. I'll get a place."

"Do you have any money?"

"I'll get a job, okay? Just..." Ivy flapped her hand. The last thing she felt like doing right now was finessing her Montana plan with some clueless rich lady.

"It's hard to get a job when you're homeless. I'm just saying. And the economy out west, well, it's tough these days." Slurp. "Have you thought about transportation? You'll need a car. Missoula's very spread out. Of course, you'll need a credit history. Hard to get credit without a credit history. That's another—"

"Would you please shut up?" Ivy jumped up and pushed the bench backward with one foot. It fell over with a loud *bang*. "I said I'd figure it out! Why can't you stop lecturing for one second? It's like a sickness with you. It's like you think you don't exist if you're not telling someone else what to do. Jesus."

"I saved your life!" Mary Ellen was raising her voice, but it sounded like she was out of practice. It came out all squeezed. "I took care of you. I fed you! You have no right to roll your eyes and ignore me and act like I'm just some kind of annoying *gnat*—"

"Stop yelling at me!"

"Well then, how else will you know I care?" Mary Ellen spit this out with so much sourness and sarcasm that Ivy did a double take.

"Jesus," Ivy said, moving over to the living room window that overlooked the ravine, putting some distance between them. The wind was squealing around the corners of the house, scraping across her nerves like a cheese grater. Her heart was beating fast, and there was an old, familiar darkness creeping around the edges of her eyesight. *Keep it cool*, she told herself. *Don't lose hold*—

"I should've known as soon as you started angling for money." Mary Ellen went for the gin bottle. "You were conning me. 'We artists have to stick together.' Yeah, right. This whole time, you were just some homeless dropout. I can't believe you would make all that stuff up about your father, and about your mom being sick. Lung disease! Oh my gosh. You got me with that one; I'll admit it. But you've never had to deal with anything like that in real life, have you? You're too young. You don't know anything about real problems."

Ivy screamed, attacking the nearest thing to her, which was the window. She pounded it with her fists and her forearms, but it was solid as a wall. It didn't even shake. She whirled around, looking for something to crush, shatter, obliterate. Mary Ellen had stopped, midpour, and was staring at her wide-eyed, the green bottle sagging in her hand. Between them stood the coffee table, piled with Mary Ellen's belongings.

Ivy lifted the thick canvas camera bag, which was surprisingly heavy, letting it swing from her hand as she glared at Mary Ellen. She could feel her heart folding in on itself over and over, growing blacker with every beat. She strode back to the window, flipped the latch, and heaved the plate glass down its track.

"Rose! Wait!" Mary Ellen shrieked. Ivy swung back her arm, then arced the camera bag up, over her head, and out into the night, feeling an intense rush of joy, like it was her inside the bag, flying through the air into the swirling darkness. She turned and grinned at Mary Ellen, snow dancing around her head and shoulders, the cold air like a first kiss.

"I'm not Rose," she reminded the lady, a lilt of triumph in her voice. "I'm Ivy."

18

Mary Ellen put a hand over her mouth. She set down the gin bottle, walked to the window, pulled it closed.

Her hands were shaking; she locked them together, willing herself to total stillness. Ivy was hopping from one foot to the other like a boxer, but Mary Ellen refused to look at her. She walled her off, set her aside, put her on her list of things to do. She took her coat from the hook on the wall and tried tugging on one of her boots, but standing on one foot was problematic. She brought the boots over to the bench and got them on, then went downstairs and turned on the deck lights.

She slid open the back door and waded through the snow to the point where the flat, white expanse dipped softly into the woods. She strained to see beyond the light's edge, but the darkness was absolute. Somewhere down there, she told herself, her camera was nestled safely in a fluffy white mound, maybe on a bed of ferns or fallen pine boughs. The Tamrac Ultra Pro camera bag—it was a splurge, but she'd bought it for just this kind of situation. All right, maybe not this exact situation. But it was waterproof. Shock absorbent.

She looked back at the house and aligned herself with

the upstairs window, then stepped off the edge of the deck, stumbling to one side when her foot landed on something hard and slippery under the snow. She caught herself and shuffled forward, squinting to see where the ground dropped off. Her foot cracked through a nest of branches, and as she yanked it out, she lost her balance and pitched forward, her leg stretching into nothingness for a moment, her rear end finally meeting the ground almost at the exact same time as her shoulders. Mary Ellen flailed her arms, one of which managed to snag itself on a spindly bush of some kind. With lots of snapping of thin, dry branches, Mary Ellen got both hands into the bush and grasped its relatively sturdy inner stalk while she twisted around and managed to arrange herself into something like a crouch.

Snow was everywhere: in her boots, in her pants, in her mouth. She was panting, shaking her head to get the snow out of her hair, waving one of her hands around in search of a thicker trunk that could provide more upward leverage. She tried crawling on all fours, but the snow wouldn't pack under her knees; it just fell apart beneath her, and she found herself sliding downward in terrifying spurts. Finally, she got one arm hooked around a pine tree and managed to seize a root with her other hand, and where her body had scraped the snow away, her feet were finally able to grab hold of the ground.

After struggling back to level ground and stepping back onto the deck, Mary Ellen rested for a moment with her hands on her knees. Her head was spinning. She did her best to brush the snow, dirt, and pine needles from her coat, then shuffled back inside and turned off the deck lights. Dropping her coat on the hallway floor, she went into her bedroom, locked the door, undressed, and burrowed under her comforter, dragging a pillow along with her.

Clamped hard against her face, the pillow couldn't prevent the sobs from forming, but it absorbed them somewhat as they hurtled past her clenched teeth. The realization had torn into her like lead shot—hot and unrelenting, spraying pain in every direction.

There was nothing beautiful in this world.

When Mary Ellen woke up the next morning, bruises humming up and down her hip and thigh, she came up with a basic plan and held it tight. Dig out the car. Go into town. Call the police. She'd say the girl had shown up during the storm, and let them deal with her. Then she would drive home and resume her life, pretending this ill-advised sabbatical had never happened.

The snow had stopped falling; it was piled precariously on the pine boughs and slathered down the sides of their trunks. She thought about her camera, just another snow-covered mound. Going after it would take too much time, and navigating that slope was too risky. She could break a leg, or worse. Hunters were probably out there, ready to shoot anything that moved. And anyway, this seemed to be just the wake-up call she needed. The camera would stay behind, in this wild and implausible place, and she would return to civilized life, newly appreciative of her house and her family and the purposeful routine of her important and well-paid job.

Mary Ellen closed her eyes and tried to conjure the soothing balm of office carpeting and purring phones and her Outlook calendar neatly bricked up with meetings. It would probably take a few late nights and weekends to get her team back on track after her absence, but that was all right. Matt and the girls would understand. They always did.

Review the physician quals... Meet with the consumer solutions team... Narrow down the direct marketing tactics. She ticked through a list of tasks in her head, but around the edges of her drowsy musing came a new sensation—a feeling like tar, spreading stickily across the clear morning, making it hard to move.

She'd been lied to. Humiliated. Worse, the entire thing was her fault. She was the one who'd let the girl stay. She was the one who'd cared for her, fed her, listened to her, believed her. She'd tried to do the right thing, as if she could somehow find a glimmer of redemption in these lonely, unforgiving woods. But of course things didn't work that way. Mary Ellen would not be let off with a few hours of community service.

She peeled off the covers and pulled her suitcase out of the closet. She began thrusting her clothes into it the way one does at the end of a trip—with sloppy ambivalence. Dig out the car. Go into town. Call the police. It was going to feel good, she promised herself, to free the car and climb out of this mess, even if she couldn't muster much excitement about what awaited her back home. Sure, it was disappointing that her photography hadn't worked out. And yes, she was probably giving up on it too easily. But that wasn't entirely her fault. By tossing her six-thousand-dollar camera into the ravine, the girl had kind of made the decision for her.

Mary Ellen sat on the bed, letting herself be pulled a little further into the tarry darkness. She was always doing that, wasn't she—letting people decide for her. What to eat, where to work, what kinds of pictures to take. "You had nothing but choices," the girl had said, and on that point at least, she was probably right. Other people—people like Rose—faced real hardship; they hardly had any choices. And okay, maybe Rose wasn't real, but somehow Mary Ellen couldn't stop thinking about her imaginary struggle. Rose had chosen something better for herself, against all odds. There was no reason Mary Ellen couldn't do the same thing.

She scrubbed her face with her hands and stood up. She went into the hall and pulled on her boots and her coat, whose folds were still wet from spending the night on the floor, the fur around the hood matted and flecked with mud. She went out the sliding door and followed the previous night's footprints, which were slashed across the deck in a not-very-straight line, and stepped down into the trampled bracken. She scanned the slope, looking for a patch of black canvas interrupting the white expanse, but the bag wasn't visible. She kicked at a clump of snow, but it offered no resistance, just exploded into a little white puff and quietly disappeared back into itself. She pounded the side of a tree with her fist, which hurt, and which caused freezing clumps to fall on her head and down the back of her collar. "Goddamn it." She grimaced, pawing the snow away from the back of her neck. "Goddamn it!"

She'd spent so much time since her father's death resenting the way he'd crushed her dreams, so much emotional energy shifting the blame away from herself. But the time for blame was long past. Wasn't this the moment—here in these lonely woods, face-to-face with all her failings—to reclaim what was rightfully hers?

Her feet made creaking sounds as she high-stepped into the forest, but otherwise the mountain was utterly silent, more silent than usual, in that post-snowstorm way, when the whole world is wrapped in cotton batting and even children lower their voices. Her boot caught on something and she stumbled, then slipped sideways, one foot skidding straight downward and leaving her in a sort of half split. She sat back on something sharp, yelping in pain.

Matt would have a good laugh at her now, she thought furiously, shifting to one side and pulling up her knees. This was where her artistic pretensions had led her—to a desolate, frozen hillside, no galleries or museums or parties for miles around. Fine. So he'd been right to make fun of her. He'd seen through Justine's hollow aspirations and correctly identified Mary Ellen's fascination as a short-lived schoolgirl crush. What had he called it? "Trying on a costume."

And what would really change once she got back home? Even if she found her camera and somehow managed to use it again, she would still be Mary Ellen and Matt would still be Matt and the girls would still be leaving home in the fall. And the two of them minus the girls would be…what?

And Mary Ellen without her father's expectations would be…what?

She hiccupped and swallowed a sob, kicking at a mound of snow with sudden, impulsive force. The mound gave way, and she went sliding downward in a mini–avalanche, her feet pedaling frantically until they came up against a fallen tree. She sat there for a moment, catching her breath and pressing the backs of her gloves to her eyes. She sighed shakily and looked around for a sturdy trunk to grab hold of. Then she saw, off to her left, caught among the inner branches of a berry-speckled bush, her camera bag.

It took a bit of downward sliding and sideways inching, but eventually Mary Ellen managed to pull herself level with the bush, which, it turned out, was covered with thorns. She grappled briefly with the branches, which bit savagely into her coat's nylon shell and the thin skin of her exposed wrists, finally looping her fingers around the strap and yanking the bag toward herself with an angry yelp.

She slung it over her shoulder and looked for a route back up to the level path, but here it was so steep that even the snow had lost its grip on much of the slope and there was no clear way upward. Below her, though, was a clear leveling off, and then a short descent to the wide, flat bank of the creek, where she could easily rejoin the staircase. Mary Ellen tried scooting carefully toward it on her rear end, but this quickly turned into an uncontrolled slide, and soon, she was sitting in deep snow with her feet resting on the creek's icy crust.

Some narrow streams of water were still moving, but most of the creek had frozen mid-tumble, curling translucently over rocks and boulders, enveloping every stick and leaf in swollen, glassy bulbs. Off to her left, a fallen tree was laced to the stream with strands of ice that started off spindly but widened as they dropped, pooling voluptuously where they met the water's surface. In another spot, a whip-thin branch had been caught in its slide over some rocks, ice bubbling and frothing aggressively over its reddish skin. And in the shallows of the creek's edge, right at her feet, she could see silver-white pearls of air hovering patiently beneath the icy shell.

Mary Ellen sat transfixed, fingering the latches on her camera bag as she cataloged the varieties of time stoppage all around her. It was like a photograph, she thought, like the creek had made a photograph of itself, and the result somehow transcended real life, becoming simultaneously more solid and more ethereal. Justine would say it was too pretty, but was it? To Mary Ellen, there was something inexpressibly sad locked inside the scene, something dark, the way every ice cube or icicle, no matter how clear, was larded with streaks of black when you really looked at it.

As the snow slowly soaked through her pants, Mary Ellen felt another sob rising in her chest. It was just too sad, all of it: her wet pants, her scratched wrists, the indifferent passage of time. Her girls, her sweet girls, waiting for the call that never came. Her father, waiting for the daughter who wouldn't visit because she was too busy with her job, her meaningless job that contributed exactly nothing to the world. Her father, who died waiting, naked and freezing in the bathtub that became his deathbed.

Mary Ellen scrambled to her feet and brushed the snow from her pants and the tears from her cheeks. She slung her camera bag over her shoulder, then decided to inspect her equipment before heading back up the slope. On first glance, nothing seemed to be cracked or dented. She took out her camera, stripped off her gloves, and took a few shots, checking them on the LCD. It seemed to be working fine; at least there was that. One of the pictures happened to catch the morning light coming through the ice formations on the fallen tree, and Mary Ellen was struck by its melancholy beauty. She went toward the tree and took another picture, and another, moving to catch the blue shine as it wrapped around one side of each stalk of ice.

Walking out onto the creek, it occurred to her that it was the invisible slide of water that had created these gorgeous accumulations, these slumping folds and swelling globes. Rather than freezing a single moment, the creek was actually revealing the slow drip of time. The drip of choices, the drip of silence, the drip of unasked questions and withheld answers. Mary Ellen crouched next to a tree branch that had dangled close enough to the stream to have a few of its brown leaves cocooned in ice; she started shooting some close-ups and then stopped, thinking. It was all being swept downstream, wasn't it? Slowly, yes, too slowly to be seen with the naked eye. But from the perspective of the boulders, the tallest hemlocks, the ravine itself, the current was swift. Mary Ellen felt dwarfed, and that, somehow, was a comfort.

She resumed shooting, feeling in the rhythmic sliding and clicking a growing sense of peace. And just behind it, a small tremble of excitement—the same feeling she'd had in that sun-drenched drawing studio, back at UNC, when she'd felt herself getting close to something real, something important, something she'd been blindly chasing without knowing exactly why. She was seeing everything in sharp, miraculous detail, each ice formation a landscape unto itself. She could see into things, through things, to the knobby bark of each stick that was layered with muscles and veins of ice.

She felt herself vanishing into the pictures and, at the same time, easing fully into herself. Her head was filled with the same buzzy lightness that was usually released after the fourth or fifth swallow of gin—only this time she was completely present, and instead of being pulled into a bottomless pool, she was being propelled forward on steady feet. All of her feelings were right there, floating on the surface, clear and bright and plainly visible: her guilt and anger toward her father, her disappointment in herself, the grief of losing her children to adulthood, the sadness of a dull marriage. It was all there, caught in the ice, and it was beautiful.

The wind kicked up, and a cloud of powdery snow swirled down from the tree branches. Mary Ellen aimed her camera upward, into the glittering haze. From somewhere within the haze she heard a loud, creaking moan, and then, with a gush of cold air, the forest slammed shut on her like a book.

She was on her back. She was lying on the ice. She was also up in a tree, which didn't make sense, but a tangle of branches was scratching at her face, and the lower part of her body seemed to be pressed against the trunk. A burst of pain stretched and cracked up and down her leg and back. She gasped and wrestled a copper-colored hemlock frond away from her face. The sky above her was like a mirror of the icy creek, grayish white, bordered by black trees and flowing toward something bigger than itself.

She cried out. Every time she moved, her left leg seemed to burst into flames. She could see where the tree trunk was lying diagonally across her thighs, but she couldn't feel the weight of it, probably because all of her senses were overwhelmed by the scorching pain in her left leg. She tried to sit up, but the pain grew too intense, and bursts of white light began eating away at her vision. She lay back on the ice, her moans tightening into a wail, trying to understand what was happening.

She could move her right leg, just barely, raising it a few inches off the ice until it came up against the tree trunk. Her left leg, though, seemed nailed in place. A tangle of branches blocked her view, preventing her from seeing how badly crushed it was. She reached through the branches with her left hand and carefully patted around the most painful area, in the middle of her thigh. The trunk, she was surprised to discover, wasn't touching the top of her thigh; a branch seemed to be holding it up and off her leg. Around the branch, her thigh felt warm and wet. She pulled her hand away and looked at her fingers and felt herself step out of the scene for a moment, calmly observing the smear of blood and then, exploring a little more with her hand, coming to a more precise understanding of the situation.

She plunged back into her body then, pain exploding in her thigh, a scream flying out of her mouth. A pair of crows tore themselves from a treetop and spiraled upward, following the sound of her voice into the empty sky.

19

I vy wasn't sure what woke her up, but it had startled her enough to get her heart going. She sat up in bed and listened for a little while, wondering if it'd been a bad dream. This place was usually dead silent; she couldn't imagine what could be loud enough to jolt her out of sleep like that.

She got up and went to the window, but there was nothing moving outside, not a squirrel or a bird or even a breeze. It was like everything had been startled into total stillness. She went down the hall and looked out at the deck, which was sloppy with footprints. The sliding door was unlocked. She hugged herself, feeling cold in the thin borrowed pajamas. She checked that Mary Ellen wasn't in her room, then went upstairs.

She must've gone looking for her camera, Ivy thought, standing in the empty living room. The night before, she'd watched the lady out the window, a little worried she was going to break her leg or something, relieved to see her come back inside, then perplexed that she never came back upstairs to finish the argument. It was so weird, the way she hadn't even looked at Ivy when it all went down, the way she'd turned all quiet and folded up. Most people would've at least yelled a little, or smacked her, or broken something. But the lady acted like she wasn't even there. It was spooky. Frustrating.

Ivy went to the kitchen and made a peanut butter sandwich but didn't eat it. She left it on the counter and went back to the window, scanning the woods. The trees had been thickened by the snow, which coated the sides of their trunks and clung to the tops of their drooping boughs, making it hard to see all the way down to the creek. She unlatched the window and slowly slid it open, the cold sucking all the air out of her lungs for a moment. The creek was silent, and even the trees seemed to be holding their breath. Somewhere down there, though, in the muffled quiet, Ivy could hear a voice. It sounded like the lady. Was she singing? Yelling? Ivy leaned forward into the cold air, turning her ear toward the woods. She couldn't make out any words.

"What?" she shouted.

The lady was definitely yelling. It started coming shrill and fast. Ivy heard something that sounded like *please please please* and *suck* or *truck* or something like that.

"What's wrong?" she shouted.

"Help!"

"What happened?"

Then the yelling faded into babbles that didn't sound like English. Ivy listened for a moment, then yelled, "Okay, okay!" and slammed the window shut. She put her hands to her cheeks to warm them. The lady must have fallen. Maybe she was hurt; maybe she just couldn't figure out how to get back up the slope. Ivy went downstairs and got dressed, helping herself to a sweater and some warm socks from Mary Ellen's suitcase. The lady had said there were no bears around here, but what if there were? What if she was

216

being eaten? Wouldn't the bear just turn around and eat Ivy too? She pulled on the rain boots and slowly slid open the deck door, stepping carefully into the snow. Was it a hunter? Had someone shot Mary Ellen by accident—or on purpose? She crept to the edge of the deck and looked down, but she couldn't see anything.

"What happened?" she called.

"Rose! Please! Come down here!"

"Are you hurt?"

"A tree fell on me. I'm... Aaahhh!"

A tree. What the fuck was wrong with these woods? These woods were a straight-up failure, shit dying and falling and trying to kill you all over the place. "Okay, I'm coming!" Ivy called. At least it wasn't a bear.

She found the zigzag path she'd come up on the first day, only now it was less of a path and more of an empty stretch between the trees. She could see little mini-avalanches where Mary Ellen had skipped the zigzag and gone straight down, probably on her butt. Ivy took the longer way, but she still slid a lot because the rain boots had zero traction. The air was colder than she could remember it ever being, the snow powdery soft.

She couldn't see Mary Ellen, but she could hear her whimpering and crying out, her voice all scratchy. She wondered how big of a tree it could be; most of them were so skinny. Ivy remembered the one that had fallen across the road, the one that made her back up and crash the car. One like that could do major damage to a person. She shuddered, not sure she wanted to see what was happening down there. What if Mary Ellen was dying? Would Ivy have to take a knife and put her out of her misery?

"Okay, okay," she said as she got toward the bottom and

Mary Ellen's cries got more desperate. "Where are you?" She saw the lady's legs on the frozen creek. A tree was lying across them, a tangle of rust-colored branches hiding the rest of her from view. Ivy got closer, slipping on the ice, then stopped, seeing blood. "Are you okay? Can you move?" She skirted the bloody ice and crouched next to Mary Ellen's head, parting some fronds to see her face, which was pale.

"I think part of it went through my leg. It's pinned. Can you see?"

Ivy turned reluctantly toward Mary Ellen's leg, lowering her head to see under the tree trunk. "Shit," she said.

"Oh God." Mary Ellen started to cry.

Ivy squeezed her eyes shut, wanting with all her heart to be somewhere else: to be sitting in math class, to be picking cans off the shelf at St. Gabriel's, to be washing Gran's hair in the sink—anything, anywhere, just not here next to this goddamned tree stub poked through the lady's leg like a toothpick through a cocktail frank. She opened her eyes and swallowed hard, trying to sound all casual and normal. "It got your leg pretty good."

The lady started flailing her arms then, breaking off the branches around her face and grasping at the tree trunk, which she basically had no hope of moving from her angle.

"Hold on," Ivy said. "Calm down." She stood up and took a good look at the tree. It was skinny, only about eight inches across, but it was long, stretching out into the middle of the stream. Sharp stubs stuck out here and there, giving it a mean, spiky look. "Should I lift it up?"

"Yes. Yes. I mean, I think so." Mary Ellen craned her neck, trying to see under the tree.

"Can you, like, push yourself away? When I get it off you?"

"I think so."

"Okay." Ivy reluctantly straddled the trunk, not really wanting to do it, not really seeing another way. "Get ready."

"Wait!"

"What?"

"What if, if…" Mary Ellen stammered. She let out a sob-sigh. "What if it starts bleeding like crazy? When the branch comes out? There's a big artery around there."

"I think you're already bleeding like crazy."

"I am?"

"Well…" Ivy held out her arms. "There's blood. Like, coming out."

"Maybe you should just walk up to the road and flag someone down."

Ivy let her hands drop. She sighed and looked up at the sky. Sure. Of course. Walk up to the road, call the cops. "I think that'll take too long," she said. "It's freezing. You're lying on, like, ice."

"I know," Mary Ellen wailed. "But I'm scared of what's going to happen when you pull it out."

"Well, I'm not exactly excited about it either!" Ivy stamped her feet, which were going numb inside the rubber boots. "Should I go get something to bandage it with? So if it bleeds a ton, I can tie something around it?"

"Okay, I guess, yeah." Mary Ellen sniffed. "You'll hurry? It's really cold."

Ivy looked at the lady's face, which was getting whiter by the minute. Her lips were the same color as her skin, making her look like some kind of statue. "Don't worry."

"Come back, okay?"

"Yeah, yeah."

Getting back up the hill was hard with all the snow, and Ivy's heart was working overtime as she kept thinking about

219

the hole in the lady's leg and how she was going to have to deal with it after she pulled the branch out. And then what? Would Mary Ellen be able to get up the slope? Would she be able to drive her car? Pretty much every scenario ended with Ivy walking up to the road, flagging someone down, calling 911. Then she'd have to explain to the cops who she was and what she was doing here and why, exactly, this lady had gone into the ravine looking for her camera. It all ended up fine for the lady and quite shittily for Ivy.

Back at the house, she searched the bathrooms and linen closets until she found a first aid kit under one of the sinks. It was puny, with nothing but bee sting ointment, a few squares of gauze, and a skinny roll of tape. Ivy huffed in frustration and threw the kit into the sink. She looked up, catching sight of her reflection in the mirror: snarled hair, lips bunched together, eyes wide and blinking a mile a minute. She really didn't look like much. Just a dumb kid who didn't know what the hell she was doing. Not somebody you'd want to trust your life with, that was for sure.

Ivy grabbed the backpack out of her room and went upstairs. She found the lady's purse and took out her wallet, holding it in her hand for a moment. Hitch a ride to Eaton. Hop on a bus. It wouldn't be hard to put the lady out of her mind; they'd only known each other—what—five days? How long had it been since Mary Ellen had shown up? Since she'd pulled Ivy out of the tree house, nursed her back to health, and basically tried her damnedest to be Ivy's mom?

Ivy leaned against the counter and put her head in her hands. "Fuck," she whispered.

She left the wallet on the counter and hurried back downstairs to Mary Ellen's room. She shoved a bunch of clothes into the backpack, then thought a minute and added some of the pads that were for pee. She went to the hall closet to get a water bottle. One of the canoe paddles fell out. She took the paddle, filled the bottle, and headed out into the cold.

Mary Ellen looked dazed when Ivy got to her; she slowly tilted her head in her direction and gave her a sleepy smile. "You came."

"Drink some water."

Mary Ellen took the bottle from Ivy and drank, but half the water slid down her neck. She started shaking—hard—which scared Ivy. She tried wiping the water off the lady's neck with her hand, but most of it had already run down into her sweater.

"Sorry," Ivy said. "I brought some stuff to tie around your leg, all right?"

"Okay," Mary Ellen whispered.

"Just get ready to scoot out of there with your good leg. I probably won't be able to hold the tree up for long."

Mary Ellen blew out a few big breaths and nodded. Ivy straddled the tree trunk, carefully avoiding the lady's leg, and wrapped her arms around it.

"Ready?"

"Mmm."

Ivy strained upward, but the tree wouldn't move. "Motherfucker's heavy," she gasped.

Mary Ellen had her hands pressed against her eyes. "Oh God."

"Let me try it this way." Ivy moved to one side of the trunk and squatted next to it. She hooked her elbows under the tree, closed her eyes, and squeezed upward with her legs. "Uuunnnhhh go go go go!"

Mary Ellen shrieked in pain as the branch lifted out of her leg. She pushed herself out of the way, and Ivy let the tree fall to the ice, keeping her eyes on Mary Ellen's grimacing face, desperate to avoid looking at the hole for as long as possible. Mary Ellen was huffing and puffing, her eyes squeezed shut. "Rose," she finally said, "bandage it up. Please."

"Ivy."

"What?"

"Nothing," Ivy muttered, as she opened the backpack and pulled out a pair of flannel pajama pants.

"Try and stop the bleeding. Tie that around my thigh, tight, up here. Like a tourniquet."

Ivy looked where the lady was pointing, and that meant looking at the hole, which was round and jagged and black with blood. Underneath, she could see the sop of blood inside Mary Ellen's coat and all down the back of her pants, which made Ivy's head go feathery, but she breathed through her nose and concentrated on threading the pajama pants under the lady's knee and tying them in a knot above the hole. "Sorry," she said, pulling the knot tight, wincing as Mary Ellen cried out. Blood squeezed out of the hole. "Jesus," Ivy whispered, wiping her hands on her jeans.

"Did you find some bandages?"

"Just these," Ivy said, pulling out two pee pads. She peeled away their backing, sticking the adhesive onto the front of a long-sleeved T-shirt. She slid the whole thing underneath Mary Ellen's thigh, then brought the sleeves of the shirt up and around, added a pad to the top hole and tied the T-shirt over that. Then she tied a pair of long socks around it all to keep it in place, and another pair of pajama pants around the socks for good measure. It was messy, but at least she didn't have to look at the hole anymore, and blood wasn't going all over the place.

"Okay, good," Mary Ellen whispered. "God, I'm so cold."

"Can you move your leg?"

Mary Ellen bent her knee slightly, her mouth stretching into a toothy grimace. She nodded at Ivy. "Yeah. Let's get out of here."

Ivy offered her the canoe paddle, but the lady shook her head. She'd gotten herself into a seated position, leaning back on her arms, and she was kind of panting and blowing air through her lips, squeezing her eyes shut and then opening them. Finally, she looked up at Ivy and said, "Some help?"

Ivy held out a hand, which the lady didn't take. She gave a long, heavy sigh. "You've got to, like, really help me."

Ivy held out both hands, not really sure what the lady was getting at.

"Put your arms around me here," Mary Ellen said, patting her sides. "Then pull me up. Watch the leg."

Ivy bent down and gingerly put her arms around Mary Ellen, turning her head so their cheeks wouldn't touch, locking her hands behind the lady's back. Mary Ellen got her good leg bent and tried rocking herself up, almost pulling Ivy down on top of her, but Ivy twisted toward the lady's good leg and somehow they kind of spiraled upward, Mary Ellen letting out a long, squeezed cry. Ivy started to move out from under Mary Ellen's arm, but she swayed heavily against her like she was about to slide back to the ice.

"Dizzy," Mary Ellen said, closing her eyes and putting her other arm around Ivy's neck. They stood like that for a few moments, Mary Ellen taking deep breaths, which she blew out in hot clouds against Ivy's neck. Ivy felt a powerful urge to push her away, but she clenched her teeth and took the lady's weight.

"Come on," Ivy finally said, "I need to pick up the paddle. Just let me lean down a second." She bent and grabbed the paddle, Mary Ellen holding tight to her shoulder. She rested the grip on the ice and put the paddle into Mary Ellen's other hand.

"My camera."

"Seriously?" Ivy could see the camera lying on the ice a few feet away, near the tree. "Isn't it kind of heavy?"

"You can put it in the backpack. Please?"

Ivy rolled her eyes. "Jesus. Fine." Mary Ellen managed to stay upright long enough for Ivy to retrieve the camera and shove it into the backpack. She slung it onto her shoulders and got herself situated back under Mary Ellen's arm. Mary Ellen clutched Ivy's neck and took a step, her full weight surging against Ivy, making her knees buckle. Mary Ellen let out a little cry as they staggered, then she got the paddle planted on the ice, and Ivy managed to straighten up in time to keep them both from falling backward. "Jesus," she said. She couldn't get used to the feeling of the lady pressed against her, so close and solid and real.

They got off the ice and started following Ivy's footprints up the zigzag path. It was narrow in some parts, forcing Ivy to turn and sidestep along with Mary Ellen, both arms wrapped around her middle. Mary Ellen was panting hard, and her face was shiny with sweat. She clutched Ivy so close that Ivy felt crushed, smothered, but she kept shuffling her feet through the snow and push-pulling the lady over each rise.

Eventually, they made it to the deck and inside the back door. Mary Ellen got herself over to the den couch and lay down with a groan. The makeshift bandage had loosened and sagged to her knee, exposing the bloody hole. Ivy turned away from it. It was too big, too dark. She wasn't ready to think about what it meant.

"Water."

Ivy went into the bathroom, dumped her toothbrush

out of the cup by the sink, and tried, with shaking hands, to scrape away some of the blobs of toothpaste that had accumulated at the bottom. Mary Ellen made another loud groaning sound, and Ivy shook her head, filled the cup with water, and rushed back to the den. Mary Ellen raised herself on one elbow and drank the whole thing. Then she dropped the cup on the floor, covered her eyes with one hand, and took a deep, snuffling breath. She started to cry.

"No," Ivy said, alarmed. "No, you have to tell me what to do; I don't know what to do."

Mary Ellen nodded and pressed her lips together. "Change the—" She gestured toward the tangle of bloody pads and clothes.

"Okay." Ivy waited for more, but the lady's eyes were closed, and she didn't seem to have any ideas. Ivy went to Mary Ellen's room and got another T-shirt and more pee pads, then took some towels from the linen closet. She came back to the den, where the lady was struggling to get her arms out of the coat. Ivy helped her, pulling the coat out from under her and bundling it at the end of the couch so the lady wouldn't see how bloody it was. Then she rewrapped the leg, biting her top lip to keep herself from going all light-headed at the sight of the wet, gaping hole. Finally, she lowered Mary Ellen's thigh onto a folded towel and carefully worked off her snowy boots.

"Get some pillows so I can elevate it some more."

"Okay." Ivy gathered some cushions and throw pillows and propped the lady's leg up, adding another cushion under the towel so it stayed pressed against the bandage.

"That's good," Mary Ellen breathed, closing her eyes. "Thank you."

"You're welcome," Ivy said, feeling for the first time

like she might actually be able to do this. The pajama-pant tourniquet refused to stay really tight, but at least the T-shirt bandage looked neat and secure; it looked like it could hold the lady's life inside her for a while. "You're positive your phone doesn't work here?" she asked.

"I'm sure."

Ivy nodded, biting her lip. "Even if I got it dug out," she said, "I can't drive your car." She wiped a hand over her mouth. "I tried, once."

The lady's head tipped to the side so she could look at Ivy. "You did?"

"It's one of those foreign-type cars. With the stick. I don't know how to work it."

"When was this?"

"You were passed out."

The lady blew air out her nose.

"I was trying to get the hell out of here."

"Leaving me behind."

"You were fine. All you had to do was walk up to the road and make a few calls. Your husband could've come to get you."

The lady put a hand over her eyes. "You can't just do that," she said finally. "You can't just leave people like they're, they're *nothing*."

"Yeah, okay. So what do we do?"

"We?" Mary Ellen snorted, wincing.

"I told you. I can't—"

"You have to walk, Ivy. You have to go up to the road and get help."

Ivy sat down in one of the armchairs and leaned her forehead on the heel of her hand. "I don't think I can do that."

"What?"

"Sorry." She got up and went upstairs, ignoring the lady's

weak protests. Her peanut butter sandwich was still sitting on the kitchen counter, but there was no way she could eat now, not with blood smeared on her pants and the thought of the hole in the lady's leg. She stared out the window into the treetops, feeling her mind darken, a familiar sensation coming on like nightfall. Why couldn't she ever seem to get out from under other people? It wasn't fucking fair. All Ivy wanted to do—all she'd *ever* wanted to do—was mind her own business and do her own thing. But she kept getting dragged down by other people's shit.

She slid the window open and listened to the cold air. The woods were so quiet, now that the creek had frozen over. It was like when the power went out and the fridge stopped and you realized you'd never known real silence before. There was no wind either, so the trees had stopped their creaking. Far away, in another mountain's stone-colored sky, crows called once, twice, then stopped.

She'd made a promise to herself: no going back. Only forward.

Ivy thought about the man with the cloudy eye, and the swinging crystal throwing light around his dirty car. She felt some comfort knowing he was out there, and probably others like him. It made things seem a little less lonely.

She pulled the window shut, the early-afternoon light washing the glass clean of any reflection. She went to the kitchen and filled a tumbler with water, which she brought downstairs to Mary Ellen. The lady was asleep.

"Hey," Ivy said, poking her shoulder. "Hey." She was really pale; too pale, Ivy decided. She shoved the lady's shoulder and was thinking about pouring some water in her face when her eyes finally opened. "Drink some water."

Mary Ellen drank slowly, weakly. Ivy checked her

wrappings. The pee pads on the top were okay, but the ones underneath were soaked through. The tourniquet had come loose too. "Did you untie this?" she asked. But Mary Ellen's eyes were rolling back, and she was groaning loudly. "What's wrong?"

"It hurts... Oh God, it... Ahhh!"

"Okay, sorry." Ivy unwrapped some fresh pads and replaced the bloody ones as quickly as she could, retying the pajama leg as tight as possible. Then she went upstairs and got the bottle of Numbitol out of Mary Ellen's purse. She came back and put two of the little blue-and-yellow pills in the lady's hand. Mary Ellen dropped them weakly onto her tongue, then jerked her head up and spat them out.

"What?" Ivy said.

"Ibuprofen," Mary Ellen said, staring at the pills in her hand. She looked up at Ivy with wide, sad eyes. "It's a blood thinner."

"Oh." Ivy shrugged. "I guess that's...bad?"

Tears were sliding down Mary Ellen's face. She threw the pills across the room; they bounced off the sliding door and fell to the floor with a light *tick-tack*. She drew a long breath and made a hopeless wailing sound. Ivy sat in the armchair and leaned her head back.

"Listen to me." The lady put her hands over her face and talked through them. "If I don't bleed to death, I'm going to die of an infection."

"You're not going to die."

"Yes I am."

"You won't."

"Please, Rose."

"Ivy."

"Go get someone. I don't want to die."

"Stop it," Ivy said sharply. "Stop talking about dying. Keep your head in the game."

"I'll give you my phone, okay? I'll give you my phone, and all the money I have, and my boots and my coat and everything else. Just go up to the road and call 911."

"I can't."

"Why not?"

"Because." Ivy took a deep breath. "I did something bad, and they're looking for me. The cops."

"What? What did you do?"

Ivy shrugged. "I stole a car. And I wrecked it."

Mary Ellen had closed her eyes. Ivy wondered if she was asleep. "Hello?"

"So you're a car thief."

"I guess. Not a very good one."

"Mmm-hmm." This turned into a little laugh. It was almost like the lady was drunk.

"You know, I think you should probably stay awake," Ivy said.

The lady gave an exasperated sigh and opened her eyes. "Listen," she said. "What about this? I'll give you my car."

"I already told you—"

"No, *listen*. I'll teach you how to drive it. It's not that hard. If you get me out of here, drive me to a hospital, and drop me off, you can keep the car. Plus, my phone and my credit card. It's everything you need to get to Montana, right? I'll even mail you the title to the car. Once I get...home."

"Oh, please. You're just going to send the cops after me."

"No!" Mary Ellen turned her head and fixed Ivy with a significant look. "This is the deal; this is *our* deal. If I get to live, you get to go to Montana. That's a promise." She grimaced and lay her head back.

Ivy thought this over. It probably wasn't any riskier than heading out on foot with no money in her pocket. "It's going to take me forever to get the car dug out," she said. "I'll wait."

Ivy thought for another moment, chewing the inside of her cheek. Then she picked the lady's gloves and boots off the floor and went upstairs.

The forest still had that wrapped-in-cotton quietness about it, so every slap of the paddle against the snowdrift sounded sharp and clear and extra loud. Ivy stopped periodically to look at the snow-piled trees around the driveway, listening for creaks and cracks. It felt like the forest was watching her too, waiting for the moment she turned her back so it could smash her to the ground.

She worked the paddle as fast as she could. She'd tried various techniques and decided it was best to use it as a sort of crowbar, levering chunks of snow away from the car's tires, then scooping the paddle under the chunks and tossing them toward the woods. More often than not, though, the snow just slid off the paddle and resettled in the wells she'd already dug. It was aggravating. Ivy kept reminding herself that the car would be hers soon, provided she could get the lady into it and delivered to a hospital. It was like a test—one of those super-hard challenges you had to pass before being leveled up in the game.

She'd been doing all right so far. She couldn't believe she'd managed to pull the tree off the lady and get her up the hill to the house. And using the pee pads as bandages was kind of smart. She wasn't sure if the lady could really die from a hole in the leg, but who knew—maybe Ivy would save her life. That was something she could carry in her pocket for a while: Ivy the hero. Ivy the lifesaver. Ivy the badass who stuck around and did what needed to be done.

She took a break and leaned against the car, her damp skin meeting the cold air a little more comfortably than before, her feet and fingers finally coming to life. She hadn't ever really thought about the tough, rescue-type stuff smoke jumpers had to do; her fantasies had mostly been about the jumping-out-of-airplanes part. But maybe she was cut out for the job in ways she hadn't thought of, in ways that proved her heart was kind of okay after all, that it hadn't completely rotted away.

After digging a while longer, she went inside to wake up Mary Ellen, give her some water, and change her dressings. The bleeding was slowing down, which was good, but the pain seemed to be getting worse, judging by the lady's shrieks whenever she moved her leg. Ivy gritted her teeth and tried to move fast, but her hands were shaking and clumsy, and she kept getting the pee pads stuck to the couch, her arm, the lady's leg.

Finally, she got everything back in place and tied up. "Okay, I think that's good," she said finally, giving the pajama pants a last tug. "I'm going back out. The tires are almost done, but I need to get to the snow under the car."

"Thank you." Mary Ellen had seized her arm and was looking intensely into her eyes. "You're doing a good thing. It's…good, what you're doing. I'll never forget it."

"Ohhh-kay," Ivy said, pulling her arm away. "I'm going back out there."

Mary Ellen was crying again. "I don't want to die here," she whimpered. "I need to get back to my girls. They need me."

"Okay, you're not going to die. Geez." Ivy pulled the lady's gloves back on. "Just give me a little more time."

Getting the snow out from under the chassis was impossible. It was mashed down, rock solid, and the paddle could only scrape little shavings from the sides. Ivy decided to go the other way and build up the ground under the tires. She searched the edges of the woods for fallen sticks and branches, which she shoved under each wheel. The branches were thin, so she needed a lot of them, which meant venturing farther and farther into the woods. The light was fading, especially under the snowy treetops, and the combination of oncoming darkness and menacing trees made Ivy extra jumpy. She walked fast, freeing branches from the snow with impatient yanks.

Eventually, she got so much stuff jammed under the wheels it was impossible to add any more. Ivy brushed her hair out of her face, pausing for a moment to admire her work, then went inside to see about getting the lady up the stairs and out the door.

Mary Ellen was asleep again, but her color looked better and she was breathing deeply, with a faint trace of a snore, so Ivy let her be for the moment. She ate the sandwich she'd left on the kitchen counter, then gathered up Mary Ellen's belongings and took everything out to the car. She went through the house one more time, putting useful things into the backpack: soap, toilet paper, a kitchen knife, extra socks.

She paused at the dining room table and picked up the journal Mary Ellen had left there. She expelled a puff of air through her lips, noticing the rose on the cover for the first time. Even now, after Ivy had come clean, the lady couldn't stop calling her Rose. She'd really fallen in love with the character. Ivy laughed a little to herself, trying to imagine soft, pink Rose dealing with this kind of situation. She wouldn't even be able to look at the hole in the lady's leg, much less bandage it up well enough to stop the bleeding. Ivy thrust the journal into her backpack, then took the canoe paddle and went downstairs.

"Hey," she said, shaking the lady's shoulder. "Time to go."

Mary Ellen moaned for a while before opening her eyes, her lips working in and out. "I can't," she whispered.

"Well, sorry," Ivy said briskly. "We made a deal. You have to teach me how to drive your car."

"It hurts."

"I know. But we've got to get you to a hospital, remember?"

"Mmm."

"Here." Ivy shook out Mary Ellen's coat, still soggy with blood and snow, and laid it behind the lady's head. "Put an arm in here." She got Mary Ellen sitting up and helped her shove one arm into the coat. She stretched the other sleeve around and got that on too. Mary Ellen was panting fast through her teeth, like people do when they're having a baby. Ivy gently lifted her leg and pulled the cushion out from underneath it, which made the lady scream. "Jesus, not in my ear," Ivy said. "Okay, now turn and put your feet on the floor so I can get these boots on you." Ivy worked the rain boots onto the lady, who was huffing and wheezing and leaning over as far as she could on her good thigh.

Getting her to stand up took a couple of tries, but eventually Mary Ellen heaved herself upward, Ivy holding her up on one side, the paddle on the other. She managed to hop weakly to the bottom of the stairs, where she halted and shook her head violently. "I can't."

"Don't chicken out on me now," Ivy said, breathing hard under the crush of the lady's arm.

"I can't put any weight on it. I'll pass out."

233

Ivy thought a moment. "So go up on your butt."

Mary Ellen sighed and sagged even more heavily against Ivy. Then she slowly eased herself into a seated position on the first stair, her hurt leg stretched out straight. The dressing had loosened, but the pads seemed to be glued in place by the thick paste of drying blood. Mary Ellen used her arms and her good leg to push herself up one step, then the next, her face opening into a pained sneer each time she moved, like she had strings tied to the corners of her mouth.

At the top, Ivy helped her stand back up and hop across the floor. "We're almost there," she said, feeling a surge of excitement when they reached the front door. This was happening; she was doing it. She was getting the hell out of Dodge, out into the world, on to the next thing. When she pulled the door open, the freezing air quenched her over-heated skin. "Come on," she said to Mary Ellen, who was hanging onto the doorframe, panting. "Come *on*!"

The snow slowed them down, but the path to the car was pretty well mashed down, so getting there wasn't too bad. While Mary Ellen leaned against the car, Ivy got the front passenger seat reclined all the way back. The lady was shivering pretty hard, so Ivy reached in and started the engine and got the heat going, then tossed the canoe paddle aside and helped Mary Ellen lower herself into the seat.

"Okay," Ivy said once she was settled in the driver's seat. "I can't wait to find out how to drive this damn thing."

Mary Ellen was still breathing hard. She put a hand on her chest, fluttering her fingers. "You've got three pedals. Clutch on the left, brake in the middle, gas on the right." As she explained, she seemed to wake up more fully, exactly as Ivy would've expected, practically brought back from the dead by the chance to teach Ivy something. She was good at it too—patient, clear. She didn't get rattled when Ivy stalled out on her first couple of tries.

Ivy finally managed to get the wheels going without the engine clunking into silence, and the car backed up a couple of inches, but then it stopped. "That's okay," Mary Ellen said. "Try first"—Ivy grabbed the shifter, and the car promptly stalled—"pressing the clutch before you shift."

"Right." Ivy tried again and got the car into first, and this time they started rolling forward. Excited, Ivy released the clutch and mashed the gas, but this, as usual, killed the engine. "Fuck's sake."

"Put it back in neutral and try again." This went on for a while, the lady repeating everything a million times, Ivy eventually getting it, the car crunching forward a few feet, then backward, but after a while, it stopped and wouldn't go forward any more, no matter how perfectly Ivy did the gas-clutch dance.

Head buzzing with impatience, she got out of the car to see what was going on. The tires had cleared the branches and were back in deep snow, which came all the way up to the bottom of the doors. Ivy didn't need to poke anything underneath the chassis to know the snow was all jammed up in there once again; the tiny car was too low to the ground. The only way up the driveway would be to spend the next five days digging out the tires and jamming branches underneath them, over and over and over and over again until Ivy died of exhaustion.

"What is it?" Mary Ellen asked when Ivy got back in the car.

Ivy didn't answer; she just started the engine and jammed the shifter into reverse. "Fuck it," she muttered. She stomped on the gas, easing up on the clutch the way she was supposed to.

"I don't think it's going to work, Ivy. The snow's so deep—"

"I'm not staying here."

The car rolled backward a few inches, then came up against something and stopped. The engine howled as Ivy harassed the gas pedal. She put it back into first and got it going forward a little, then reversed and tried turning the wheel to start getting the car faced the right way. It wouldn't cooperate, though, the tires not even spinning anymore, just grinding against the screaming engine, the heat pouring out of the vents, Ivy's hands like teeth biting the steering wheel. She screamed as she urged the gas pedal toward the floor, feeling the rage burn through her heart like it was paper, the thinnest tissue just evaporating in the blazing heat, black shreds of hope floating languidly into the freezing air.

20

Honey. Sweetie. Rose. Shh." Mary Ellen had been making comforting sounds for a while now, but the girl was so immersed in her fit of rage that nothing was getting through. Mary Ellen put her hands over her eyes and waited for it to be over. Finally, the girl stopped screaming and racing the engine, and the car became quiet.

"Rose—"

The girl pounded her fist on the steering wheel one more time. "It's Ivy, okay? *Ivy.*" Tears were streaming down her face.

"Ivy. I'm sorry. I keep forgetting." Mary Ellen felt her own voice fill with tears.

Ivy sniffled loudly. "I hate this fucking car so fucking much."

"I know, but listen, it's going to be okay. You can still walk up to the road and get help."

The girl slowly rocked her head back and forth. "*No,*" she said, choking on her despair. "I already told you I can't."

"Take my phone. Call somebody. Then you can just leave. They don't need to know—"

"I need this car. You promised I would get it, but now the deal's off, okay?"

Mary Ellen put her hands back over her eyes and drew a deep, shuddering breath. Could it be? All the girl cared about was the car? The gash in Mary Ellen's leg throbbed, beating out its warning. She was really on her own now. She was on her own, and she was probably going to die. It wouldn't be an easy death either. It would be a prolonged slide into fever and vomiting and blackening skin and the systematic surrender of her organs, one by one, until she was nothing but a bag of poison, useless and rotting. No one would hear her screams; she'd be the proverbial tree falling in the forest, silenced by solitude. Matt, Sydney, Shelby—they were already used to her being gone. What was another week, year, decade, eternity? A mere stretching-out of the distance that already yawned between her and them.

"Stop it. *Stop it.*" Ivy raised her voice to be heard over Mary Ellen's sobs. "Calm *down*. Jesus."

"If you're not walking up there, I am," Mary Ellen cried, hoisting herself up on one elbow and shoving the door open. She gritted her teeth and used her hands to swing her hurt leg sideways. It was almost dark, but she could just see the canoe paddle lying in the snow a few feet away. She gripped the sides of the car door and heaved herself up onto her aching, trembling "good" leg, a yelp squeezing through her clenched jaw. She hopped toward the paddle, one hand on the car door, then stopped, gathering her courage to let go and move forward without support. She heard the other car door slam.

"Don't be a dumbass," Ivy said, snatching up the paddle and coming to Mary Ellen's side. She ducked under Mary Ellen's arm and took up some of her weight, pushing the car door shut with her free hand. "We're going back in the house."

"I can't stay here. I need help." Mary Ellen grabbed the

canoe paddle and tried to pivot toward the driveway, but Ivy jerked her in the other direction.

"You can't make it up that hill," she hissed.

"Well, I can't stay here and—"

"Can we not do this out here? It's almost dark."

Ivy took a step toward the house, and Mary Ellen sagged against her, emptied of courage, and allowed herself to be led inside.

Ivy deposited her on one of the living room sofas and piled some cushions under her leg. Then she lay down on the opposite sofa, an arm flung over her eyes, looking exhausted. A pang of guilt complicated Mary Ellen's feeling of despair. The girl was so small, and she'd done so much already.

"You know," Mary Ellen said. "It's incredible, everything you've done. Getting me out from under that tree and all the rest."

Ivy said nothing.

"You're so strong. I never would've expected you to be able to do all that. Helping me up the hill. Digging the car out."

Silence.

"I'm sorry if—"

"I'm not going out there."

Mary Ellen squeezed her eyes shut. It was hard to think clearly; the pain in her leg was like deafening heavy-metal music. "If it's money you want, I'll give you my ATM card and my credit card. You can take as much as you want. Use them to buy a car—"

"I'll go in the morning."

"Tomorrow morning?" Mary Ellen stared at her in disbelief. "That's, like, twelve hours from now. I'll be dead of an infection by then, or I'll bleed to death. Don't you understand?"

The girl didn't move. Was she asleep?

"Ivy?"

The girl sighed and turned her face to look at Mary Ellen. "Is it the dark? Is that why you won't go?"

Ivy turned her face away. Mary Ellen blinked away tears, wondering if she could make it through the night. The pain wasn't getting any better; if anything, it was worse. Was that the infection setting in? She wished, for the first time ever, that she worked in a different division of Gallard—on something like surgical products, which required actual medical knowledge.

She felt a sudden stab of hunger. "Do you think you could bring me something to eat? Please?"

The girl sighed loudly and went to the kitchen, where Mary Ellen could hear the rattle of cereal hitting a bowl. She realized she was actually ravenous; the hunger was coming over her like a fast-moving storm. When Ivy brought her the bowl, she gulped down the sugary slurry as fast as she could in her semi-reclined position, milk streaming from the corners of her mouth. "Thank you," she moaned, letting the bowl drop to the floor.

Ivy sat opposite her, eating her own cereal. "My signature dish," she said, her mouth full.

"You know," Mary Ellen said, "I think you're actually going to do all right. Out there. In Wyoming."

"Montana."

"Montana. You're tough."

"Thanks."

"You just have to work on things like impulse control." Mary Ellen couldn't help adding this.

"What do you mean?"

"I mean, you get really angry sometimes, and then you act…irrationally. Like throwing my camera out the window." She let silence fall, then said quietly, "Why? Why would you do something like that?"

"I was pissed!"

"It's a six-thousand-dollar camera!"

Ivy was silent for a moment. "That's insane."

"Throwing it was insane."

"Six *thousand*? My ma's car cost that much, and it can't even take pictures."

"Well."

"Can I ask you a question?"

Mary Ellen turned her head to look at her.

"Does a six-thousand-dollar camera make you better at taking pictures?"

Ivy was trying to get a rise out of her, but Mary Ellen felt too tired to oblige. There was no point in arguing, no point in keeping up appearances. "No," she said.

"'Cause, I mean, phones are so good at taking pictures these days, I can't imagine what a six-thousand-dollar camera could do. Looking at those pictures must be like, I don't know, going into another dimension or something." Ivy laughed.

Mary Ellen felt a long sigh of pain wash up her leg. She groaned and pulled at the dressings Ivy had tied around the wound. Her skin was red and tight. "Oh my God, it's getting infected," she whimpered. "I can tell it's starting; my skin is all hot."

"What's it like, anyway?" Ivy asked.

"It's like there's not enough room inside my leg for everything, like my bones and my muscles and my veins are going to burst through the skin."

"No, I mean having all that money. How does it feel?"

"What?" Mary Ellen lay her head back against the sofa arm. "I don't know. It doesn't feel so special." She tried to ignore the pain in her leg and think about her money, her relationship with it. "It feels safe. Warm. Like a blanket."

Ivy didn't look impressed by this answer.

"Okay, no." Mary Ellen closed her eyes. "It feels...slippery."

"Like, in a sexy way?"

"No. I mean you never really know how much you have, whether you have enough. Some days you feel good about it, proud of it...those are the days you buy expensive cameras. Other days you freak out because you hear how much your friend paid for her stove, and you realize your perspective is all off. You don't have anywhere near enough."

"Oh." Ivy thought about this for a minute. "My sister, Agnes, is like that, but with her body. One day she's prancing around in short shorts like she's a Victoria's Secret model, and the next day she's literally crying in front of the mirror about her cellulite. She always looks the same, but her opinion changes every five minutes."

"I don't know why we do that to ourselves, always comparing and worrying and feeling inadequate."

"I don't," Ivy said.

"You don't compare yourself to other people? Come on."

"Well, yeah, of course I do. But it doesn't make me feel worse about myself. It usually makes me feel better."

Mary Ellen laughed a little at this, surprised by how happy she was to hear it. Then her burst of happiness abruptly tipped over into tears—as bursts of happiness always did when they were unexpected and sorely needed.

"What?"

"Nothing. I love that about you. It's great."

Ivy stared at her for a moment, her mouth open. "I'm sorry," she finally said. "About the camera. I didn't know all this was going to happen."

Mary Ellen wiped her cheeks and flapped a hand at her. "You couldn't have known."

"I do have a temper. I get it from my gran."

"Yeah?"

"It feels good, you know? It's such a rush, getting mad and doing something crazy. But then there's the hangover afterward when I feel bad."

"Hangovers are the worst."

Ivy lay down and pulled her knees into her chest.

"You know, it actually wasn't that bad, going into the ravine today," Mary Ellen said. "Before the tree fell on me, I mean." Remembering the ice formations on the creek filled her with wonderment all over again. "I had this moment of clarity, this moment when I finally had real perspective. And that felt like the beginning of something. Of being able to let go." She sighed and pulled a throw blanket from the back of the sofa, covering herself.

"Let go of what?"

"Just, bad stuff that's been weighing me down. Nothing."

"Yeah, but I want to know. Like, you have everything you need, right? Nice car, nice camera, probably a really nice house full of nice stuff. I'm just curious what's bad about your life."

"Oh, come on, Ivy. You're not that naive, are you? You know a car can't make you happy, a camera won't give you a reason to get up in the morning."

"I guess."

"You can still end up lonely. You can still feel like your life hasn't added up to anything. And…things can still happen. Things you feel bad about."

"Like what?"

Mary Ellen shook her head.

"No, come on. I'm not being nosy. Remember last night? You said I've never had to deal with real problems. I want to know what you think real problems are."

Mary Ellen sighed. Would it help—putting her pain out there between them, on the coffee table, to be looked at and commented upon? Would it make her seem more human to the girl? Would it give Ivy a reason to care whether she lived or died? "Fine," she said. "My father passed away last year. And it was my fault."

Ivy rolled on her side and propped her head on her arm.

"I hadn't been visiting him as often as I should have. He lived alone, about twenty minutes away from us, and I used to check in on him every few days. If I couldn't go out there, I'd call. Just to, you know, make sure everything was okay." Mary Ellen felt tears coming on, but she dammed them up. She just needed to get through the story. It was complicated, though, and she didn't really know where it began. College, probably—wasn't that when her father had pressed the lever that set her life rolling down a track that ended in emotional paralysis and a lethal separation?

So she told Ivy everything. She told her about her joyful, short-lived stint as an art major; about her sudden redirection; about her utter failure to rebel in any way, ever. She explained how her growing dissatisfaction with her job had built up inside her over the years, secretly, shamefully, until it all came to the surface in the form of resentment and blame as soon as her father died.

"I mean, who blames their father for something like that? It's awful. I should have just taken charge of my own happiness." Mary Ellen blinked furiously at the ceiling. "I don't know why I've had this constant, obsessive need to put it all on him." She covered her eyes with her hand, the pain in her leg all mixed up with the pain in her heart. "God, I'm just the worst," she moaned.

"No you're not."

"I am, though."

"Everybody does that shit to themselves. I do it." Ivy folded a throw pillow in half and shoved it under her cheek. "I hate my ma for being sick. Okay? I am *literally* the worst."

Mary Ellen tilted her head to the side. "She's really sick?"

"Yeah."

"I'm sure you don't *hate*—"

"Yes. That's how I am. She feels awful and that makes me feel awful and that makes me mad. I know I'm going to be stuck at home taking care of her and my gran for the rest of my life, and that pisses me off worse than anything. For a long time, I hated myself for being that way, but now I just accept it. It's who I am: a shitty person. A shitty person who does shitty shit." Ivy sat up abruptly, grabbed their cereal bowls, and went to the kitchen. Mary Ellen heard the clatter of dishes being tossed in the sink, and it occurred to her that this was the first time she'd ever seen Ivy pick something up and put it away.

"Ivy," she called toward the kitchen, "you're not a shitty person. It's normal to feel angry at people you love. It's just the feelings you have... It's not who you are."

"Says you." Ivy flopped back down on the sofa.

"Yes." Mary Ellen felt confused. "Well, I told you I was going to start letting go of things. I'm trying."

"So?"

"So what?"

"What happened to your dad? How did you kill him?"

"Oh. Lord, it wasn't like that. It's just..." Mary Ellen shifted her position on the sofa ever so slightly, which caused a jolt of pain to travel up her spine. She gasped and tried to focus her mind on the story, which was helpful in terms of taking her away from the situation at hand. "I started avoiding going out there. I kept coming up with excuses, because there was all this stuff building up inside me, and seeing my father just... I don't know. It threatened to bring it out. Stuff I didn't want to deal with." An aftershock of pain made her wince.

"So how *did* he die?"

"In the bathtub," Mary Ellen whispered. "He'd gotten so weak. I didn't realize it; he never wanted to admit how frail he was. But he couldn't... He couldn't..." She pressed a hand over her eyes. "Oh!"

Ivy was quiet. Mary Ellen took some deep breaths, trying to get herself under control, but it was too much, she was too worn out, she was in too much pain. The image of her father, naked, alone, trembling, dying, was more than she could bear. And now—now! Her punishment!

"He couldn't get himself out?"

Mary Ellen nodded. "The neighbor called the police, when the newspapers started piling up. He died of hypothermia."

"That sucks," Ivy said.

"Yeah." Mary Ellen took a long, shaky breath. "It does."

"But I mean, it's not like you did it to him. It was an accident."

"I should've checked in on him. I should've realized he was too weak to live on his own. I should've called."

"Well." Ivy twisted her fingers around themselves. "I guess we have something in common, huh."

"Yeah." Mary Ellen extended an arm toward Ivy, pointing a finger at her. "It doesn't mean we don't love them." She let her hand fall to the floor beside the sofa. She felt so tired. "I wasn't very good at taking care of him, but I never stopped loving him." She closed her eyes.

"I'm no hero, you know," Ivy said, sounding far away. "I get scared."

"We all do," Mary Ellen murmured, swiftly dropping off to sleep.

Mary Ellen felt herself melting into the earth like a dead leaf under the snow. Would Matt be able to see her, she wondered, if he came now? Or would he pull back the blanket to find her turned wet and black, smelling like rain, old lettuce, and ripening snowdrops, a few veins still visible, the rest sinking swiftly into her bed of soil? Matt. She pulled him close, tucking her nose under the nape of his neck, drawing her knees into the backs of his knees, slipping her ankle into the hollow just above his heel. There he was, solid and real, her companion under the snow, ready to fetch some water if she asked, ready to bring the shaky glass to her lips. Just as he'd wiped applesauce from the girls' reddened cheeks, always able to find that last dry spot on the bib, he would dab at Mary Ellen's thin skin too someday, and she would stir honey into his tea. He liked it that way.

The ice was still flowing. She could see its molten, sensual progress over the stones, and she gave herself to it. She flowed toward the bend in the creek, and it was so smooth and gradual and soft that she thought, *What a lovely way to travel*, and wondered why she didn't do this more often.

When she awoke, the world was gone. The only thing that existed was the pain, like a black hole sucking everything into its insatiable depths. Mary Ellen realized she'd been moaning for a while; now, she began expelling long breaths with a louder *aaahhh* sound. She tried moving her leg, but it seemed to be glued to the sofa. It was hot, tight, pulsing. Mary Ellen's *aaahhh* sound squeaked into a higher register as she awakened to what this might mean.

It was dark. "Ivy?" she called. "Are you there?" She was desperate for some water. How late was it? Was the girl asleep? "Ivy!" she shouted, the girl's name surfing on a wave of pain. "Ivyyy!"

Mary Ellen twisted her neck and fumbled for the floor lamp, flicking it on. The coffee table and the floor next to the sofa were cluttered; she blinked rapidly, trying to sort out the mess. Towels. Incontinence pads. Scissors. Three or four water bottles. A loaf of bread. A bottle of orange juice. A jar of peanut butter. Her purse. Her camera. A pair of rain boots. A canoe paddle. A bottle of gin.

She stared blankly at it all, pain fizzing on the surface of her thoughts. She seized one of the water bottles and drank, furiously at first, then stopped herself and put it back on the floor. "Ivy!" she cried. "Ivy, please." She choked on her tears. "Did you really go? Did you really leave me here?"

She peeled back the blanket and looked at her leg. Its entire length was swollen; her skin bulged around the make-shift bandage, shiny and red. She couldn't see her foot—she still had her socks on—but it felt huge, tight, immobile. The wound had bled through the bottom of the bandage and soaked the towel underneath. Mary Ellen knew she had to re-dress her leg, to keep it clean and dry, but she felt so weak she wasn't sure she'd be able to sit up enough to reach all the supplies Ivy had left beside the sofa. She let her hand drop down beside her, where her fingers found the gin bottle. She unscrewed the cap, hoisted herself up on one elbow, and brought the bottle to her lips. She drank, then immediately spat a mouthful of liquid onto the floor.

She sniffed the bottle just to be sure.

"Very funny," she muttered under her breath, then shouted into the darkness, "Very fucking funny!" Something white stuck out from the bottom of the bottle, which was no longer a gin bottle; it was just a stupid water bottle. She yanked away the note that was taped there:

You drink too much.

Mary Ellen collapsed back onto the sofa and cried softly for a few minutes. She longed to tell someone about the pain, to seize their hand and look them in the eye and explain what it was like. But of course, even if someone were there to hold her hand, there was no way to really make them understand. "On a scale of one to ten," she would weep, "it's a ten," and the very act of assigning a number to the pain would squeeze it into a package that was absurdly small and tidy.

She clapped her closed fists three times against her forehead, then sat up as well as she could and steeled herself to work on her leg. She loosened the pajama-pant bandage, and the feeling of flames washing over her skin suddenly became more pointed, more searingly focused. She lay back, panting *hee-hee* and *hoo-hoo* the way they'd taught her in Lamaze class. Her eyes were wide with amazement—amazement at the profound force of the pain, amazement that something so boundless and strong could come from inside herself, amazement that the violence of it wasn't exploding her body into a million tiny shards. Tears streamed across her temples and ran into her ears.

Gritting her teeth, she peeled the pad away from the wound, which looked angry and red, oozing pus. A foul smell rose from it, sweet almost, like rotting fruit. Gritting her teeth, she peeled away the two pads under her leg, which were glued to her skin with dried blood. With several breaks for Lamaze breathing, she managed to replace the pads and the towel under her thigh, noting, with mild relief mitigated by the sight of her grotesquely swollen limb, that the bleeding underneath her leg had stopped.

She reached over to the coffee table and snagged her purse with her fingertips, pulling it close so she could take out her wallet. She opened it and rubbed her thumb over the plastic window protecting the photo of Matt and the girls. She wanted so badly to talk to them. She turned the wallet over, unzipped the pocket, and tipped her wedding rings into her hand. She slipped them on. She noticed that her credit cards and her ATM card were still tucked into their pockets, but the cash was gone.

So Ivy had abandoned her. The supplies she'd left were a clear enough message that Mary Ellen was on her own. She was just going to have to summon some of the courage that had sent her down into the ravine in the first place; she had to get herself up and walking around. If she could get to the bathroom, she'd be able to clean the wound, and eventually maybe she'd be able to get into some warm clothes and get herself up the hill to the road. If she wanted to live, she had to move. She couldn't stay under her blanket on the sofa, in the comfortable nest Ivy had left for her. That would only lead to hopelessness, dementia, sepsis, death.

She took a deep breath and lowered her good foot to the floor, then reached for the canoe paddle. Gripping it with one hand, she used her other hand to pick up her hurt leg and swivel it over the edge of the sofa. She couldn't bend her knee, so she had to put her leg down at an angle in order to avoid the coffee table. The pain made her gasp; she pushed air in and out through pursed lips. When the dizziness subsided, she gripped the paddle with both hands and levered herself up onto her good leg.

She moved the paddle to the other side, waited a moment, then inched the hurt leg forward, hanging as much of her weight as possible between the paddle and her good leg. Her foot touched down, her weight shifted, and pain exploded like a galaxy being born, unfurling its arms infinitely outward. The light dazzled her, and then she was falling, so slowly but actually quite fast, into a deep, velvety, smothering cushion of oblivion.

vy shut the door softly and stepped out into the snow. She'd spent too much time indoors all geared up in Mary Ellen's thick sweaters, socks, coat, boots, hat, and gloves. Now the cold air struck her sweaty skin like a clapper hitting a bell. She stood for a moment waiting for her eyes to adjust to the darkness, but the world remained hidden. No moon, no stars. No streetlights, storefronts, porch lights, or passing cars either. Ivy realized she'd never experienced a complete vacuum of light before. She was totally blind.

She hugged herself, bracing for the wave of terror she knew was rolling toward her. Somehow, knowing it was coming never seemed to help. "Put yourself on the outside of it," Colin used to say, whenever she would crawl into bed next to him, sweaty and shaking. "Stand outside yourself and say, 'Look what a scaredy-cat I'm being.' That's what I always do when I'm scared. You see yourself, and you see your fear, and it kind of gets smaller. Because you're not inside it anymore; you're off to the side kind of, like, checking it out."

That never really seemed to work, probably because Ivy didn't try very hard. It was enough to have the big, muscled mass of Colin next to her. This time was different, though.

This time she really needed to be able to put her mind over fucking matter.

There were sounds all around her—little sounds made big by the light vacuum. The forest was swishing and ticking and creaking. For once, there weren't any crows flying around, but she knew there were other kinds of animals that only came out at night: hunting animals, the kinds with glowing eyes. She could hear their feet pricking the snow; she was pretty sure she could hear them breathing.

She closed her eyes and tried going outside herself, off to the side and up in the air a little way, but in this kind of darkness, how exactly was she supposed to look back and examine the situation? You couldn't see a damn thing. Maybe, she told herself, that was good. She nodded, twisting her torso back and forth to keep the blood moving. She was invisible. Whatever was out there couldn't find her, couldn't touch her, because she was like smoke.

She opened her eyes, stretched out her hands, and aimed herself in the direction of the car, moving slowly, her legs tensed up, ready for the strike of a log or a rock or a car bumper. The distance to the car stretched like a rubber band, then snapped shut when she came up against the cold metal body. She felt her way to the front door lock, stabbing it with the key until she finally got it open and the dome light flooded the whole world with its brilliance. She swiftly grabbed the backpack she'd left in the back seat, then tossed the keys onto the dashboard and shut the door, the orange glow staining the backs of her eyeballs for another full minute.

With trembling hands, Ivy opened the backpack and pulled out the kitchen knife. She would slice her way through the dark. She thrust the blade out ahead of her, and somehow this persuaded her legs to move as well.

She thought she'd memorized the shape and size of the driveway, the way it curled into the first switchback, then scribbled its way up the slope. But the picture in her mind was useless now, the reality of the physical world as formless as a just-forgotten dream. She'd have to use the incline as her guide, keeping her feet moving uphill. As long as she did that, she was bound to reach the road eventually.

She was in the woods now; branches scraped her face and thorns tore at her jeans. She stumbled a few times, nearly stabbing herself in the face with the knife as she pitched forward. She was pretty sure she was headed uphill, but it wasn't always easy to tell in the confusion of the snowy undergrowth. Her foot hooked itself under something, and this time she flew forward, letting go of the knife just in time to break her fall with her hands. She patted around herself in all directions, but the knife was gone. She struggled to her feet and turned back toward the house.

Something yellow was glowing down there, at the bottom of the hill and off to the left. Mary Ellen must have woken up and turned on a lamp. Ivy exhaled slowly, grateful for the shred of light, glad to know the lady was still alive. Earlier, Mary Ellen had started talking nonsense, her skin hot with fever. When Ivy changed the bandage, she'd seen that the wound was weeping yellow stuff and was starting to give off a whiff of death. She'd known then that waiting until morning would probably mean the end for Mary Ellen. Ivy's fear of the dark was going to have to take a back seat.

Keeping the light behind her—checking its position from time to time—she could kind of go in a straight line, even though she was as blind as ever, and trees kept jumping out in front of her. It was a little easier on her brain just knowing the glow was there, like the little bare-bulb night-light in her room back home. It helped her stay on the outside of the fear, looking back at herself.

And what she saw when she did that was a girl who wasn't all bad. She saw a girl who could take care of herself and sometimes even other people, a girl who'd stopped running away, because running away was for scaredy-cats. She was running toward something better, something that might turn out to be harder. But that was okay, because doing hard things gave her life a shape she hadn't been able to see before.

Her hands found something that felt like a frozen wall, and after feeling along it, trying to find its beginning or its end, she realized it was the bank of packed snow left by the plows. She scrambled over the wall and hopped down onto the asphalt, grateful for the smooth, hard surface.

She could see the sky now, padded with light-gray clouds, and she could just make out the difference between the flat road and the humped banks that lined it. She looked up and down the road, waiting for headlights. There weren't any for a while, so she started walking toward Agloe, looking over her shoulder from time to time, listening for the hum of an engine. Finally, she heard one coming up the hill from town, the headlights just a glow from behind the switchback. Ivy took a deep breath and stepped into the road. She raised her arms, making herself as big as possible. When the car stopped, she slung Mary Ellen's scarf across the lower half of her face and pulled her hat down around her ears. The headlights made her squint, but she moved toward them, over to the driver's side window. She said what she needed to say, pointed toward the break in the trees. Then she moved off to the side of the road, hopped back over the snowbank, and vanished into the woods. Like smoke.

22

Justine loved the accidental photos Mary Ellen had sent her. Birgit turned them down, but Justine said she had other galleries in mind, and a friend at the Fleischer who owed her a favor. She told Mary Ellen all of this in her hospital room after the first surgery, when Mary Ellen was out of intensive care and finally seeing visitors.

"We'll find a home for them, I promise," Justine said, her eyes roaming the teal-and-beige room.

"Don't worry about it," said Mary Ellen, somehow embarrassed, in spite of everything, to be seen in this state—no makeup, haircut grown out, dirty lunch dishes still sitting on a tray across her lap. "I'd rather not do anything with those pictures. Bad memories."

Justine ripped off her glasses and polished them with the hem of her threadbare sweatshirt. Mary Ellen had never seen her so uncertain, so at a loss for words. But she understood what Justine wasn't saying, and had, in fact, already accepted this apology in her head, eager to put the confusing question of blame behind her.

Matt came in the room then, and Mary Ellen saw immediately that he hadn't put anything behind him. Without a word of greeting, he took the lunch tray from Mary Ellen's bed and cast about for a place to set it down, eventually choosing the bathroom sink. Then he busied himself unpacking the bag he'd brought, slamming through drawers and cabinets.

"Can I bring you anything?" Justine asked Mary Ellen. "I'm sure the food is terrible—"

"She has everything she needs," Matt said.

Justine watched him for a moment as he folded and refolded a sweater. "I heard good things about your surgeon. They say she's the best."

"Mmm-hmm," Matt said. "So tell me… Have you paid that snowplow bill yet?"

Mary Ellen reached for the morphine pump.

Justine leaned an arm on Mary Ellen's bed, edging Matt out of her field of vision. "They say it's an art, surgery," she said. "Unlike the art world, though, women actually have a chance in medicine."

"How are you feeling, Mary?" Matt asked, coming to the other side of the bed. "Tired?"

"I am a little, yeah."

Justine stood up. "All right," she said, giving Mary Ellen a weak smile. "You have my number. If there's…anything."

When she was gone, Matt draped himself over Mary Ellen's torso, pressing his face to her neck. "I hate her so much," he moaned, and Mary Ellen closed her eyes, feeling something pulse between them. She dropped the morphine pump and hugged him back, wishing there were space in the bed for Matt to stretch out beside her. At the moment, though, her leg, encased in plaster and bristling with tubes, seemed bigger than the two of them put together.

"I know," she said into his hair. "She won't be back."

Matt straightened up and sat in the chair next to her bed, hands open in front of him. "How do you forget to pay the snowplow company? Hasn't she heard of bill pay?" He lowered his head for a moment, then raised it and looked at Mary Ellen. "Don't get me wrong, I hate myself just as much. For letting you take the Mini. Even the ski trip, the girls getting in trouble. I shouldn't have let any of you leave home."

"This wasn't your fault, Matt. And it's behind us now. All of it."

"Well..." He gestured toward her leg with his chin.

"I just mean we'll get past this. A year from now, we'll be thinking and talking about something different." Mary Ellen closed her eyes. "I used to feel like every moment was going to end up being the permanent state of things...like, if I was sitting in my office writing a report, it felt like the rest of my life would be spent in an office writing reports. If I was walking down Sansom Street feeling annoyed by all the construction, then it seemed like Sansom Street would be under construction for all eternity, and I would never stop feeling annoyed by it."

She turned her head to look at Matt, who was squinting at her. "I only saw, like, a fixed version of things. But there's this huge amount of movement happening all around us, and when you start looking at it that way, you..." She held her arms out in front of her. "I don't know. You feel better. Things open up."

"You been hitting that morphine pump a little hard?"

"Matt! It's hard to explain. But I feel like life has this, this fluidity about it now that wasn't there before. And it's a good thing. For us."

"Okay." He nodded slowly. "Good."

Mary Ellen did her home exercises on a yoga mat in the den. At first, it was just a matter of lifting her foot off the floor and raising it to meet Sydney's hand. After a week of that, Sydney began lifting the foot higher in the air, ever so gently, stretching Mary Ellen's hamstring and the thick scar tissue that had knotted itself all around the muscle. This hurt so much that Mary Ellen would cry, which felt strange, because she'd never cried in front of her daughters before. Sydney would press her lips together and hold the stretch for another few seconds, then gently return Mary Ellen's foot to the floor and stroke her shin, saying, "Good job, Mom, good job." That also felt strange, but not in a bad way.

Matt and the girls had initially taken turns driving Mary Ellen to her physical therapy appointments, but before long, Sydney took over, sitting in on every session and pestering the therapist with questions. She took charge of Mary Ellen's home exercises, keeping her on a strict schedule and recording her progress on her iPad. Mary Ellen stuck with the exercises, as painful as they were, because she loved seeing Sydney come into her own. She learned to breathe through the stretches, riding the pain like it was a fiery wave, not fighting it but joining it, letting it carry her to the place she needed to go. It got easier as the summer went on. It got less painful too.

Shelby seemed as directionless as ever, refusing to discuss possible majors or areas of interest beyond the World Cup. Then one day over breakfast, Sydney tearfully announced that the University of Pittsburgh had a better physical therapy program than Penn State, and that she'd like to give up her spot at Penn State to go there. Matt and Mary Ellen watched apprehensively as Shelby absorbed this news, as if she'd just been told she was going to have a leg amputated. But Shelby took a nonchalant bite of her English muffin and said she was fine with it.

"You're sure?" Matt asked, getting his worried German shepherd look.

"Yeah," Shelby said. "No problem."

And just like that, the twins were separated.

—⊸⊷⊶—

Walking with a cane, Mary Ellen realized, was so psychologically wounding as to be counterproductive to her recovery. Once she made up her mind to stop using it, she began venturing out more, going to the occasional happy hour after work, rejoining her book group, even enrolling in a new class at the University of the Arts—printmaking this time. It was taught by a young Tyler student with ink-stained fingers who seemed intimidated by his middle-aged pupils.

Walking without a cane allowed Mary Ellen to start using her camera again, which she did on her short walks around the neighborhood. She found herself spending more and more time at the Logan Circle fountain, photographing the water as it spewed from the mouths of the bronze turtles and frogs, accelerating her shutter until it raced along with each droplet, creating fleeting sculptures in the air. It was the only thing that could stop the obsessive slide show that had been strobing in her mind day and night—coppery hemlock fronds, blood on the ice, the beam of a penlight shining in her eyes. The looks on the paramedics' faces as they shouted at her, urgently wanting to know what year it was and who was president. Taking pictures, she found, brought her peace.

A show opened at the Institute of Contemporary Art that sounded interesting, but Mary Ellen hesitated to go, not trusting herself, or maybe just not trusting the art, but she finally went on a Sunday in late summer. Rather than walk through all the galleries, she forced herself to sit for a long time in front of a single abstract painting, her hands folded in her lap, waiting patiently for her thoughts to soften into feeling.

It was hard to focus, though, because she had too much on her mind. There was the long list of things to buy for the twins' dorm rooms, and the luncheon she had to plan for her book group, and a mammogram she'd already rescheduled three times. Taking deep breaths, she trained her eyes on the painting's lines, following them as they charged forward in energetic angles and plunged downward in great, graceful swoops. She imagined herself holding the hand of the painter, stretching her arm up to the very top, then jaggedly dancing across the upper corner and back to the center. Gradually, her thoughts began to relax into images and memories, charging and plunging along with the lines—jazz, pistachios, a golden afternoon with a single red leaf floating in the pool—until she could almost feel the painting in her chest, like the beat of loud music pulsing across a row of roof decks late at night.

While Mary Ellen was sitting there, Cheryl Jones, a fellow Penn Charter parent, came over to say hi, saying she'd seen the article about Mary Ellen's accident in the *Inquirer*. It turned out Cheryl's son was also going to start at Penn State that fall. On top of that, she was going to the same physical therapy practice as Mary Ellen for a knee problem—a pair of what-a-small-world coincidences that led to them having coffee, and later, lunch, and eventually a concert at the

Tower Theater with a group of Cheryl's girlfriends, one of whom worked at the Philadelphia Cultural Alliance, which had just launched a search for a director of marketing.

⸎

On move-in day, Matt took Sydney to Pitt, and Mary Ellen took Shelby to Penn State. Shelby was nervous; she kept her earbuds in for the entire drive, barely speaking. On the walk from the parking lot to the dorm, she struggled to carry two trash bags of bedding while her rolling suitcase refused to cooperate, forever twisting onto its side. Mary Ellen limped along behind her, carrying an armful of hanging clothes, longing to take the suitcase but knowing it would be too heavy. She kept quiet, her heart aching along with her leg, wishing it didn't have to be like this, knowing there was no other way.

Shelby's suitemates hadn't arrived yet. Mary Ellen explored the common room with wonderment, exclaiming over the flat-screen TV, the kitchenette, the sleek furniture. "How can you call it a dorm without cinder blocks and This End Up furniture? This is nicer than my first apartment!"

"This is how they are now, Mom." Shelby was pulling pillows out of a trash bag, keeping an eye on the hallway, where some loudly chattering girls were broadcasting their social proficiency to the world.

"I bet you're going to love your roommates," Mary Ellen said, reading the names posted on the door. "Aaliyah, Brooke, Madison—they sound nice."

"Mom," Shelby complained, "you're being ridiculous. Those are just names."

"Okay, okay. Where do you want your shoes? In the closet or under the bed?"

"Wherever."

Mary Ellen helped Shelby unpack in silence until a short brunette entered the suite and introduced herself as Brooke. While Shelby made awkward small talk in the common room, Mary Ellen stayed in the bedroom putting things away. In a pocket of the suitcase, she found the wooden nameplate that had hung on Shelby's bedroom door since she was a baby. Mary Ellen took it out with a fond smile, running her finger over the colorful carved balloons and prancing cats that decorated the letters of Shelby's name. She found some pushpins and mounted it on the outside of Shelby's room door, then turned to Shelby and Brooke with a wide smile. The girls stopped talking, and Shelby's face fell into the kind of deathly slackness she reserved for moments of fury or despair, or both.

After retreating to her room and slamming the door, Shelby hissed, "I can't believe you," her face working hard to maintain its mask of indifference.

"I don't understand… It's cute! Why did you bring it if you didn't want to hang it up?"

"*Mom!*"

"So take it down!"

"I can't now. *God.*"

"Then I will."

"Don't touch anything. Don't do anything, Mom; just stop, I swear. You're just…uhhh." Shelby squeezed her eyes shut. "You're ruining everything."

"I'm sorry. I—"

"Shh!"

What was it about being shushed that was so infuriating? Mary Ellen crossed her arms, tamping down her anger, struggling to find a calm, reasonable way to defuse the situation. "Now, Shelby—"

"Shh!"

"*Don't shush me!*" Mary Ellen's breath caught up in her throat. Shelby's eyes flew open. "Excuse me." Mary Ellen pinched the bridge of her nose. "No, actually, don't excuse me. I'm on your side, Shelby. Can't you see that? You have no reason to hate me."

"I don't hate you."

"You have no reason to *act* like you hate me, even if you're stressed out." Mary Ellen paused, breathing hard. "You should treat me with *respect*, damn it. I'm your mother."

Shelby's face folded in on itself, and after taking a moment to recover her senses, Mary Ellen sat beside her on the bed. "I know it's hard, especially with Sydney going to Pitt. But you'll make friends. It's going to be amazing. You'll see."

"I know."

"Just…try not to get sucked into the party scene, okay? No more fake ID shenanigans."

Shelby looked down and away.

"I know we never really talked about it, with everything that happened, but Shelby, come on." Mary Ellen searched for a way to say what seemed so obvious that it shouldn't need saying. "Don't do stuff that'll get you in trouble with the police. And aside from all that, don't drink too much. You start doing it for fun, but later on, it becomes, like, an excuse to avoid dealing with life. And then it's not fun anymore. Okay?"

"Okay."

"Okay." She patted Shelby's knee. "I'm sorry I didn't call you after you got sent home. I was caught up in things that were happening up there, and I don't know. I don't really have a good excuse."

"Did they ever catch that girl? The runaway?"

"I don't think so." Mary Ellen played with her wedding rings for a moment. She hadn't told Matt or the girls very much about Ivy. "She was a pretty determined person. If I had to guess, I'd say she's in Montana by now."

———

Matt wanted to sue Justine. "Dale says it's winnable."

"Dale the tax lawyer?" Mary Ellen slid a letter into an envelope and passed it over to Matt, who stuck a stamp on it. She'd joined the board of Greensgrow and was helping with their annual appeal.

"He went to law school."

"I really don't see the point in suing her."

"She sends you to this place in the middle of nowhere, no land line, no reception, and doesn't bother paying the snowplow bill? She's liable. Sorry."

"Okay, but I think I just want to move on. Don't you?"

"This is *how* we move on. By making the responsible party pay." His jaw was tight—she could see the joint twitching under his second-day bristle.

"I guess I see it more as a mistake," Mary Ellen said. "I mean, yes, what ended up happening was horrific. But I blame the woolly adelgid more than Justine."

"The what?"

"The bug that's been killing all those trees."

Matt stuck a stamp to an envelope and pounded it with his fist. "I'm sorry, but that bitch—"

"Matt!"

"—has to pay."

Mary Ellen squinted at him disbelievingly. It had been building for months—the muttering, the door slamming, the parking ticket he'd ripped to shreds and thrown to the ground. She'd never seen him like this. "Why are you so angry?"

"Why are you so *not* angry?"

She sighed and picked up another letter, folding it carefully and drawing her finger along the crease. In the beginning, she'd been touched by Matt's fury. It had seemed protective, gallant even. But now it felt like a weight around her neck, pulling her into the past. She wanted to go the other way. Her leg was better; her new job would be starting in a month. She'd been taking new classes and making new friends. Why couldn't Matt—

She put down the letter. "Oh."

"What?"

"Is this really about Justine? Or is it about something else?"

"No, it's definitely—"

"My father used to do this. It was like anger was his proxy emotion. Whenever he was anxious about something, he'd take it out on Mom. Or the reading lamp... He was always yanking the chain right out of the socket."

"I don't do that."

"Are you worried about something?"

Matt rolled his eyes and pounded another stamp into place.

Mary Ellen took a long, fortifying breath through her nose. "So, I know we haven't really talked about this, and I don't want you to feel like I'm pressuring you."

"What?"

"I guess I'm just wondering if you have any plans. Now that the girls are gone and all." This felt terrible coming out of her mouth. Nagging. Hectoring. "It's okay if you don't want to say."

"You care about my plans?"

Mary Ellen blinked at him. "What?"

"Yes. I have plans."

"Okay, good ⸻"

"Which you would know if you'd ever bothered to ask."

"Oh, come on, Matt. I was trying to leave you alone! I didn't want to pressure you!"

"Well…" He shrugged, looked at the table. A lock of hair fell into his eyes, and he tucked it dolefully behind his ear.

"Matt, honey—"

"I get it. I realize I'm kind of useless at this point. My work here is done."

"I never said that."

"You're probably thinking it."

"You're not *useless*." Mary Ellen went back to folding and stuffing. She'd never thought that. And anyway, she wasn't married to Matt for his usefulness. It was his friendship, his constancy. It was also, she was beginning to realize, his resemblance to her father. That steely dedication to the status quo.

"I know you've been through a lot, Mary, even before the whole tree-falling-on-you thing. You've been questioning things. And I just… I hope you're not questioning me. Us."

"Oh, Matt." Mary Ellen squared a stack of envelopes, tapping them on the table. "I mean, sure, I've been trying to move things in a different direction. I haven't been happy for a long time. And I've reached a point in my life where it feels kind of urgent to make changes."

"And?" Matt was staring at her with wide eyes.

"What?"

"This is the part where you reassure me."

Mary Ellen slid the stack of envelopes across the table to him. "I don't know," she said softly.

"What?"

"I don't know if I can reassure you." She looked down

267

at the table, then raised her eyes to Matt's confused and frightened face. She supposed her face looked the same, because she was finding this out at the same time Matt was. "It's the honest truth, Matt. I feel different about things now. I feel like just because something has been a certain way for a long time doesn't mean it's going to be that way forever... or that it has to. I mean, when did we get so frozen in place? Remember what it was like to be a teenager, when every minute of every day was a chance to try things out, to try being this kind of person or that kind of person, to walk through all these different doors and see what was on the other side?"

Matt looked lost. "Yeah," he said. "It sucked. I mean, at least now I know who I am."

"Do you really, though?" Mary Ellen sat back in her chair.

"I know that I'm your husband, and I'm a father, and I don't want those things to change."

"I know you don't."

"Are you leaving me?"

Mary Ellen searched Matt's face, seeing its contours as if for the first time, as if she were back in the drawing studio, teasing the physical world into shapes and shadows and lines. She saw the way the light from the kitchen window settled along the center of his forehead and down the ridge of his nose, skirting the hollows under his eyes and the recesses of his cheeks. She saw the worried dents in his forehead, the way his eyelids retreated into his brow. She saw the uncertain set of his mouth, the stubborn smile lines, the tiny fans at the corners of his eyes. She saw fragility and joy, pain and pride. The exhaustion of age and the anxiety of love.

Ivy was right—Mary Ellen had nothing but choices. It was easy to ignore the multitude of futures arrayed before her, harder to open her eyes and imagine wandering into the wilderness or going to the sun. Staying in one place could be a trap, or it could be a declaration of love. It all depended on how you looked at it.

Mary Ellen reached across the table and took Matt's hand, which was warm and limp, waiting for her answer. She shook her head.

"No," she said. "Not today."

—⚬⚬⚬—

Mary Ellen Googled "Gardner Funeral Home," just trying to sort the real from the made-up, and possibly to find an address to send a letter to. But there was no such business anywhere in New York. She supposed Ivy didn't have any way of finding her either. Maybe she'd glimpsed Mary Ellen's last name and address on her driver's license, but it seemed doubtful that she would have memorized it.

She browsed some Montana smoke-jumping sites and considered calling them all to ask if they had any rookies named Ivy. For some reason, though, she never found the time to sit down and do it. Maybe she didn't want to find out. Maybe she didn't need to.

It wasn't until years later, after the girls had graduated and she and Matt had downsized to a trinity in Northern Liberties, that she saw a report on the news about a forest fire outside Missoula. She grabbed the remote and hit Record, but no matter how carefully she scrutinized the footage, she couldn't spot a familiar face among the smoke jumpers boarding a plane behind the reporter.

There was so much Mary Ellen wanted to tell the girl. She wanted to let her know that she'd rewound the news report three or four times, searching for her blue eyes and freckles and wispy blond hair. That she'd followed the story of the fires for the next few weeks. That she'd found an article online about a group of Missoula smoke jumpers who had died fighting those fires, trapped in a canyon between two walls of flame.

She wanted to say that when the paramedics arrived at Justine's house, she'd been close to death, that another hour or two would've been the end of her. That she understood how hard it was for Ivy to walk into those dark woods, and that she longed, more than anything, to thank her for it.

She also wanted to say she was sorry for doubting Ivy, and that she didn't doubt her anymore—that she knew for certain she'd accomplished everything she set out to do. In fact, Mary Ellen had been carrying that certainty around like a talisman, rubbing it between her fingers from time to time, drawing courage from it, and hope.

Finally, she wanted to tell her that she hadn't read the names of the smoke jumpers who'd died; she hadn't needed to. Because somehow, she could feel Ivy's presence, still blazingly alive—not just in the big skies over Montana, but inside herself. Where a small part of her, she realized now, had always been.

READING GROUP GUIDE

1. Why does Ivy think she has a black heart? Do you agree?

2. Mary Ellen feels excluded from her family's life. Do you think this is an inevitable consequence of her choice to have a career, or has she brought it upon herself in other ways?

3. Why do you think Justine goes out of her way to help Mary Ellen?

4. How does Mary Ellen's product, Numbitol, reflect her life choices?

5. How does Mary Ellen respond to the art when she first visits the Institute of Contemporary Art with Matt?

6. Why do you think Mary Ellen has trouble taking pictures in the beginning of her stay at Justine's house?

7. Why do you think Mary Ellen loves the "accidental pictures" so much?

8. Why does Ivy have so little empathy for Mary Ellen's midlife crisis?

9. Does Mary Ellen's privilege make her unsympathetic? Why or why not?

10. What does Ivy learn about herself when she helps Mary Ellen after her accident?

11. What are some similarities between a teenager coming of age and an older person having a midlife crisis?

12. Do you think creating or experiencing art can help navigate life's difficult passages? Have you ever had this experience?

13. Have you ever pretended to be someone you're not?

14. Have you ever run away—from home, from your feelings, or from something else?

A CONVERSATION
WITH THE AUTHOR

How did you get the idea for this book?

My friends have a beautiful vacation home in the woods of northeastern Pennsylvania, and sometimes they let me go there to write. While I was there one winter, working on my first novel, *The Objects of Her Affection*, it occurred to me that the house would be a great setting for a story. I loved the contrast between the modern, glassy house and the rough, blighted forest... I was also inspired by the ice formations on a nearby creek. Whenever I had writer's block, I would walk to the creek and take photographs of the ice, and as I became absorbed in the pure, physical beauty of it, I found myself becoming more open to ideas and emotions. That experience became the core of this story.

Have you ever gone through a midlife crisis?

I don't know if I would call it a crisis, but in recent years, I've definitely been thinking a lot about how to lead a more authentic life. I've decided to prioritize artistic pursuits—a choice I realize is only available to people of privilege. I've been reflecting a lot about that privilege, feeling simultaneously grateful and guilty—something that probably comes through in the way I've written about Mary Ellen and Ivy.

Was it difficult to write from the point of view of a teenager?

It was so much fun! I spent some time reading my diaries from high school, which was cringe-y but also really helpful. I was struck by how actively engaged I was in forging my identity and how obsessively I tried to view the results through the eyes of other people. I really felt like I was in control of my own actualization—a feeling that quickly disappeared after college, but which returned, in a milder way, later in life. Inhabiting Ivy's character was a fun way to revisit that time of intense self-invention.

Mary Ellen becomes obsessed with art theory and something called "criticality." Do you feel that these pursuits are a waste of time or even a destructive influence?

For the most part, I think the academic study of art theory is a worthy and important discipline. For someone like Mary Ellen, however, it can be tempting to use theory as a barrier to a more intimate and visceral experience of art. Being too caught up in theory can also make it difficult to create art, because it can get in the way of raw, honest emotion. In Mary Ellen's case, it has a paralyzing and distancing effect, which is only exacerbated by her tendency to run away from her feelings.

Have you gone through a struggle similar to Mary Ellen's in your writing?

Absolutely. The most difficult part of being a writer (or

any artist) is learning to access uncomfortable emotions and channel them into your work. Like Mary Ellen—like anyone, really—I'd rather avoid those feelings than dig around in them. I've also had my share of writer's block, which can come from insecurity, and second-guessing myself, and trying to be someone I'm not. Overcoming all of that stuff is hard work, but in the end, it hasn't just made me a better writer—I think it's made me a more honest, self-aware, and empathetic person.

ACKNOWLEDGMENTS

I would like to thank Kirsten Bakis for her tireless support and astute ass-kickings, always delivered when I needed them most; Dana White for her kindness, insight, and inspiration; and Curious-On-Hudson for introducing me to these two remarkable women, without whom this book would never have seen the light of day. I would also like to thank my early readers: Ed, Eulalia, and Jodi Cobb; Amy Conklin; Greta Cowan; Karen Engelmann; Holly Fiss; Susan Kleinman; Nell McClister; and Kelly Simmons... You all shone your light into the shadows, and for that, I'll be forever grateful. Much gratitude also to my even-keeled agent, Adam Schear; my always thoughtful (and patient) editor, Shana Drehs; and the entire hardworking team at Sourcebooks. And finally, my deepest thanks to Brett and Maia Cucchiara for giving me a place to confront my demons in solitude. Your house was more than a beautiful place to write; it was a spark of inspiration, and I can't think of anything more precious than that.

ABOUT THE AUTHOR

Sonya Terjanian lives and writes in New York's lower Hudson Valley. Her previous book, *The Objects of Her Affection*, was published under her maiden name, Sonya Cobb.

Photo © Christy Knell